PRAISE FOR
TWILIGHT OF THE GODS

"Timely, hilarious, and wildly original, *Twilight of the Gods* is unlike any book you've ever read and finds Baumeister at the top of his game."
— Jonathan Evison, author of *Again and Again*

"Forget what you think you know about Norse gods and modern history. Irreverent, humorous, and packing a gut punch of reality, Baumeister has invoked perhaps one of the most memorable Lokis of the 21st century, an unlikely guide down America's gritty streets toward a topsy-turvy examination of good vs. evil. One might be tempted to invoke Gaiman or Grossman, but *Twilight of the Gods* carves out a genre-bending and metafictional journey that is undeniably Baumeister."
— Sequoia Nagamatsu, National Bestselling author of *How High We Go in the Dark*

"Big, sprawling, smart, epic in every sense of the word - Baumeister's *Twilight of the Gods* mines ancient ground and comes up with something wonderfully vivid and new to say about mythology and our modern era."
— Amber Sparks, author of *And I Do Not Forgive You*

"If the MCU--or, better, D'Aulaires Book of Norse Myths--was redrawn by Martin Amis, you'd arrive at Kurt Baumeister's *Twilight of the Gods,* a book that combines Nabokovian grace with sardonic, hardboiled snap. The result is a total delight."
— Matthew Specktor, author of *Always Crashing in the Same Car*

PRAISE FOR PAX AMERICANA

"Hang on tight, because the thriller's been reinvented, smartened up, and rendered blazingly funny in Kurt Baumeister's wild, raucous ride of a novel. Spiritual, sly, and so fast-paced you could get whiplash. Truly, *Pax Americana* is hilarity with heart."
—Caroline Leavitt, author of *Is This Tomorrow* and *Pictures Of You*

"Ambitious, fearless, and frequently brilliant, *Pax Americana* is a speedball of religion and politics delivered in a steel syringe of adrenalin. In the mad, mad world of a not-implausible future, Baumeister posits the larger question of which deity we're destined to worship: The God of The Bible or the God of Technology?"
—Chuck Greaves, author of *Hush Money* and *Tom and Lucky (and George & Cokey & Flo)*

"Kurt Baumeister has more fun with language than any novelist since *Money*-era Martin Amis. I haven't read such marvelously obsessive prose in years."
—Darin Strauss, author of *The Real McCoy* and *Half a Life*

KURT BAUMEISTER

TWILIGHT
OF THE GODS

STALKING HORSE PRESS
SANTA FE, NEW MEXICO

CONTENTS

WICKED IMPULSES - 13

THE DREAM THAT WASN'T - 29

THE LAZY LATE-NIGHT PARADE - 33

TRAGICOMEDY FOR THE FALLEN, PART 1 - 45

WHITE GUY SOUL SHAKE - 50

YOU DOUBT MY RAVENS? - 62

ALWAYS BRIGHTEST BEFORE THE FALL - 69

THE ASGARD KISS - 80

CAN WE STOP WITH ALL THE HITLER? - 85

TRAGICOMEDY FOR THE FALLEN, PART 2 - 101

THING IS - 106

TRAGICOMEDY FOR THE FALLEN, PART 3 - 121

MY NONFICTIONAL EXISTENCE - 125

KEEPING DESTINY'S BEAT - 136

HEL'S WACKY FACTS - 140

TRAGICOMEDY FOR THE FALLEN, PART 4 - 149

CALLING YOURSELF MEPHISTOPHELES - 155

LIKE FUCKING FATE - 165

A PAIR OF TAILORED BEHEMOTHS - 169

I ASSUME ASGARD DECADES - 181

CONTENTS (CONT.)

AS FOR KURT - 185

THE BIFROST CONVENTIONS - 193

UNLIKE THE EVIL GENIUSES - 198

TRAGICOMEDY FOR THE FALLEN, PART 5 - 206

A SORT OF BEMUSED CONCERN - 210

THE ANSWER THAT DOESN'T EXIST - 220

A STATUE OF YOU - 225

TRAGICOMEDY FOR THE FALLEN, PART 6 - 238

TO LET FATE MAKE YOU A LIAR - 244

TRAGICOMEDY FOR THE FALLEN, PART 7 - 255

GODDESS OF THE NIGHT - 260

KNOWING YOU'RE REAL - 269

YOU AND ME - 273

FANTASYLAND - 284

RAGNARÖK - 288

THE BABE IN A BASKET - 305

LIQUID IN HIS VOICE - 309

HEART OF AMERICA - 323

DRAMATIS PERSONAE

Loki—*aka Trickster; God of Evil, Mischief, Strife, Murder, and Betrayal; Interests: helping humanity, pro wrestling, economic theory, demolition derby, Valkyries, and first-person narration.*

Sunshine: *One of three Norns (Fate's Handmaidens); Loki's long-lost love; Interests: antiquities, psychotherapy, political strategy, and serving Fate. Sisters: Halflight and Darkness.*

Hel: *Goddess of Death, Disease, Pestilence, and the Underworld; Interests: Joan Didion, chess, computer hacking, and French cigarettes. Daughter of Loki.*

Odin—*aka All-Father; God of War, Wisdom, and Sorcery; Interests: Totalitarianism, being worshipped, interplanar travel, magic, and TV gameshows; Loki's foster father.*

Kurt: *Tax attorney; Writer; Amateur addiction counselor; Friend of Loki, Interests: Sunshine, Loki, Norse mythology, Dad rock, and fantasy football.*

Surtur: *Fire Giant King; Brother of Thyrm; Henchman par-not-quite-excellence to Loki; Interests include Monsieur von Mayhem, DnD, smoking, drinking, and (maybe) killing Kurt.*

Thyrm: *Frost Giant King; Brother of Surtur; Henchman par-not-quite-excellence to Loki; Interests include Monsieur von Mayhem, DnD, smoking, drinking, and (maybe) killing Kurt.*

Fen—*aka the Fenris Wolf; child of Loki; Expected to eat Sun and kill Odin at Ragnarök; "Biggest sweetheart on four paws"; Interests include sleeping, eating, and being petted.*

Thor: *God of Thunder, Lightning, Storms, Strength, and Fertility; Son of Odin; Interests: flexing, homophobia, and biting holes in aluminum cans.*

Heimdall: *God of Foreknowledge and Vigilance; Parentage unclear; Expected to kill Loki at Ragnarök; Interests: Surreptitiously following people, bad disguises, and rainbows.*

Baldur: *God of Beauty, Light, and Purity; Son of Odin; Expected to be slain by Loki before Ragnarok.*

Greta Bruder—*aka the German Washington, former general, current politician.*

Reinhold Vekk: *German industrialist and politician.*

Fate: *Fate.*

TWILIGHT
OF THE GODS

KURT BAUMEISTER

1

WICKED IMPULSES

A DOUBLE-STEEPLED, bronze-bricked Gothic at the cross of Warren and Dartmouth, Blessed Savior has been on that corner for more than a hundred years. Through world wars and great depressions, terror scares and countless recessions—through an American Century of money, blood, and long-forgotten love—Blessed Savior has been there. Or, rather, it's been here, hawking its wares, doing its do.

Spires climbing into the starlit dark, searching for whatever it is spires have always been searching for, the church has taken its age gracefully, façade barely betraying the slower, deeper decay, the architectural osteoporosis, lurking beneath its skin. Working that corner, rain or shine, snow or sleet, Blessed Savior has always reminded me a little of a pusher standing his beat, selling the lies he bought himself once upon a time.

You think that's wrong, right? Bad? Evil? But it's only logic. Because no matter how bad life gets, no matter the flaming slings and venomed arrows good old Fate pitches our way (more on that one in a minute), we cling to what we have, whatever that is. What Blessed Savior has is the Father, Son, and Holy Ghost, even though none of them are real. And what I have is you, even though you don't think I exist.

I TAKE the steps two at a time. Sure, they're iced over, badly—this is winter in Boston—but that doesn't bother me, not really. I've still got talents, skills, *bona fides*, if you will. Not that I'd measure up to what you've learned to think of as a god. None of us would.

Between your jacked, spandex-packed comic book heroes barging across the silver screens and your sitcom gods clogging up the little ones, you've tricked yourselves into believing we can't possibly be real. We're creatures of blue screen, phantoms conjured from the narrative ether, nothing more. That's where you're wrong, though. We're not ghosts, not us. At this point we're very much flesh and blood, more like you than we've ever been. More like you than you could possibly imagine.

Take me. I've got no horned helm or black, flowing mane, no ever-present smirk or scheme-furrowed brow. I have dark black skin, a shaved head, and a friendly, trustworthy face. Truth is, I look a lot like a cross between a young Denzel and a young Taye Diggs. And, man, does it piss Odin off. No, not looking like a movie star. It's the black skin that gets him. Not that I can really take credit for it. Fate gave us new, static forms after Odin and the rest of them fell. Who knows why? I mean, that's the thing with Fate, isn't it? We never really know what she's up to until the Norns tell us, but the Norns are gone, have been for centuries.

Don't misunderstand me: It's not that I want or need you to care about me or how I look. Loki's here if you want him, and if you don't, you don't. Odin on the other hand…well, he's roiling, has been ever since…honestly, I can't remember a time when One-Eye hasn't been seething with miscast rage at all the "slights" you guys have laid at his sanctimonious boots. No, the

All-Father is not your pal, no matter the snowscape wishes and fairytale dreams you feed yourselves time and again.

Hanging from a magic tree to bring wisdom to humanity? Enthroned in far Valhalla, granting boons to the most valorous of warriors? Magic spears and talking heads? Sorcerous ravens and preternatural wolves? Eight-legged horses? I mean, seriously… how did he come up with this stuff? Don't answer that. Please, don't. I know exactly how he came up with it because I helped him. And I'm sorry, little ones, oh, so sorry.

But isn't that what you'd expect of real evil? Not some pat, cartoon devil twirling his mustache and muttering a caustic "drat" every now and again, but an avatar of light, a pretense of good, honor, and nobility when the truth is the opposite, when Odin is the source of pain, both yours and mine. If he hadn't started meddling in your lives way back when, if he hadn't cast me out of Asgard time and time and time again, what a wonderful world it would be.

FRESHLY WAXED linoleum floors of pale spearmint-green and walls of saffron-yellow cinder block: Blessed Savior's basement is an interior decorator's acid trip gone completely to shit. Shuddering fluorescents loom overhead, emitting a low-grade buzz as lonely motes circle the spindly silver bars suspending the lights from the ceiling. The lights remind me of bug traps at some backyard soiree waiting to go zippety-zap on uninvited guests. Heavy, floral perfumes and 100-proof colognes linger from the Council for American Purity meeting that broke an hour ago. I know those people, those CAPs. They're hell on two legs, Odin's own special angels. And they're everywhere these days. Yes, it's true, my dears: even in America.

Hooting about the taxes they don't pay, and the welfare other people shouldn't get, howling about their inalienable rights to Social Security, Medicare, and a white, Christian America. Something about being in the People's Republic of Taxachusetts, maybe, that makes the right wingers veer even farther right. That's how it is, though. That's how it's always been.

Back in the past, back in those last days of Valhalla, I always felt queasy when we were all together, like I was out of my element. And I was. I just didn't realize how bad Odin and the rest of them had gotten until Hitler came goose-stepping out of the grand old Weimar, a cancer of ego and animus, desperate for life.

See, what's true for you is true for us, too. Fate can still surprise us: It can still take the hope, love, and happiness we thought we'd found, ball it up and send it streaking into eternity's ever-ready abyss. Yes, we may be immortal, but Fate still rules our lives. Fate can still make us cry.

A PAPER cup of coffee in my left hand, a translucent-amber, plastic stir in my right, I watch the floes of un-dissolved creamer bob and weave across the caramel-colored whirlpool I've just raised to life. Forget about reality for a second—forget about everything you've ever known—and this cup of coffee could almost be magic. The way the liquid becomes a tiny vortex, the way it beckons eternal sleep, it's almost enough to make you, or me for that matter, dive right in...

I set down the stir, bring the cup to my lips and sip. Scalding, the coffee tastes like it always does at these basement shindigs, same as it did at the Gambler's Anonymous meeting I just left in Brookline. Burnt and flavorless at once—yes, it's a mystery even to me—Blessed Savior's coffee tastes of the irony implicit in repetition; it tastes a little like fascism to be honest, the fascism you keep buying even though you know you shouldn't.

"All right, Gustav, why don't you kick us off?" says our facilitator, Kurt, turning my way.

Kurt's my boy, my latest in a long line of human reclamation projects. Hair a dirty gold, slate-blue eyes, average height and build, good-looking in an unthreatening way (or maybe unthreatening-looking in a good way), once upon a time Kurt might have been the all-American boy. These days, he looks like a personification of various forms of privilege, though not enough to piss most people off. Like his looks, Kurt's vibe is chill. He goes along to get along.

In addition to running this unsanctioned Sexaholics Anonymous chapter—they all are, unsanctioned I mean—and his somewhat lackadaisical practice as a tax attorney, Kurt fancies himself a writer, a novelist in fact, a pursuit we share. Yeah, I've been at it a minute, since before Cervantes even. Man, have I got a few pages to drop on an agent someday.

Kurt's writing? Oh, it's not bad. Sure, he gets carried away with his prose and has a subconscious fear of plot, but it could be worse. Trust me, I've seen worse, centuries of it, not least from Don Miguel himself. You should have seen the fireplace fodder he penned on the way to *Quixote*.

Kurt's working on one of those serial-killer-thrillers these days, something he calls *The Mists of Seeking*. Minimalist prose, queer, female profiler as a protagonist, supernatural elements. His agent, Suzy-Sadie, swears "Mists" is going to be the commercial hit that has thus far eluded him. And maybe she's right. Though this isn't the first time Kurt's literary career has, at least according to him and Suzy-Sadie, been on the rise. One thing I'll say for the guy: He is prolific.

There was the satirical spy novel about religion. Suzy-Sadie shopped that to what seemed like every editor in Manhattan, from the ones she knew personally (not many) to those she followed or stalked or whatever they're calling it now on social media (lots more). Nothing. Next came the cozy mystery set in outer space and populated entirely by otters. That, too, Suzy-Sadie assiduously proffered to contacts, and non-tacts, near and far. Nada. Then there was the urban fantasy trilogy in which all the magic had to do with the ability to make fast food appear and disappear on command. No luck. The western, the contemporary relationship novel, the YA, the MG, the *Harry Potter* knockoff, the *Goosebumps* knockoff, the *Lee Child* knockoff, the parody about knockoffs, the farce about knocking off knockoffs, the pot-boiler, the spine-tingler, the tour-de-force-r, the catch-all, the be-all, the end-all, the catch as catch can all. Like I said: prolific.

Sure, the stuff gets published—most of it, eventually— though I wouldn't call Kurt famous by any stretch. That's the thing non-writers don't get. You can be successful—ok, *comparatively* successful—as a writer while making almost no money, maintaining a second career to pay your bills, and having no one know who the fuck you are. Funny, I know, but all too true.

No, Kurt has no idea who I am. That would spoil the fun, wouldn't it? But we have spoken about me on occasion. Dude practically gushes over "the Loki construct," tells me without a shred of irony how much he loves "the character," as he refers to me.

Imagine someone deploying earnestness when it comes to me. What a twist, right? Honestly, it's kind of embarrassing. I try to avoid the subject as much as possible, but he keeps bringing me up, says there's this novel about Norse mythology he's been meaning to write for years, decades even. I know, with that output you'd think there'd be nothing left in his poor little noodle. Apparently, there is.

"Happy to, Kurt. 'My name is Gustav, and I'm a sex addict,'" I offer with all the diffidence I can muster. See the down-turned gaze? See the batting lashes?

"Hello, Gustav," the group responds in a sort of echoey semi-synchronicity.

I cut my gaze as though about to divulge something so dark you'd have to stuff Secret Squirrel in a wood-chipper if he found out. "I had a situation this week."

"Yes?" ask various members, interest piqued. Others nod, smile, and/or avert their gazes. All I've learned, standard responses from Twelve-Steppers.

"I was at my dad's house, and I started having urges," I say.

"What brought on these urges as you call them?" Kurt asks.

"It was the Valks."

"What's that, a new dick pill?" asks a guy in a white Oxford. The sleeves of his once-immaculately-starched, now-immaculately-wrinkled shirt rolled up, jacket and tie dispensed with somewhere between the underlit anti-glamor of his corporate veal pen and the bright, Siberian chill of this basement, he looks vexed, distressed even. He looks like a politician surveying a disaster site he's about to get blamed for. "Like bicockatrix?"

Kurt cuts in, "No, no, no...Come on, gang, it's an

indigenous tribe, like the Anangu. But from Europe." He nods to me for confirmation.

I don't correct Kurt even though he's wrong. How could I? I'm the one who dished him this aboriginal fib a few weeks back.

"Valkyries?" he asked at the intake. "You mean like Norse mythology?"

I laughed, guffawed really, voice full of good humor and a touch of dismissiveness. "Naw, dude, totally different spelling. And we usually call them Valks. It's a lot easier. I mean, it sounds like a 'v' but it's more like an 'fsth' when you write it out."

"That doesn't—"

"In their language," I added authoritatively. "Trust me, Kurt-o, I'm only trying to make this as easy as possible."

He nodded and, of course, bought it. Yeah, I know I'm a Dickens, but what can I say? I may not be "evil" anymore, I may be good 24-7 (close at least), but I still have a few tricks up my sleeves. Fore- and first-most, I am one hell of a liar.

"Somewhere in the Carpathians," Kurt adds confidently. "No value judgments here, Gustav, but you've talked about these Valks before. Does it occur to you that this isn't just a simple indiscretion, that it's more like an abuse of power?"

"They don't work for me."

"They work for your father, though. You can't get around the fact that you're having sex with the household staff."

"What are they? Maids, cooks, charwomen?" asks the politician.

"Charwomen?"

He offers up his palms, tilts his gaze noncommittally.

"They're imported...I mean, guest workers, Einstein visas... Like I said, low cost of labor. Economic decision."

"You mean like slaves?"

"Slaves? God, no, they're like, they're...more like nannies," I add, smiling wide and white as punctuation.

"Nannies who get Einstein visas?" he asks.

"And you turn them out?" asks a woman with a buzz cut. Dressed in a red plaid shirt and a black, polythene vest, she looks like so many of you do these days. Woodsy and citified all at once, she looks as if she can't decide whether to hug a tree or blow one up.

"He's a pimp," says the politician, smiling, an understanding reached.

"No, I told you, I don't turn anyone out. I just had a threesome. If anyone's a pimp it's my stepfather. You should see how he treats them."

"Mm-hmm," he says skeptically, "Sounds like envy."

"Trouble dealing with authority," offers the woman.

"Control issues manifesting as wicked impulses," says Kurt, grouping the barrage of accusations into one manageable rhetorical missile.

A hush falls, as though Kurt's crossed a line, but the group can't decide which line he's crossed. What Kurt said doesn't bother me, mind you. How could it? He's responding to pure fabrication, mine at that. But it seems accusing a fellow groupie of something as base and Biblical as wickedness may have rubbed a few of us the wrong way. Which implies a fair amount of guilt circulating through our little gang.

Two beats without a sound and three and four, finally, the silence is broken by a woman's voice. "If you ask me, your father sounds like a freak, y'know?" The voice is smooth, light even, the tone matter of fact. 'Sounds' comes off as though it has a subscript z lurking within, like something from a German lullaby.

I turn to three o'clock and the voice's owner. A sun-blushed redhead with cheekbones that seem to go on for decades, she wears knee-high boots and jeans just this side of melodramatic. Long, straight hair, eyes of frosty midnight, honestly, she looks like a Valkyrie—a real one I mean, from back in the old days, not the invented version that has so recently run amok. And for the record, as far as I know, they haven't been around since we fell. Yeah, sure, I saw all of them eat concrete, that day in Berlin nearly a century ago. I didn't see any Valks, though, not one. Maybe that's why I make up silly stories about them. Maybe I miss Asgard and my once-beloved Valkyries more than I can even say.

That's not all of it with the redhead, though. I get this feeling looking at her, this feeling of progressive déjà vu, as though I've seen her before even though I'm sure I haven't. Yes, I realize that makes no sense. Still, I get this feeling.

"It's not like you forced them, right?" she continues.

"Of course not."

"So?"

"Exactly. Thank you."

"All right, all right," says Kurt, busting in. "That's a good start, Gustav. Sabrina, why don't we go with you next?"

"Sure," she says, surveying the crowd. "My name is Sabrina, and I'm a sex addict."

"Hi, Sabrina," they say.

"Hi, Sabrina," I whisper a second too late.

You wouldn't think I'd still be attracted to you guys after all these centuries, but there's just something about the human form, male and female both—the combination of energy and fragility, tragedy and optimism—that I can't get over; something about a pretty girl or boy, that can still turn my head and heart to mush. I'm smitten with you guys, it's true. And I always have been. This feels different, though; sends my mind spinning back, down a tunnel of *deja vu*: I don't know what it is about this woman, but it's something real, deep, and ancient, something that makes me think of the old days; of Asgard, Valhalla, and Fate. More specifically, Fate's servants. There were three of them them; three sisters named Sunshine, Halflight, and Darkness. We called them Norns.

"Why don't you give us a little backstory, Sabrina?" Kurt asks.

Sabrina replies, "Well, I used to be a therapist."

"Psychiatric?" asks the politician.

"Yeah, sure," Sabrina says, winking at me. "I had a whole gaggle of patients, practically an entire pantheon of personality disorders."

"What do you do now?" the politician asks.

"Not therapy, that's for sure."

"So—"

"Antiquities," she says.

"What?" he asks.

"I deal in mystical antiquities. Primitive totems with purported magical powers, stuff like that."

The politician opens his mouth, and I'm sure he's about to ask for examples when Kurt cuts him off.

"Okay, okay," Kurt says, "I think Sabrina's shared enough for the moment." He turns to the politician. "Let's go with you now, Percival."

The politician looks down, face tinting a bashful red.

"Have you done what we talked about last time, Percival," Kurt continues, "Y'know, forced yourself to stay out of the chipmunk costume for the entire week?"

"Well...," says the politician.

AFTER THE meeting breaks—after we sit through the sadly titillating tales of Percival the politician's shadow existence as a full-contact furry and Granda the bisexual exhibitionist's lapse as sandwich-middle in an unsuspecting deli's walk-in—I'm still surreptitiously checking out Sabrina, trying to figure out who she is and where I know her from. My other support groups, my various pro bono odds, and philanthropic ends... I scan my semi-fake life in my supposedly real mind, searching for the connection, looking for Sabrina. Nothing concrete, though, just that faint, lingering feeling of forgotten history lurking beyond reality's veil. Before I know it, though, Sabrina's up on me, electric, beautiful, and standing way too close. I can almost hear Sting's sandpaper contralto name-dropping Nabokov.

"Let's not play any games," she whispers.

"I'm sorry?"

"I need..." She slits her eyes insistently, scans the room, a spy at a meet making sure she hasn't been tailed.

"Yes?"

"I need..." More eye-slitting and side-glancing. More spy at meet-making-tail-check-ing.

"*Yes?*"

"I need to talk to you," she explains, without actually explaining.

I wonder then if I'm being catfished. I mean, it's happened

to me a lot online, but never in RL. At least, not yet. Not that I'm making a value judgment. All I do is catfish people. Y'know, roam the world, making up and using fake identities.

The key difference between me and the standard catfish(er?) is I'm trying to help people. Always have, always will. But maybe someone else doesn't feel that way? Maybe someone thinks ol' Gustav done done 'em wrong and this is the beginning of some grisly campaign of payback? Maybe it's Odin even, wondering about me over there in New Valhalla, deep in the Black Forest? Maybe he's sent some minion of his to make a little trouble?

"Kurt's sponsoring you himself, isn't he?"

She glances at Kurt. He waves way too gregariously, like a five-year old trying to flag down Mommie at pickup. Oh, poor Kurt. He needs more help than I could possibly have imagined. I'm getting it done, though, don't worry. Kurt's my latest and greatest challenge, and I shall not fail him.

"Sure, but it's not about that."

"What?"

She brings one delicate hand to her mouth. "I know who you are," she whispers.

"Yeah, I know who you are, too, sis'. Don't worry. Outside these doors, mum's the word."

"I mean it, *Trickster.*"

I grunt in subhuman double take. I remind myself of that misogynistic chimp-impersonator fro *Suburban Monster.* Honestly, it's embarrassing. I'm not sure how that guy has managed to spend his entire adult life making that chimp sound and making money at it, not just little money either, but heap big money.

"I have no idea what you're talking about."

"You still don't recognize me?"

"From a few minutes ago, of course.."

"It's me, Sunshine."

"As in Sunshine the…?"

"Norn? Right!"

"How come you look so different? Whither the cowled face and pervasive attendant shadows?"

"I'm different now. I guess we changed. We were gone a long time, y'know?"

"Oh, I remember begging you and those sisters of yours to stay. What was that, eight centuries ago?"

"I should have anticipated this reaction. Not about my looks, though."

I shrug.

"You've changed a bit yourself, Loki. I mean, you're black now, y'know? Or is this just a disguise?"

"No disguise. This is my new, static state."

She smiles.

"I'm still not saying I believe you, whatever your name is."

She frowns.

"For starters, how'd you recognize me if I don't look like I used to. Which I don't."

"I'd know you anywhere, Loki. I'm surprised you didn't recognize me. I should probably be hurt."

"But how?"

"Your eyes."

"My last form's eyes were blue."

"Not the color. The energy."

"Are you sure you're not just some actress Odin's putting up to this?"

"Of course not. How can I prove it?"

"I really don't know. Give me a little while to check you out."

"Check me out? You've been checking me out for the last hour."

"You know what I mean."

"Oh, the giants, right? And Hel? Still running around with them?"

"They're my family."

"A pretty sordid lot if you ask me."

"They've changed, too. Just like me. And, supposedly, you."

"I'll give you twenty-four hours, but that's it."

"What if I say that's not enough time?"

She reaches for my wrist, grabs it tightly, and I feel something like a shock of electricity as she looks me in the eye. Yes, they're blue now, but somewhere, somehow, I can see the black gaze Sunshine used to have. Is this proof? No, it's not proof. But it's enough to freak me the fuck out, that's for sure.

I reply, "There's an Irish bar called McMurtry's a couple blocks back on Boylston."

"You mean the one you go to just about every night?"

"Have you been following me?"

"You go to a lot of support groups, don't you?"

I squint. "I'm trying to help people."

"And that writing workshop. What's the story with that?" she chuckles at her own pun.

"I'm helping them, too."

She slides her gaze down and to the left, as though she doesn't believe me.

"Really, this has been very encouraging. It's obvious you've already investigated me. We'll see how you like it."

"I'll meet you at McMurtry's day after tomorrow, ten p.m."

I leave ahead of Sabrina/Sunshine, then linger outside, blending into the shadows. A few minutes later I watch Kurt and her leave together. Never mind the Norn or un-Norn of it all, I'm beginning to wonder whether I can trust Kurt, my supposed buddy, fellow writer, and Sexaholics Anonymous shepherd.

THE DREAM THAT WASN'T

HAVE YOU ever had a dream you were falling? I know, right? They're the worst, leave you convinced you're about to die. Arms and legs cycling wildly, the ground grows beneath, you grit your teeth, brace for impact, only to wake a split-second later, panting like a hunted fox, sweating like a drugged racehorse. *Phew*, you think, grinning and shaking your head. *Good thing that wasn't real…*

I've had the falling dream myself. What, you think gods don't dream? Of course, we do. You'd be amazed what about. Actually, you wouldn't. It's become pretty tame. These days, I dream about things like going to Home Depot with my wife (I don't have a wife.) and hanging out at Starbucks pretending to write a novel (a little closer to reality, but not much). But every now and again, I have that same-old, scary-old falling dream, the one that wakes me cold, leaves me panting and shaking my head, thinking, *Good thing that wasn't real…*

There was this one time, though; this one time I had a different sort of falling dream, one I'm fairly sure you've never had because it wasn't a dream at all.

I REMEMBER floating, drifting through the boundless silence of space. I saw novae and quasars, wormholes, and comets. *Hmm,*

I thought, *this is nice.* You know, relaxing. *Maybe if I just chill here for a while, I could really sort some shit out.*

All of a sudden, though, almost as if in response to my sense of relaxation, I began moving, picking up speed as I went. No, there was no floating anymore, no lazy afternoon on a hammock in the Hamptons.

I'd been pushed, shoved, catapulted...pick your verb, whatever it was, something, or someone, had acted upon me. The speed grew: galloping horse to accelerating racecar to supersonic fighter. It didn't stop there. It kept increasing until finally I was moving faster than light, bounding seas of space in seconds, crossing eons in instants, flying through entire dimensions in the time it took to blink. Which was when I realized what was going on.

I remember screaming at the realization, screaming in a voice that probably sounded more than a little like Rosemary Woodhouse, "This is really *happening...*" before passing out.

WHO KNOWS how much time elapsed? Minutes? Weeks? Years? Eventually, though, I woke when I thudded to a stop on snowy Midgard, which you guys have taken to calling Earth. Physically unharmed—I am a god, at least I still was then—my chief reaction was one of surprise. Up until then we'd all gotten along swimmingly in Valhalla.

Which was when it came back to me. It was Odin who'd tossed me out on my ear. I still didn't know how. But I did know why. He blamed me for his eye, even though it wasn't my fault. It was the giants. Hell, I even warned him before it happened...

"Better watch it with the giants."

"Oh?"

"Check out Surtur's castle some time. He's got a whole room filled with miniature battlegrounds."

"Everyone needs a hobby."

We were in the throne room at Valhalla. This was after all the rest of them had gone home for the night—y'know, back to their individual castles, citadels, and what-have-you. We had just opened this fantastic cask of honey mead Odin had gotten in tribute from the elves, and he was feeling talkative. Nothing used to cheer Odin up like tribute, especially from the elves.

This was before the Norns left, before the Great Integration, before Odin decided to help Hitler, and they all fell to Earth. Yeah, it was before all the shit, the shit I will absolutely get to. Just give me time.

"Most of them have you in the middle."

"I'm right here." Like so many ageing patriarchs, Odin is a literalist, maddeningly so.

"They're miniatures, oh wise one. One for you, one for Thor, plenty of Valkyries." I left out the part about me in black armor leading the charge.

"Leches," he said, smiling faintly...or was that leering wistfully? It's always been hard to tell with Odin.

"You know how those giants are."

He nodded. Because he did. Forget the PR. Back in the bad, old days, long before this even happened, Odin and the giants were buddies. I mean, we're all the same ultimately, all descended from the same gene pool, much as we hate to admit it, much as we all try to turn life into a deadly game of 'us' and 'them.'

"Worst part is you only have one eye."

And that was when he laughed. He roared more like,

bending double and flapping his arms like some great bird. "If there's only one eye, how do you even know it's me?"

"It looks exactly like you and 'Odin' is written on its base."

"Hmm," he said. Negging his avian act and rising back to full height, he eyed me with both right and left for one of the last times. "Sorry, son, but I just don't believe you."

"Why not?"

"Let's say you've developed a bit of a reputation...Trickster... Sly One...Mischief Maker..." he said, tousling my hair.

"But I'm serious this time. I swear it on, on," I looked around, gaze settling on Sleipnir, Odin's magical eight-legged horse. God, how he loved Sleipnir. "I'll swear on Sleipnir."

"You are not swearing on Sleipnir," he said, clucking his tongue a couple times.

"Sleipnir's my child, Odin. If I feel like swearing on him, I will."

"On the contrary, son. Child or not, you gave me Sleipnir to settle a debt. You remember the time I saved you from being the main course at Trollfest, don't you?"

"I guess."

"You can swear on the wolf or the serpent if it means that much to you."

"It's not the same."

"Oh, I know." He chuckled.

"Odin, I'm completely serious about this. The giants have been plotting for centuries."

"Maybe you're being honest and maybe you aren't, Loki. The truth—the real, universal *All-Father's* truth—is everybody loves me, even the giants. I am the All-Father. What could go wrong?"

2

THE LAZY, LATE-NIGHT PARADE

WALKING HOME that night, Boston's sidewalks are empty, the streets clear but for the lazy, late-night parade of cabbies and cops, the whoosh and whirl of automotive glass and chrome that accompanies them. With the reduced foot and car traffic the city seems lonely, peaceful.

This is why I like the city at night. It seems pristine, shiny lights freely reflected in the icy, black glaze that covers its streets. So quiet it makes me think of my family, of what I've lost, of what I keep losing again and again.

Why do I try to forget Odin and the rest of them? The memories are painful, that's why. Even though they're evil. Even though I know they're evil; maybe it's not the sheer evil I abhor. Maybe it's their hatred of me, the litany of failed relationships, of lost chances at love, the millenias of lost love I see behind my eyes.

Don't let anyone tell you being on the outs with your family, even your foster family, is a good time. I mean, I still have Hel and the giants, but I miss Odin and all the rest of them. It's true.

THE MOON hangs neon bright against the diamond-studded black. Electric and relentless as a two-dimensional spotlight, it hides behind the north tower of the whitestone I call Chateau Loki. See it, there, peeking out, waiting to say hi.

Sure, I own the building, all seven floors of it, nine if you count the basement and sub-basement. The ones next door, too. Not that I occupy all of them, or any of them, in toto.

The top floors of Chateau Loki, though; yes, I live there with Hel and the Fenris Wolf, to use his Christian name. The giants stay there more often than they do at their own place and eat like termites who just discovered wood. Servants? Staff? No, man. The gross symbols of class or caste or tribe—those are Odin's things, not mine.

Not that I am without guilt about the way I live. I guess I'm a lot like one of your limousine liberals at this point. Shopping at Holistic Nutrition and Amazon Feedbag, ordering twenty-dollar beers and ten-dollar coffees, driving my Lokimobile—a white custom Tesla—hither and yon.

Seriously, in the face of all the privation I see around me, even in wealthy America, never mind the refugee camps that seem to be in every other country now, it makes me wonder. It makes me wonder whether any of us are going to make it. I mean, I believe chances are we, or at least you, will.

You keep surviving the seemingly un-survivable, gods help you. Sometimes it's not pretty watching you soldier through, though. I mean, if I weren't spending so much time trying to help you, I probably wouldn't be able to pry myself out of bed. As is, I still need my own space, a lot of it at that.

Thing is I don't really have to do anything to live like this. These days, in America, I seem to attract money. But it hasn't always been like that. During and after the war, I was homeless; first in Berlin, then Paris, Rome, and Athens. In spite of all the culture and history and wealth Europe had once held, there was only poverty and decay, every day a new adventure in want... Finally, I got so cold, tired, lonely, and hungry I did what I'd sworn I wouldn't. I went back to Germany.

Once I was there, Odin was easy enough to find, primarily because he found me. Oh, he gave me the usual two-step about making up, about being a family again, and I bought it, the way I always seem to. It didn't last long, though, that new era of good feeling.

Soon enough, I realized the reason Odin had sought me out. It wasn't paternalism, friendship, familial piety, or any of that horseshit. No, Odin was back at it with the magic. And he wanted my help. Paltry as his powers had become, he was trying every ritual he could remember, trying to turn the Nazi gold he'd slunk off with into, as he said, "Something I can work with."

No, I absolutely did not help him. No doubt that was one of the reasons I wore out my welcome so fast. Not that there weren't plenty of others willing to try. Frigga, Thor, Baldur, Heimdall, Tyr, all of them were in on it...Anyway, it was in the early fifties by the time I left Germany for good, by the time I headed back out on my own.

MIDNIGHT BY the time I'm inside. I find Surtur and Thyrm racked-out on one of the black leather sectionals in my cathedral-ceilinged great room, staring at the sprawling wall screen as it flickers in greens and whites and blues. Ever the elemental homebodies, a fire whispers in the stone hearth beyond. Sure, I had it put in. The giants insisted. Stones from Norway, remnants of castles long fallen, it reminds them of Jotenheim I guess. It reminds them of their, of *our*, eternal home.

A word on the giants before we go any further. They're not. Giants, I mean, not anymore. Sure, I still call them giants out of deference—those guys were kings once upon a time, they're owed some respect—but when they fell, they changed. We all did, but the giants more than most, more even than black-skinned me. The giants shrank...a lot, so much that they became, well...little people. You know, dwarves.

Their stubby, blue-jeaned legs and pudgy, work-booted feet up on the coffee table, the guys are drinking Bombay Sapphire martinis and smoking Don Carlos #4 maduros. They look like a pair of construction workers who just hit the numbers.

"Loki," I hear, in near chorus.

Fenris perks his head up, peers over the back of the couch. Sighting me, he leaps to the floor, rushes up for a quick game of Sniff-and-Slobber, collar jangling as he moves.

"I see you let yourselves in," I say, giving Fen a couple pats and moving towards the sofa. "Do I even need to ask whether you used your keys?"

Bashful smiles from both. If they weren't so cute, I don't know what I'd do. Give them a stern talking to? Box their ears? To bed with no dinner?

"You guys realize every time you do that there's a chance someone will call the cops?"

"Yeah, but you'd just get us sprung. Like you always do," Surtur replies.

"You're so sure?"

"Or we'd get ourselves sprung. Same difference."

Not that I really care. It's good for the giants to keep their skills fresh. After all, you never know what's going to go down and when. Take this situation with Sunshine/Sabrina. Who knows the who/what/where/which/when/why of it? That was true when I was a god, and it's true now that I'm a semi- or demi- or whatever I am.

I plonk down in the couch's big middle section. Fen follows, settles in next to me, and lolls his head in my lap, stares at me upside down, waiting to be petted. As I scratch the silvered fur on his chin, I realize what the giants have been watching, and I want to get up, walk back out the door and keep going until I hit, oh, Tahiti or so.

That's right: It's MSNBC International. The Germanic babble submerged beneath simultaneous interpretation and studio talking heads can mean only one thing: the German Chancellor's election everyone is obsessed with, the campaign to replace Merkel. It's basically down to former NATO general Greta Bruder, the so-called German Washington, and her opponent, neo-fascist businessman Reinhold Vekk.

Yes, you'd have thought they'd outlaw fascism in Germany after what happened with the Nazis. You'd have thought they'd outlaw fascism *everywhere* after what happened with the Nazis. Apparently, they haven't.

Vekk is ahead by a mile. But everyone over here, everyone in America, is still hoping somehow Bruder can pull it out. It's terrible to see an ally go so wrong—heart-breaking and terrifying in equal measures. I hate to think what it would be like to see a country as powerful as America go that way.

I think back to the war at times like this. I think about how you came through that. It wasn't nearly as clean as your documentaries make it seem. Hitler could have won. Perhaps even would have won had he kept his crazy in check and left Stalin alone. But he didn't, or maybe couldn't, in spite of all Odin's help.

Hel walks in, clocks the TV, and squints. "What's 'The German Washington' up to today?"

Petite and olive-complected with jet black hair, high cheekbones, and a big mouth (in more ways than one), Hel has one of those lineless, cherubic faces—now that she's got an actual face—that's a constant source of bemusement for her, consternation for me, and confusion for the rest of the material world.

Her favorite act is to cop the persona of an ambiguously aged twen-teen-something. Hair in a perky ponytail, smirk ever on, Hel walks the world ironically chain-smoking Gauloises and seriocomically chain-quoting Joan Didion. Her shtick routinely leaves bystanders wondering whether I'm beleaguered dad, deplorable cradle-robber, or some hitherto unexposed (sorry…) super-perverse admixture of the two. Honestly, it can be He-…oh, never mind…

"Immigration crisis," Thyrm replies.

"Four-part plan," Surtur adds.

"Any good?" Hel asks.

They nod. "Yeah, it's incredible."

Hel adds, "Not that it'll do her any good. We've seen this all before, right? Turkey, Poland, France. Vekk is gonna take it, and the Germans are gonna go back to being Nazis."

Why is Germany doing this to itself again, 20th century history still so close and clear in the rear-view? I could give you all kinds of explanations about changing demographics, the climate crisis, religion, and wealth concentration—and maybe those things are part of it—but the real problem is it's hard to tell yourself the truth about yourself.

Sure, it's easy to see the flaws in others. They practically scream at you, so loud you want to shake people, ask what the fuck they think they're doing. For some reason, when it's all about us, like in Germany today, people just don't want to hear it. They don't want to hear about authoritarianism or fascism, toxic nationalism, racism, or antisemitism. And they absolutely don't want to hear anything about Hitler or Nazis.

They're convinced they could never fall a second time to that sort of evil; so convinced they lie to the pollsters, so convinced they beat the hell out of reporters when asked why not enough of them lied to the pollsters, so convinced they talk about how bad it is in other countries. France, Britain, even Canada: the Germans think everyone but them is on the verge of falling to fascism. But they're the ones falling. Oh, yes, Germany is quickly becoming something they spent a century thinking they'd never be again.

"Second thought, can you just turn it off, guys? I'm not in the mood."

"Sure, I guess," Surt says, grabbing the remote, tapping Power with something approaching ceremony. When he looks back at me, he's got that glint in his eye, that spark that's come to portend drunken nights and skull-fucked mornings. "We've actually been waiting for you to get home anyway."

"Yeah, I'm not up for a night out, guys, not tonight."

Thyrm smiles. "Ha, no, it's not that."

Surtur winks at him and turns to me. "You're never gonna believe who called."

"A Norn?"

"A what?"

Sometimes, I forget what the giants and Hel know or, for that matter, don't. Sometimes, even for me, it's hard to keep all the lies, truths, and half-truths straight. I was the only one of us who ever lived on Asgard, who ever actually met and interacted with the Norns. And I don't talk about the bad, old days much at this point. Honestly, I do my best to forget them.

"Never mind."

"OK—"

"Shh," Surt says, hitting the remote's message button. "Let him listen for himself. Go ahead, Loki. Listen."

"Fine. But, in the meantime, how about one of those for me?" I ask, nodding at Thyrm as the messages queue up.

"Which?" Thyrm asks, gaze sliding from cigar to martini.

"Right," I reply.

Hel clears her throat and plops down in an armchair to the side of the hearth. She pulls out a Gauloise, lights up, takes a long drag, and exhales. She's smiling which I know means she already knows who my mystery caller is and that I'm not going to like who my mystery caller is.

Thyrm says, "I thought you didn't want to go out."

"Doesn't mean I'm not going to drink and smoke."

Both giants "meh." In chorus, they sound like sheep.

Which is when I hear this, "Son! How've you been?" It's Odin—Who else would call me son, right?—He's completely loaded, slurring liberally.

"Son?" Thyrm chuckles as he hands me my drink.

"Grampy!" says Hel. She sneers. "Fuck you, Grampy!"

Caught in mid-puff, Surt laugh-coughs, pulls the Fuentes from his lips. "How long's it been since he called you that?" he barks between hacks, like an anthropomorphized seal.

"I know, right?" I drain the glass, hand it back to Thyrm. "Another, barkeep."

"Coming up."

I take a Fuentes from the humidor in the center of the table, guillotine the tip, toss the nub in the tray.

"Wait, though, it gets even better. Way better." This is Surt.

"We need to meet," Odin adds, sniffling a little near the end.

"We?"

"Just wait," says Thyrm as he reaches over to pat Fen's flank.

"By we, I mean the whole family: Frigga, Thor, Heimdall, Baldur…"

"Baldur," Surtur says, practically spitting this time. "That prancing prick's got a lot of nerve showing his face."

"Least he didn't mention Tyr."

Fen raises his snout, grumbles. I pat him. Fen relaxes, drops his chin back onto the sofa.

From here Odin descends quickly and only marginally comprehensibly into a tearful jag of Old Norse. There's talk of Valkyries, blood oaths, and maybe even a giant chinchilla. He begs and begs for me to come, like it really is time for Ragnarök, aka the Big R. None of us are sure what exactly he's saying, but it's easy enough to tell when it's over. Once he hits click so do I.

"He's a mess," Hel offers.

"Always has been. What should I do?"

Hel: "You have to go see him obviously."

"I know."

"Even though it's probably a trap."

"I know that, too."

She nods.

"But I haven't given you guys the kicker yet."

"Kicker?" asks Hel.

"Supposedly…I met a Norn tonight."

Hel: "You mean one of those fate chicks you never let me meet, the ones you fell in love with?"

"Indeed, Hel, that's precisely who I mean. One of the fate chicks I never let you meet. But there was only one I fell in love with. Her name was Sunshine."

NO ONE'S impressed with news of the Norn, not even Fen. Which is disappointing. Fen is usually like a plant at a comedy show. He's a super-sentient support animal. I'd say he might as well be my kid, but he is, technically speaking.

The next day, I have Hel flex her Dark Web chops. Oh, yeah, Hel is the darkest, the web-iest. Is it her "pretend" age, the whole twen-teen thing? Or is it that the Dark Web is like the virtual underworld, her former namesake?

IDK. What I do K is that Hel can hack databases, security cameras, and just about anything else. She can also determine whether this Sabrina/Sunshine is a real human. Once Hel gathers her intel, I'll send out the giants in disguise, tell them to post up near McMurtry's and watch for Sunshine.

But there's one last thing that might help, one more potential data point. I need to call Kurt. Yeah, right, I don't know why I didn't think of this before. But Kurt's the line, in a sense, between me and Sabrina/Sunshine.

"Gustav," he answers, a sea of static warring with his voice and the ambient Dad Rock soundtrack. What is he listening to? Dave Matthews? John Mayer? Yeah, he plays guitar, not terribly well. But I'm not Van Halen either. Talk about gods.

"On the move?"

"That bad? You want to call me back later?"

"Nah, I can hear well enough."

"Sorry, man, this new uPhone sucks. IDK why I even bought it."

"Send it back."

"Probably should." He pauses. "You know, this is actually fortuitous."

"What is?"

"Your call."

"Oh?"

"Yeah. But you go first."

"I called to talk to you about Sabrina. I saw you guys leave together last night."

"You've got your eye on her already? Jesus, dude, do you ever stop? I was just giving her a ride home. You should be writing, not chasing women."

"It's not like that—"

"Because I was clear, wasn't I, Gustav? No romance with group members."

"It's not that. She just said some really weird stuff to me."

"Like what?"

"It was personal. But you can't, like, give me any more background on her, nothing at all? We're friends, aren't we?"

"We're friends." He pauses. "Fine. I guess there are a few things I can tell you if it will make you feel better."

"It will."

"She's from the north country."

"Norway?"

"Maine. Describes herself as a Sunday River snow bunny."

"And you believed that?"

"I guess."

"Where'd you find her?"

"Actually, she just called the helpline out of the blue the other night. We talked and I told her she should come to group. That's about it."

"How old is she?"

"Too young for you, that's how old she is."

"Man, you don't know the half of it."

"What?"

"Never mind. So, that's all she said? She's a snow bunny form Maine."

"Listen, buddy, I hate to say it. I mean, I'm not trying to make you feel bad, but besides being what, like a third of your age, she's completely out of your league."

"You think she's in yours?"

"Mine? I mean…"

I sense a 'maybe' lurking somewhere in Kurt's conversational substratum. I want to tell him he has no chance, like he just did me. But I can't bring myself to do it. Fortunately, he bails us both out.

"Whether I do or don't doesn't matter. She's been to group now, and there'll be no shenanigans. Don't you have enough problems with all these imported maids anyway?"

I laugh. You guys are so gullible. "True. Alright. Fine. I guess that will have to do. What did you want to ask me?"

"I need some help with my fantasy football lineup again."

"I don't know."

"There's no money on the line. It's just a bunch of guys pretending. Come on, man. Just one more time. Help a bro out."

"The whole lineup?"

"No, just the skill positions."

"You're sure there's no money on this, right?"

"Of course not. Just for fun."

TRAGICOMEDY FOR THE FALLEN, PART 1

ODIN'S SPEAR struck Valhalla's golden floor with a mighty thud, silvered veins of sorcerous power erupting from the point of contact, energy flying electric and jagged to the four corners of his throne room. This was One-Eye's signal for quiet, and I went along. We all went along.

"Mr. Hitler has a proposition," spake the All-Father, clearly pleased with himself.

1933, and it had been a long time—ages, literally—since his failed Great Integration, nearly a millennium since the Norns had deserted us. Finally, though, Odin could see himself back on top. He was practically giddy.

"Ahem," Hitler cleared his throat.

The would-be Master-of-the-Thousand-Year-Reich smiled fully—disturbingly so given his uneven, copper-tinged teeth. But behind that smile, I could see the rage in Hitler's gaze, the malice not so much masked as controlled. The ruddy-sweaty speed-freak complexion, the dark stains under the arms of that baby-shit-brown shirt, that weird shiny hair, and ridiculous half-stache. As the cops say, the guy was wrong, so wrong.

"Ah, right," Odin explained, sounding flirty, submissive. "He prefers 'Führer.'"

"Führer of what?" I asked, wriggling free from a couple Valkyries, Helvetica and Nonchalance if memory serves. Yeah, I know, strange names. Strange Valkyries, by the way. One-Eye never let me play with the ones I really had something in common with, Peace, who plays a mean game of chess, and Silence, who can really sing.

I swayed to my feet, grabbed a fresh tankard, and drained it as I composed my thoughts. I hadn't seen any of this coming, though I should have known there was a reason for Odin bringing me back after so many years on the outs. There always was. At the moment, though, I was just so happy to be home. It had been centuries.

"The Fatherland," Hitler replied.

"Father...what? Was this your idea?" I asked turning to Odin who threw up his hands in reply.

"Germany," Hitler said, as if he meant reality.

"You mean the Weimar Republic? There are no Führers, no Kaisers. Anarchists, Marxists, socialists, democrats, that's what you've got...it's a fucking fractious mess."

"That's all going to change. That's what Mr.—"

Hitler cleared his throat again.

"The *Führer* wants to talk to us about."

Odin was being so deferential, so polite. It was surreal, and I couldn't take it. I started breaking up, laughing. Practically, yeah...OK, fine, I was cackling by that point. Cackling like a mad scientist alone in his lab. Odin Asgard, Lord One-Eye, Mr. Hotshot-Topshit King of the Gods Himself, was groveling to this sweaty, little, Viennese weenie.

"Well, by all means, let's hear what...*the Führer* has to say."

"Ah," Hitler said, a grand mystery solved. "You must be Loki, this Jew the All-Father has told me of."

Man, did that little weenie have some guts, let me tell you: talking smack to a god, any god, what mortal does that? But then in my estimation, crazy will do that. I mean, look at this Vekk guy over in Germany. He's talking about Jews again, talking about how great they are at math, how great they are with money, how much he loves them. No one's standing up to him either, not even in Germany. I guess one of his daughters is married to a Jew—a Jew who incidentally has had enough plastic surgery to make him look a perfect Nazi. Apparently, that's Vekk's out. As long as you have a Jewish son-in-law who looks like a Nazi you can say whatever you want.

"Jew?" I asked, turning to Odin, who feigned surprise. "I'm a pagan deity, you nitwit."

Hitler sneered; the hate no longer masked. If only I'd done more that day, if only I'd been able to stop them. I tell myself I tried, and I did, but I could have done so much more. We all could have, including you. And not just then, but now. Today.

I turned to Odin, "You're not actually thinking of helping this schmo, are you?"

Odin raised his tankard, the sign for a refill. "We'll talk later."

HITLER FINALLY disappeared, dematerialized really, dissolving in a waterfall of dying light, like Princess Leia telling Obi-Wan he's our only hope. Which is when Odin hauled me into one of the throne room's antechambers and closed the door behind us.

"Son," he began.

"Oh, here we go."

"The reason I called you back is this Hitler guy."

"Yeah, I get that from the meeting we just had."

"I need your help. If we're going to make this work, we need everyone on board. And…"

"What?"

"I don't know. I was hoping you'd tell me. Aren't you supposed to help me with image consulting?"

"I already told you," I said. "I'm not helping with this."

"Will you at least give it some time, watch what he's doing down there, the way he's unifying them all? It could really work to our advantage. He could get them to worship us again. Wouldn't you like that?"

"Not really. I've never had many worshippers, remember?"

"Oh, sure you have."

"A few. But nothing like you. And I don't really care whether I have them or not. I never have."

"But I care. Can't you see how much it matters to me, your dear old dad?"

There was Odin's "real" emotion. He was playing me for the thousandth time and even then, even when I knew it was happening, I couldn't stop it. What is it with family, that makes you want to try again and again?

"But he's evil."

"So are you!"

"Says you."

"Fine, maybe you're not. But, son, I need you. Will you at least give it a little time? Watch him, see how things go. Help me make it work. I know we can do it."

"Yeah?"

"Yes. And if we do well enough maybe that will even get the Norns to come back. Wouldn't you like to see Sunshine again?"

"Of course, I would. But it's been eight centuries. I hardly think us helping some strongman preach 'law and order' will bring the Norns back."

"Couldn't hurt," Odin said. Gaze going wide, he looked down and away, as if saddened by the very fabric of reality, still more by the eternally disappointing family of flunkies who surrounded him, our current situation a perfect example.

"That doesn't make any sense at all, but you know how hard it is for me to say, 'no,' to you."

"I do," he replied, looking up, his eyes completely dry.

"I'll do what you want, this watching and waiting thing, at least for a little while."

"Sure, sure, give it a decade or two, tops. I'm telling you, this guy is top-notch, a fine human if I've ever met one."

And there I was, a victim of Odin's real emotion, yet again.

3

WHITE GUY SOUL SHAKE

OWNED BY a Lithuanian with ties to the Russian mob and managed by a Polish ex-body builder named Israel, McMurtry's is your typical slice of Americana: a place where languages, religions, and races collide, money acting as simultaneous interpreter. It's the sort of place that once you're a regular—which I am—they'll let you do pretty much whatever you want—which I do. I go there to write and drink, mostly to write. Oh, who am I kidding? I go there mostly to drink.

I arrive at ten, fresh off a check-in with the giants. They're outside, in position, ready to follow Sunshine, Sabrina, or whoever she is once our meeting ends.

Of course, I came. Even if I'm not what you might call "game," this woman has something, and I need to know what it is. Is she a full-on Norn? Is she my once-beloved Sunshine?

No, she doesn't look like the Norns did back in the day. Their appearances were essentially identical, so close in fact that I wound up in awkward situations with Sunshine and her sisters more than twice. Most of the time, they wore dark, flowing gray robes, with cowls that left their faces obscured, but for the scantest view of neck.

No, the Norns weren't always the most aesthetically

pleasing trio back then, but they didn't need to be. These were Fate's handmaidens! They knew things, things no one else did or could. That was what they did all day, just sat around spinning threads on The Wheel of Fate, learning about the lives of every creature: Animal and vegetable, giant, god, and man.

As special creatures will, they tired of being part of the parade of failures our religion became. And they put it to Odin, told him if he didn't get things moving, they were gonna walk. They gave him plenty of warning, too, well over a century. And he tried. Well, mostly I tried. At any rate, trying was involved. Failing, too.

So, they left, finally, unceremoniously. Sure, Sunshine stopped by to tell me she'd return, someday, when it was time for Ragnarök. Of course, I cried. I begged and pleaded even though I'd seen it coming for a while. But Sunshine and her sisters were serving Fate, and Fate had told them we were a waste of energy.

Fast forward eight-hundred-some years, and I think you'll understand why I need more details. Because, either way, the fact that Sabrina or Sunshine or whoever she is thinks I'm the Norse god, Loki, is…troubling. Primarily because I *am* the Norse god, Loki, and that's not something I've been looking to feature here on Earth. Like I keep telling you: I'm not the horn-helmed lunatic popularized in comic books, films, and even the basic, half-baked mythos Odin's been pushing since he could get anyone to listen. I'm good. I'm here to help.

MCMURTRY'S IS dark, as usual, a weak, molasses hue fallen across the entire scene. The scents of spilt beer, illicit cigarettes, and fried cod permeate the place—stale and sugary; smoky and sulfurous; burnt and oily. To tell you the truth, it smells a lot like Valhalla in the old days.

A frowning Sabrina/Sunshine waves me over. "Some place," she offers, "I was starting to think you wouldn't show."

"Then this must be a pleasant surprise." I plant myself in the captain's chair across from her. Its frame squawks in something like protest.

"You want one?" she asks.

"A pleasant surprise? I'd love one."

"A drink." She nods towards the flute on the table in front of her. Half full of a pale, golden liquid, bubbles bunch at the bottom of the glass. Every now and then one shakes free, floats upward for a millisecond, and explodes.

"What is that?"

"Champagne spritzer."

"Ch-what?" I squint. "They actually let you order that?"

McMurtry's is a Jameson's and Guinness joint all the way. Still, I guess if you look like Sabrina/Sunshine, you can get whatever you want wherever you go. I should know that already, though, shouldn't I? Come to think of it, so should you.

"Meaning?"

"Never mind," I say, nodding to the bartender Yuri, mouthing 'usual.' "Let's get back to the reason you brought me here."

"I already told you, Loki. It's simple: I know who you are. That's why I brought you here. The more important question is why you came."

"Hey!"

"What?"

"You just flipped that on me."

52

"I did."

"Alright, maybe I'll tell you. After you tell me where the Jotenheim you've been for the last eight hundred years?"

She nods. When she doesn't say more, I nod, too.

"You mean now? Oh, OK, fine." She takes a sip of her spritzer, sets it down, and spills. "We wandered after we left Asgard. We were interstellar nomads, moving from plane to plane, looking for a spot in the space-time continuum where we might make a difference, serve Fate again."

"Which I assume you did?"

"Sure, after a few centuries."

"That long?"

"It's a big multiverse. We were aimless at first, depressed, dispossessed."

"I'd say escaping One-Eye was the smartest thing you ever did."

"It's not as easy as you're making it sound, Trickster. What do you think it's like being an afterthought in a religion only to see it fail?"

"Yeah, well, I've got a little experience with stuff not working out, too."

"But you always had a place in the religion, a high place."

"As the force of evil?"

She mehs. "The humans had completely forgotten us by the time we left. You remember how many Norns there were when we started out."

"Sure, there were even more of you than the Valks. You were as common as fur on a cat or sand at the beach."

"You can stop agreeing."

"I don't know what you expect. Odin stripped most of my

powers the last time he launched me from Asgard. Then most of the bit I had left…er…*left*…when Hitler killed himself and the rest of them fell. I can barely make a cup of coffee at this point."

"I'll get to that. But let's start off with this Hitler fella. Tell me about him?"

"You don't know about Hitler?"

"Of course, I've done the research. But I need to hear it from your lips. I want to know what really happened between you guys and Hitler?"

"Odin just kept getting worse. The decades went by, then turned to centuries, and the worship kept dwindling. He blamed me, of course, kept launching me from Asgard for this or that infraction."

"And I suppose you weren't doing anything wrong? No legitimate reasons to be 'launched?'"

"OK, maybe I wasn't always perfect, maybe some of it was legitimate."

She nods.

"But since I've been here on Earth this last time. I'm…"

"You're."

"I'm—"

"What?"

"Good."

"Even though you helped Hitler?"

"Helped Hitler? Did Odin tell you that?"

"It wasn't Odin. But, yes, someone suggested it. And, umm, you're known by your reputation, Loki. Of course, you know I've always been on your side." She reaches across the table, pats my hand. "But my sisters are sure this is all your fault."

"All what's my fault?"

"Everything that's gone wrong since we left."

"Everything? It's Odin's fault. Odin and all the rest of them. They were desperate for power. When Odin found out Hitler was intrigued by Norse myth, he had his in."

"But that doesn't sound like something Odin would do. Sure, he was never as good as he made out. But he is the All-Father. And you were…?"

"I was what?"

"Well, OK, this isn't me talking. You know I always cared about you." She pats my hand again. I pull it back. "But my sisters…they're sure you're still the force of evil."

"Force of evil?"

"Right."

"I just played a few tricks."

"They don't see it that way. They're convinced helping Hitler was your idea, that you lured the other gods in."

"It was Odin's idea."

"I believe you. But they're going to take a lot of convincing."

"Why does it even matter? There's no way we could put on a decent Ragnarök at this point. There aren't even any Valkyries anymore."

"They were everywhere at New Valhalla."

"No?"

"Yes."

"You've been there?"

"Of course. My sisters are there now with Odin."

"And you saw Valkyries?"

"Lots of them."

I catch Yuri's eye, mouth, 'double.'

"All right, Sa-…Sun-…er, whatever, fair is fair. Let's hear a little more about this supposed tour of the cosmos."

"We wandered a long time, finally wound up in this pocket dimension that…y'know, felt right. A place we thought we could be happy, make ourselves useful."

"Pocket dimension?"

"Like a parallel dimension, just smaller."

"If you say so."

"It was dreamy there, low stress. The entire reality was populated by sentient, bisexual plants. They were like, 'Do whatever. Just don't hurt anyone.'"

"What did they want in return?"

"Nothing. They just let us hang out. Said we could stay as long as we wanted."

"What about serving Fate?"

"Oh, there was Fate there. We had things to do."

"So, why leave?"

"No idea. I thought things were going great, then all of a sudden one day my sisters disappeared…Poof!"

"They're dead? I thought you said they were with Odin."

"I didn't say dead. I said, 'Poof!' They disappeared. You know, into the cosmos." She waves her hands as though preparing to break into some serious kung fu. "I had no choice but to follow them here, to Midgard."

"They call it Earth now."

"What sort of name is that?"

"It's just what they call it. If you go around saying 'Midgard-this' and 'Valhalla-that' somebody's going to rat you out to Homeland Security."

She squints. "Don't."

"Don't what?"

"Don't ask, 'What does any of this have to do with me?'"

"OK."

Jenni, the waitress, arrives with my Jameson's. Yuri must have picked up on my situation. The thing's a triple, maybe even a quadruple, amber liquid sloshing over the edge of the glass. I slurp at the rim, bring the contents to a reasonable level before setting down the glass. Sabrina/Sunshine brings the flute to her lips and drains it.

"You want another?" Jenni asks.

"I shouldn't. This champagne stuff is tasty, but it gives me headaches."

"Why don't you just rejoin your sisters?"

"You don't understand. I ran away."

"Why?"

"Odin wants us to help you get your powers back."

"Me?"

"All of you. And he's convinced my sisters."

"How?"

"Ragnarök, obviously. They believe it's time. And Odin's reformed. That's what he says."

"He's spent the last seventy-five years helping them. He still is."

"Helping who?"

"That Vekk guy over in Germany for one."

"The National Front candidate? The one who keeps a book of Hitler's speeches by his bed?"

I nod.

"But can you prove it? Because he's got my sisters convinced."

"Maybe with some work."

"Good," she says, "That's a start."

"A start of what?"

"Odin's going to invite you to New Valhalla. He wants you to help him."

"Help him do what?"

"Find me, among other things."

"And what are the other things?"

"I don't know exactly! You'll need to figure that out."

"This is all...I don't know, Sa-...Sunshine...whatever. You guys roll out eight hundred years ago, now you're back with with some kooky story about arboreal pocket dimensions. I'm going to have to give this some more thought."

"I told you we'd be back. You remember, don't you?"

"The last kiss? How could I forget?"

She smiles.

"Don't look so pleased with yourself. I haven't said I'd help you."

"Why not?"

"I like being human. Close to human, at least."

"Oh, you do not?"

"I do. It's like what you said about the Plantiverse or the Arboreal Dimension or whatever it's called. It's relaxing. All that cosmic destiny, gotta-do-this-gotta-do-that, Ragnarök maybe tomorrow, maybe the next day stuff is a bad trip."

"You can have a little time." Nodding crisply, she opens her purse, pulls out paper and pen, and scribbles for a few seconds. She hands me the paper.

I look down. 'Tonight, midnight,' is written on the paper.

"I'll come to where you live. Start thinking now," she says, rising, staring down at me. "Because I'll expect an answer."

"Why didn't you just say that?"

"I felt like writing it down. Is that OK with you?"

"I guess."

"Now, stand up, I need to try something," she says.

"What?"

"Just do it."

"Yes, mistress," I stand there, smirking at her.

All she does is glare at me. For five seconds, then ten, fifteen. Honestly, I'm beginning to wonder if she's gonna take a swing. Y'know, test my chin. But she doesn't. She steps around the table, swoops in, and kisses me full on the lips. No tongue, not even an open mouth. But the electricity. *Zamm-o.*

I close my eyes, draw in the sensation. I feel like I'm spinning in darkness, like the old days. And that's when I realize this is Sunshine, no question. A few seconds later I open my eyes and catch a glimpse of her leaving, the night air bracing as the door swings shut.

"Go after her," says Yuri.

"Timing's all wrong."

"Timing looked pretty right to me."

I WALK out the door and run right into someone, nearly knocking us both to the ground. I look up, and it's Kurt.

"Gustav," he says, "Did you see where Sabrina went? She was supposed to give me a ride home."

"Sabrina? Oh, right, yeah, I thought you said you weren't involved with her."

"I just said she was giving me a ride home. I didn't say we were going to an orgy together."

"Sure, you did."

"Is that mistrust I'm catching?"

"Could be."

"Look, Gustav, we've been over this, right? One, I'm not lying to you. Two, no fiddling around with other group members. And three, she's about fifty years too young for you and way out of your league besides."

"That's actually four," I say, turning to the glass front of McMurtry's where I see our reflections there staring back at us. Yeah, sure, Kurt's mildly good looking, but somebody's getting a little (or a lot) carried away with himself. "Seriously, though, dude, do your eyes still work?"

"What's that mean?"

"It means, look at us."

"Look at us. Objectively speaking, I'm quite handsome. I look like Denzel with just a dash of Taye Diggs. And you, well…"

"Me, well, what?"

"At best, you're a middle-aged James Spader."

"Middle-aged? I've still got hair," he says, running his hand through it. He's not lying. He's got a lot.

"Fine. Pre-TV James Spader."

"I like James Spader. Some people find James Spader very attractive."

"Sure, man. There's nothing wrong with James Spader. But he ain't Denzel."

"And you are?"

"Shit, man, just look."

He does. "OK, fine, I can sorta see it. I shouldn't have said the thing about you being fifty years too old."

"Thank you."

"You're thirty years too old, tops." He smiles.

"Touché."

"You really didn't see where Sabrina went?"

"I didn't."

He shakes his head. "Guess I'm walking home."

"Call an Uber."

"I could use the steps."

We team up on a white guy soul shake and head our separate ways. Once Kurt's out of earshot I'm on the phone with the giants. I tell Surtur to keep following Sunshine. I tell Thyrm where to pick up Kurt's trail.

YOU DOUBT MY RAVENS?

VEINS OF LIGHT, luminous as molten silver etched a frosty, alien language across Valhalla's golden walls. More than heat or pure, physical energy, these were the signatures of ancient magics, sorceries abiding since before Odin's time, powers even he didn't understand.

I was back on his home court, seeing Valhalla for the first time in centuries, and maybe I should have been scared. I wasn't, though, not a bit. I was happy to be home, soaking it all in. This was my first of many homecomings. And I thought, as I always seemed to, that I was back for good.

1000 A.D. give or take. I was to one side of the throne (*Odin's* Golden Throne), lounging on a pile of furs—Asgardian lynx and Jotunheimian bear, Niflheimian mammoth and Midgardian fox; the product of One-Eye's multifarious hunts.

Valks fluttering hither and yon, I was on my fourth Mead of Poetry; and I was more than a little snockered. In spite of that, I was, at least as I remember it, reeling off a mean bit of iambic hept. I was staring at Odin's golden ass-holder, thinking how good I'd look sitting there, watching its silvered reliefs writhe with the magic within, just like the walls, when Himself piped up.

"What is the purpose of wisdom?" he said, his glare

imperious. Dude is always so serious, so self-absorbed, like the meanest of his intellectual farts represent high fucking art.

"To bring triumph in battle," boomed Thor, flexing, always flexing.

If you have siblings, particularly a lot of siblings, you know there's always one who's the favorite, often in spite of having few redeeming qualities. A lot of the time, favorites are lazy, stupid, and talentless, but somehow, in spite of those reasons—or, perhaps because of them—they become the apples of their parents' eyes.

"To make us just rulers," said Tyr, rubbing his stump, for all the good Odin's brand of "justice" ever did him.

"To protect beauty from the decay that is evil," said Baldur, tossing his hair, stroking his beard.

Baldur had a point. He's a long story is Baldur, the one of my "brothers" with whom I have the most complex relationship. Me being a shapeshifter and liar, the God of Mischief; him being undeniably beautiful and non-gendered in his way...sure, there was bound to be something between us. Was it love? I'm not sure I'd go that far. I mean, it wasn't like what I felt for Sunshine. But there was something well beyond liking that went on.

Who was the top, you wonder? We took turns, of course. How do you like them apples? Sure enough, though, Thor and Odin were bound to wreck it. Whatever it was we had, they were bound to turn it into things it never was. And in the end to turn love into hate and sex into murder: those are some of Odin's greatest tricks.

"Hmm," said the All-Father, scanning the main hall of fair Valhalla. Our eyes locked. Squinting gravely—and perpetually monocularly by that point—he asked, "Loki, what is *your* answer?"

I rose to my feet and stepped towards the throne, passing a sleeve across my lips as I did. These were the bad, old days; and honestly, it was a necessary precaution. Sometimes when I got too close to the throne I'd actually start to drool.

Was I evil, then? A thief? A usurper? A murderer? No, no, no, and no. OK, maybe a little, but mostly not. I just wanted what Odin had *made* me want, what he *wanted* me to want. But he wanted something else, something I was unable to ken till much later; something that has always eluded poor, blundering Thor.

Odin found the best way to maintain his power—the best way to make himself feel good—was to have two heirs and to make them fight with each other, make them fight so much, so bitterly, and for so many years, that they never had time to focus on him, let alone band together and take him down.

"Wisdom? Meh…Wisdom's not my thing. I do tricks, not wisdom."

"You must have an opinion. You're my heir."

"Supposed," Thor whispered, too loudly. Which is a complete understatement. Thor's whispers hit the air with the force of crashing waves.

"Sorry, I don't. Really."

Odin stared at me with disbelief, disdain, and probably a few other dis-es. That one, that dis-ing look of his always used to work on me back then. And maybe it still does. You and I both, *all of us*, spend our lives looking for the approval of our fathers. But approval comes in many forms. Sometimes the approval you want is to make the father in question so angry he takes action.

"What does this have to do with anything?" I asked in response.

"The birds," he whispered, lips pursing with cryptic effect.

"Birds?"

"The black ones," he added, the pitch of his voice rising as he motioned vaguely towards the ceiling. Far above, hanging on gilded perches, loomed two dots of feathered jet, Odin's ravens, Knowledge and Afterthought.

You'd think with all the power he had, and all the extra knowledge, that he would have been better at explaining things. Not so. Used to fly off at the slightest challenge to his logic. And he's only gotten worse since we fell.

"Oh, the ravens? Did they tell you something again?"

He nodded solemnly, and I knew where this was going. At that moment, the last thing I wanted was to leave Valhalla, to go on some sort of vague "quest for wisdom"—especially based on a game of avianic telephonics One-Eye had drunken delirium-ed into being.

For their part, the birds gazed blankly into the distance, enthralled by this or that beam of golden Asgardian oak, squawking dumbly from time to time. Clearly, Odin's cherished ravens were not engaged. I was sure that, as usual, Odin had made the whole thing up in his head; that he was insane or careless or both, telling us to jump, listening hungrily for, "How high?"

"I'm really not feeling anything. You sure about this?"

Odin rose from his throne. Claiming *Gungnir* he slammed its butt on Valhalla's golden floor. *Krangg,* spake the spear.

"You doubt *my ravens*?" he roared, the two birds squawking once more then taking flight.

Circling the hall, they flew crying, screaming, shitting, and pissing, generally making a hell of a racket and even more of a mess. Out they went, finally, into the white light beyond, and I began to get this sickening feeling. I was going to have to follow, and there was nothing I could do about it. Which didn't mean I was beyond trying.

"They are just birds. You have to admit."

"*Just birds*?????" By this point he was squinting at me again. His face scrunched up and flushed, he reminded me of a Cyclops with conjunctivitis. Yes, I've seen them, and it's not pretty. I knew it was time for damage control. I knew it was time to dance.

"All right, all right. Super genius spirit ravens...?"

"With prophetic powers," he added, nodding in that self-satisfied way he's always had.

Like I said, birds. It's always struck me how susceptible to language the rest of the gods are. Not just from me, either. How do you think they wound up falling under Hitler's spell? I mean, the weirdest part of how everything went down with the gods and Hitler was how symbiotic it became in the end. It really did feel almost like fate in a sick way; like he was destined to be the conduit for their (for our?) demise.

"That's better," Odin said.

I turned back to Helga the Valkyrie, held out my horn so she could pour me another Mead of Poetry, hoped Odin would forget what he'd been talking about. He tended to do that, you know, even back in those days. A lot of irons in the fire, a lot of spheres of influence. All-Father and all that.

Odin's voice thundered through the hall, "What are you waiting for, Christmas?"

"Christmas?" I asked.

"The Christians," he said, "It's their holy day. One of them."

"How many do they have?"

"A lot, apparently."

"More than a week's worth?"

He nodded somberly. "Yes, now get going." He glared, his grip tightening on *Gungnir*.

"I feel like you want me to go somewhere or do something, but I'm honestly not sure what it is."

"You must seek wisdom. You must seek the Norns."

"You want me to go see the Norns?"

"Yes."

"Alone."

"Yes."

"And, what, you're going to have Thor attack me once no one can see?"

"Really?" Thor asked, twirling *Mjolnir* for effect.

"There will be no attacks. But you must go see the Norns. They have…"

"What?"

"Requested it."

"Requested?" asked Thor. "You sure you don't just want me to attack him? Modi and Magni, you up for it, sons?"

They hopped to, of course, reflexively flexing like dear old Dad. Have you ever been to a bodybuilding event? You know at the end, where all the finalists have a posedown? Yeah, so that's what it's like seeing Thor and his two sons together. So much flexing, so little thinking.

"There will be no interference with the will of Fate," said Odin. "Now, go, Loki, you have been summoned. The ravens have spoken."

"Fine, fine, I'm going."

"Better hurry, too," he said, smacking his lips. "I can taste snow in the air."

Back on Asgard, it always tasted like there was snow in the air, even though it rarely actually snowed. When it did, it was a great portent, a sign that the Norns were at the height of their powers.

Well, that day, that time, I'd barely gotten outside when it started coming down. Yes, I knew I was in for a long, torturous trip to Mount Norn, unless I sped things up considerably. I did what anyone would have done in my position: I turned myself into a giant Asgardian eagle. Yes, it was cold; but it was also fast.

4

ALWAYS BRIGHTEST BEFORE THE FALL

THE SIDEWALK'S narrow, and there's a young couple in front of me doing that walking and making-out thing people do when they're so in love they don't see anyone else. I'm on the verge of crossing to the other side of the street when Surtur calls.

"Speak," I tell him, stopping flat.

I must say it too loudly because the couple turn and look back as though I just goosed them with a fire hose. When they see it's only little, old me—and not a goose with a fire hose—they laugh and go back to walking and making out.

"You're not going to like this, but they're in cahoots."

"They who?"

"They Kurt and the Norn."

"Kurt, seriously? How? Why?"

"Her room is cleared out. Only thing I found is a match book from The Genetic Impossibility."

"The strip club?"

"Yep, just peeking out from beneath the bed."

"What does that prove?"

"It's got your buddy Kurt's address and phone number inside."

"I still don't know what that proves. She knows Kurt. He's the reason I met her."

"If you say so."

"It's not, 'If I say so.' It's how it is."

"If you say so."

"Fine, I don't have time for this back and forth. You said the room is completely cleared out?"

"Yep."

"What about Thyrm?"

"Still tailing Kurt. Dude's wandering around aimlessly over by McMurtry's, doing laps. It's sort of sad."

"I guess Sunshine really did stand him up."

"There's something else: Heimdall is following Kurt."

"My brother, Heimdall?"

"Yeah. He's disguised but it's obviously him. You remember how terrible his disguises are, don't you?"

"How could I forget? I'm the one who taught him to do everything wrong."

"That was a good one, Loki. Top-notch."

"OK. I want you to go rifle through Kurt's apartment while Thyrm keeps an eye on Heimdall. You should have at least thirty minutes before he's home. And tell Surtur to make sure he's not being followed by somebody working with Heimdall."

"Is there something specific I should be rifling for?"

"Anything that has to do with me or Sunshine."

"And he thinks your name is what?"

"Gustav Johansson."

CHATEAU LOKI. The great room is right below the building's formerly three-level North Tower. I had the tower's floors blown out to create a vault. When the fireplace is going, and the lights are off you can't beat the shadows. And I do love shadows. Let your mind, soul, and memory go and you can see just about anything in the mass of shadowy shapes: a ballet, a murder, a ballet of murders, people fucking, people fighting, people screaming. Yeah, you can see the whole universe in those shadows if you look hard enough.

Hel and I are smoking a joint, talking strategy, and playing a fake game of chess when the knock comes at the door. The chess game is for Sunshine's benefit. Hel's killing me.

I've lost my queen, both bishops, a knight, a rook, and six pawns and taken nothing off Hel in the process. I imagine this is how the board would look if Kasparov were playing a chimp. Yes, of course, Hel set it up this way, but it was my idea.

"Go get it, Fen."

Fen gives a short, happy bark, jumps down off the couch, and jogs across the floor in the direction of the foyer. Jingle-jangling all the way, he bangs the tip of his ample snout against the automatic opener.

I always think, man, that must hurt. But he just keeps doing it, so it must not. Seems to love it, in fact. I guess it's hard to understand the advantages and limitations of large dog snouts if you don't have one. I mean, sure, I've done time as a canine on occasion, back in the old days mostly. Memories fade, though, even for gods.

The doors swing wide, and I see Sunshine standing there, backlit by the hall lights, the private elevator's golden doors beyond. She's wearing a tan shearling coat and knee-high boots. She's carrying a suitcase, one of those metallic smart-bag type things actual airports won't let you use. She's got a big, underfilled duffel slung over her shoulder.

"Ladies and gentlemen," I offer, rising and moving towards the door. "This is Sunshine. She's a Norn."

Fen grumbles.

"You're the gentleman, Fen."

He yips.

Sunshine steps inside and the door closes behind her. She curtsies, sort of. Fen looks up at her and wags his tail. "The Fenris Wolf, I presume?"

Fen licks her hand, nuzzles up to her.

"I see you've changed quite a bit, too," she adds.

He wags his tail, wags it so hard it goes thump-thump-thump against the wall.

"Maybe you were telling the truth, Loki?"

"Sunshine. You've…brought so much stuff. Were you planning on staying a while?"

"I'm not going back where I came from, one way or another."

"That sounds ominous."

"It's meant to."

Sunshine follows me back across the room, her heels tapping out an echoey morse code. Yeah, the vaulting effect gave the great room good acoustics, too. Sunshine sits, crosses her legs, and eyes the board. Fen stops short, stands gazing at her.

Looking down at the board, she asks, "Who's white?"

"That would be me."

"But you used to be so good at chess"

"He's met his match," Hel offers.

Sunshine nods gravely.

Hel surveys Sunshine, "So, this is a Norn? You always said they were fearsome. She doesn't look so tough."

"You described us as fearsome?"

"Well, you did look a bit different before."

My phone vibrates and I check my DMs. It's Surtur.

"Kurt implicated further. Found a phone number for 'H.' scrawled on a piece of note paper from a Gothic Lodge Motel. Called it from burner. No answer, but H. must be Heimdall, right? Busting through the doors in 3, 2, 1…"

As I look up, several ungainly thumps come at the front doors. A few more seconds and they swing wide, the giants stumbling in. They hit the lights as they do. Squints all around.

"Loki," they say, tripping deeper in as the doors close behind them.

Once they're close enough, they pretend to just notice Sunshine. "Oh," they say.

"This is Sunshine," says Hel, "She's a Norn. You know, those fate chicks Loki never let us meet."

"Nice to meet you," the giants say, bowing, blushing.

Hel shakes her head.

"So, that's everyone, then? Except…what about the Serpent?"

"Jormungandr is still MIA."

Fen grumbles. I mean, that's his brother, and Fen wonders where he is. We all do. The simple answer is nobody knows. Sure, we located Jormungandr at one point, found him hanging out in Loch Ness goofing on people. Remember all the stories about how Nessie was growing? There is no Nessie, never has been. But there was a Jormungandr there for a while.

Yeah, people think being the Midgard Serpent and all, having a role like squeezing life from a dying world, you wouldn't be that bright. But it's not true. Oh, he's not as smart as Hel, to be sure, but it's a dead heat between him and Fen. Anyway, I have no place to keep him. Jormungandr didn't change nearly enough to be manageable. And, so, he pretends to be Nessie or any other number of mythical sea creatures. You'd think not knowing exactly where he is at any time would give me some comfort that Ragnarök's not going to happen in the next ten minutes. Not so. If history has taught me one thing, it's not, "It's always darkest before the dawn." My history has taught me, "It's always brightest before the fall."

"Fine, then, do you have a decision? Maybe you'd like me to go for a walk so you can confer with your…advisors?"

"Oh, I'm going to Germany."

"Excellent. When do we leave?"

"We don't. You'll stay here with the giants and Fen. Though not here exactly. Apparently, you're being followed."

"Oh?"

"By Heimdall."

The giants nod in unison.

Sunshine nods slowly in return. Yeah, she doesn't look terribly surprised by the revelation. I could construe that as evidence I can't trust her or evidence she doesn't trust Odin, couldn't I? Both?

"You have someplace safer than this? Someplace Odin and the others won't be able to find us?" she asks skeptically.

"Absolutely, places upon places. The giants and Fen will guard you, make sure you're safe from both Aesir and Vanir."

"What about me?" asks Hel.

"You're coming with. In case I need backup."

"Ooh, a chance to spar with Grampy. I thought you'd never ask."

TWO A.M. I'm packing, and you wouldn't believe what a pain in the ass it is. Packing, you think, come on?

Imagine never having to pack a day in your life. Imagine always being able to wriggle your nose, say 'poof,' or whatever other kooky thing you feel like saying and having whatever you want blip into existence. Then try losing that ability without any warning. It would suck, right? And it does.

Besides which, Sunshine insists on watching me pack. Which, currently, involves perusing the contents of my bedroom and commenting on them as I throw a few days' worth of duds in a carry-on.

"It's not like things were perfect before, Trickster."

"Right. Odin was running everything into the ground."

"It wasn't just Odin."

"Oh?" I ask.

"OK, fine, it was mostly Odin, but it was all of you."

"Even me?"

"I know you've always thought you were good, that all Odin's 'PR' as you call it has been 'fake news,' but my sisters never trusted you. You did help him, didn't you? You helped him quite a lot actually."

"Not even when we were together?"

"Not even what? Oh, my sisters trusting you? No, especially not when we were together. And they still don't."

"It's been centuries!"

"You remember what happened, I know you do."

"Which time?"

"Precisely."

"This is getting too heavy," I say, staring at the bag.

"Take something out."

"I meant the conversation. Anyway, haven't we already gone over all this? Isn't this why I'm going to Germany?"

"OK, fine, pick something lighter."

"Alright, what's the deal with you and Kurt?"

"That's lighter?"

"Depends on your answer."

"I read the beginning of his book."

"What, that serial killer thriller thing? Yeah, it's not bad. Might make a few shekels."

"No, this is something completely different. It's new. He just started it."

"And?"

"Actually, it's really good. I was surprised how good. You really never know with humans, especially writers. They can fuck around for decades then write one thing and it's all people remember."

"Sounds like you're getting pretty chummy. Is there anything else you're swapping other than reading materials?"

"Well, I didn't say we swapped anything. But I think I know what you're talking about and, ew!"

"So, you're saying you're not attracted to him?"

"I'm not saying that. I'm saying, 'I'm not attracted to this line of conversation with you.'"

"Fine, I'll quit being vague."

"That's actually pretty vague, but OK."

"Are you involved with him or what, Sunshine?"

"Involved?" She pauses to glare at me. "Sort of, but it's not what you think. I thought maybe I was gonna have to use him to get in touch with you."

"You did, didn't you?"

"Oh, yeah, I guess so." She crosses the room, takes my hand. "Relax," she says.

"Why, what are you doing?" Much as I want her…and I do, I don't need some Norn messing with my head as I go off to reckon with Odin. Even though she probably already has.

"I'm going to give you a reading."

"A reading of what?"

"A palm reading."

"I don't think that will be necessary."

"You're telling me what's necessary now?"

"Fine. But this isn't gonna get all spooky, is it?"

"Not a bit."

"Alright, if it will make you happy."

"It will." She lowers her gaze, concentrates. "I see you taking a trip across a vast ocean."

"Insightful."

"Seriously, though, I see it. I see a woman. And another woman. And another. One of them is me."

"Obviously. Who are the others? Hel? Frigga? Sif? Freya? Valkyries!? There are only so many possibilities."

"Actually, Trickster, there are billions of possibilities. I guess that's just something you'll need to figure out. Don't forget, though. You're refusing to take me with you. I'm entitled to withhold a little information if I feel like it."

"That doesn't sound very friendly."

"Neither is leaving me here."

"Au contraire. The giants and Fen are exceptional hosts."

"If you say so. Remember: Look for two women."

"Oh, wait, that must be your sisters, right?"

"Could be. Then again, I could be lying." She lets my hand

fall, but keeps holding onto it, our fingertips coming to touch. Then her other hand starts moving slowly up my arm. The feeling is at once, scintillating, chilling. "I've been thinking," she adds.

"Yeah, I think I have a fairly good idea what you've been thinking based on that kiss before. You're thinking you're going to sleep with me, mess with my head, and leave me little more than a pawn."

"Pawn? It's not like you're some chess master. I think we established that a little earlier."

Success.

She shakes her head. "And you used to be so good? Remember when we used to play back in the old days?"

"When you used your powers or didn't?"

"Didn't, of course. There's no way you could beat me otherwise."

"You still haven't answered about Kurt."

"Haven't answered what?" she says, letting my hand go.

"Are you having an affair with him?"

"An affair? I don't remember you being so uptight about stuff like this. Next, you'll be asking me if I'm his 'kept woman?'"

"Well, are you?"

"Don't be stupid," she says. "You're really killing the mood here."

"That's probably for the best."

"Where am I supposed to sleep?"

"Hel!?" I yell.

"Loki!?" Hel yells back, from somewhere deep in the penthouse.

"Sunshine needs a place to sleep!" I yell again.

"OK!" she yells back again.

"Go to Hel. She'll get you set up."

"If you're sure that's what you want," she says and turns to go. I catch myself checking her out. So does she when she wheels back around.

Here it comes, that thing I've been trying to avoid in spite of wanting it ever since that kiss in McMurtry's. Honestly, ever since that last kiss on Asgard, I've been gaming this out. And she got me once already. I can't let her do it again.

She's within inches before I can move, her breasts grazing my shirt. So heavy, deliciously heavy, even with the barest of contact. Fuck. I'm stuck. A couple seconds and I'm the one kissing her. Lips, tongues, hot, full, slippery, wet. Again, again, again, again. I'm a mess. It would be time for me to appeal to my higher power if I had one.

She pushes away. "But you don't want me to distract you, so I guess I'd better just go to bed."

I watch her leave. This time, there's no turning back.

THE ASGARD KISS

IN THE end, it turned out Christianity absorbed us, not the other way around. Did that change Odin? No, not at all. Well, maybe I shouldn't say that. It did change him obviously, psychologically, made him even more bitter than he had been, probably paved the way for his involvement with old Adolf. But as for any sort of magical changes—as for Thor's grand theory about how Odin would actually become Jesus—or maybe Jesus would become Odin—no, nothing.

The good part of this failure, the compensation if you will, was how much time I got to spend with Sunshine. Yeah, she was a regular guest at my Asgardian citadel, though Odin and the others showed up unannounced often, so we had to be careful. Let's just say I had an entire pack of "alarm wolves" roaming that castle. Fen was in charge of them. Sunshine and I didn't always meet in my citadel, though. We went places.

A weekend in Alfheim, a fortnight in Jotenheim. We were *together*. But our favorite spot was the Glade of the Norns, the place we'd had our first date if you can call the beginning of a torrid triste between the God of Mischief and one of Fate's Handmaidens a date. It was also the place I'd see Sunshine for the last time on Asgard.

SHE'D BROUGHT Darkness and Halflight with her. It was my first time seeing them all together in decades, and I have to admit I had some not-so-wholesome thoughts dancing in my noodle. Which, admittedly, was pretty sketchy since they were, all three of them, wearing dun-hued robes, the robes' hoods obscuring their faces. They looked like some sort of netherbeings—you know, from the Dimension of Shadows—but that was the guise they were going for in those days. I knew what lurked beneath those robes.

"There are three of you again."

"That's right, Trickster," said Sunshine, pulling back her hood as the others did, too. Before me stood three coal-haired beauties I couldn't tell apart, physically, at least not at this distance. The voice, Sunshine's voice, was the only way I knew it was her. "We've come to talk to you about something. Have a seat."

"I'm already—"

"We're leaving." This was Darkness taking over, mean, old, domineering Darkness.

"Leaving?" I looked at Sunshine. She looked down, away. "Leaving where?"

"Leaving here," said Halflight. "You will not see us for many years, Trickster. When we return, you will not be expecting us, and we will not appear as we now do."

"That sounds very confusing."

Darkness replied, "Great changes will come while we are gone. This will be a time of testing, one in which the gods must prove themselves."

"But we're working on this Great Integration thing you wanted. Please. Odin's putting his heart into it. I've honestly never seen him like this."

"We have seen him like this before, Trickster, before even your time. It will not work."

"Why not?"

"Mixing lies with truth can never produce truth."

I have to admit that last statement had me feeling attacked, like they were telling me everything was my fault. "But—"

"Look for us on Midgard. That is where we will come to you when next we meet," Darkness said, lowering her black-eyed gaze.

"You have a special purpose, Loki, one ordained at the making of the Nine Worlds. If you fail to fulfill it, untold innocents will suffer," Halflight chimed in.

"Especially your beloved humans," this was Darkness, of course.

"Wait, wait, you're not talking about the Big R., are you? We're all getting along back at Valhalla. The giants are quiet. The elves are pacified. The dwarves have even started to come around. There's no need to worry, really."

Darkness replied, "Ragnarök is not what you or the All-Father believe it to be."

"What is it then?" I asked.

"Fate will tell you when she is ready," Halflight replied.

"How? Fate only talks to you. Once you're gone, there'll be no way for us to find anything out."

Sunshine smiled. "He has a point."

Halflight nodded. "We should talk to Fate, make sure she hasn't changed her mind."

Darkness turned to her sisters, her lower lip curling downward slightly. "You realize he's doing it again, right?"

"Doing what? I just want the truth," I replied.

"The truth?" they said, as one.

Darkness added, "That's a rather odd request coming from you."

"I meant the facts."

"Fine, Trickster," said Darkness, looking down in that long-suffering way she had. "We will pose your questions to Fate. You will wait here."

SO, I waited. Hours, days…Who knows precisely how long? Eventually, only Sunshine returned.

"Are you here to say goodbye?"

She exhaled heavily, as though my words had taken the breath from her. "Something like that."

"Shouldn't you at least tell Odin before you guys leave? How will we get in touch with you if something really goes wrong?"

"We already gave him the ultimatum. A long time ago. What more can we do? He's just going to beg and plead, scream and cry, promise to do better, then not. Like you just did."

"That's probably true, but we both know this is going to fall apart without you, without Fate."

"It already has fallen apart. You just don't realize it." I guess I started to tear up. "Aw, don't cry, Trickster. Listen, and this is the truth: we will be back someday. When it's time."

"When Fate commands?"

"Exactly. When Fate commands."

"I thought you loved me."

"*I do.*"

"So?"

"You know I have to go where Fate says. You know I can't be parted from my sisters until the end, until Ragnarök. These are the rules, the laws. Come on, don't cry. We'll be together again someday."

She kissed me then, in a way she never had before. Or was it, more likely, that I just felt emotions I'd never felt before; that a permanence had attached to this loss in a way Odin tossing me from Asgard time and again never had.

She brought her hands to my cheeks, held my face. And I felt something like pure love then, coming through her fingertips. I wanted to pull away, to ask her what I was feeling, but I knew parting from her would end whatever it was.

Was that kiss so long ago, what she conveyed in it, why I believed her all this time? Or maybe it was the idea, once the Norns had left, that they didn't even necessarily know what was going to happen?

Or was it the idea that Fate really had changed, completely and inexorably, when the rest of them fell? Maybe, after they fell, I started to think Fate didn't have to be Fate, that even someone like me might have a chance in spite of what had been "ordained."

5

CAN WE STOP WITH ALL THE HITLER?

THERE'S TOO much history in Munich, too many of humanity's recent failures that begin and end there. Not that Berlin is better in that respect, but at least flying into Tegel serves another purpose. It keeps Odin and his bunch from having any idea where I am. What? You think I travel under my own name? Oh, come on. Loki Trickster? God of Disguise? Master of Lies? Even if I'm not evil you know there's got to be at least a little to that...

Jack Crawford, import-export consultant, touches down at Tegel by way of Schiphol by way of Heathrow by way of JFK by way of Logan. He's here with his teenage daughter Becky—aka Hel, Goddess of Death. Baggage claimed, customs cleared, Jack and Becky head for the Sixt counter, where Jack spends the next half hour assuring a kid named Heinrich that, yes, he does want *that* bright-cherry, brand-new 6-series coupe. Becky spends her time looking annoyed, chewing gum, and chain-smoking Gauloises.

Hel's making a scene, of course, alternately goggle-eyeing Heinrich and huffing around like this is the worst inconvenience she has ever endured. You have to give it to Hel: She has the overprivileged American teenager down cold.

"Germans drive fast," Heinrich cautions, wagging his finger as though I shall, indeed, have no pie. Which is especially galling given his peach fuzz and preternaturally bright eyes. I think he must be trying to impress Hel.

"That's not a problem. I want fast. Look, kid," I confide, "I *need* fast."

He stops wagging, smiles a shade more threateningly. "Fast," he says, with mustard, the "s" getting plenty Germanic.

Either this is the German equivalent of the waiter asking whether I really want that curry "hot," or he's considering putting me on some sort of watch list. Of which, I can only guess, there are plenty what with all the fear and loathing sweeping Europe, particularly Germany, these days. Odin has been a busy bee, yes, indeed. His boy, Reinhold Vekk, is leading in the race to take over for Merkel, the only other candidate with even a remote shot, this upstart, so-called "German Washington," Greta Bruder.

"Right. Got it. Fast, fast, fast. But I want fast, kid. I mean, I'm American, right? Need for speed, cradle to grave, *Go Dog, Go*, and all that."

He stops typing. "Dog Go-Go?" he asks, looking at Hel with the young man's signature blend of thinly veiled lust and abject confusion.

"No," I say, "*Go Dog, Go.*"

"What is this Dog Go-Go?"

"It's a book," I say, the continued perplexity of his gaze causing me to add, "With pages, for children. It's about dogs driving cars."

He squints. "But this is preposterous. Dogs cannot drive. They have, uh…pfotes." He makes what I ascertain to be a dog face—nose scrunching, mouth puckering—pretends to drive with hands incapable of gripping, then holds up his mitts as though I just got the drop on him. "How in English?"

"Paws?"

He nods briskly, point proven, though he's only halfway done shaming me for my stupidity. "The dog, he cannot even..." he pretends to shift gears, "schalten?"

You have to love the Germans, their national sense of humor at least. One part British stodge, one part French aloofery, they're unmoved by the banal jokes Americans love. But give them a hulking sexecutioner in black polythene and a Hello Kitty mask, and they'll yuck it the fuck up. Dogs driving cars, though? In Germany? Please, don't be foolish.

"Shift?"

His eyes light up. He points at me like I just won the bonus round at Sixt. "Yes, shift!"

"Just, never mind about the dogs driving. You gonna give me the car or what?"

Heinrich's smile disappears. He eyeballs me for a few more seconds, leaves me considering watch lists once again. Not that they'd even locate the real me amid all the fake identities.

He eyeballs Hel one last time and hands me the key.

THE 6 isn't an electric, or even a hybrid. But I'm justifying that to myself, thinking the two hundred and fifty miles between Berlin and Bavaria will straighten my noodle, help me figure a few things out before I have to talk to Odin. And if I'm going to drive that distance on the Autobahn, I don't want to spend it with an endless stream of sportscars flashing their beams at me.

We're barely out of the airport when Hel pipes up. "Dad," she says, "when are we going to get there?" She's got her shoes off, feet on the dash, smirking so hard it's practically a leer.

"You realize we're alone, right? There's no benefit to you playing entitled American teen anymore."

"Au contraire."

"Yeah?"

"Practice."

"I guess."

"So?"

"Maybe later."

"Aw, you're no fun," she replies, lips curling into a pout. She hits the SatRad, starts bopping to some sort of neo-metallic German techno pop reggae fusion. Within sixty seconds she's talking again.

Did I mention Hel had five espressos before we left Tegel?

THE GREAT thing about BAB 9, besides the speed, is all the green. And more than that, all the black. If you saw the way Germany looked in '45, you'd know what I mean. Crumbling buildings; battered, ashen roads; and soot-covered soil everywhere. I'll never forget those first few days, how odd it felt when those bullets hit and more than that, hurt. Sure, they couldn't kill me, gunshots feel more like flea bites do to you, but when you haven't felt human pain your entire existence, any measure of it comes as a big, unpleasant surprise. Having to walk places? Having to ask for things? The hunger? The thirst? The cold? The need for sleep? Let me tell you, the trip out of Germany was no hoot. But I made it. So did Odin and his crew. But they came back. And stayed.

I guess I was hoping there'd be less blatant symbols of fascism here in Germany, less of an obvious imprint, that it would be more like…well, America. But even without the visuals, listening to SatRad disabuses me of those notions. True, Merkel's still in charge, and she's always been reasonable, but every other story is about immigration, violence, or immigration and violence. Never mind the billboards everywhere: Vekk's perma-tanned face and flaxen, slicked-back hair looming over reality, like an Instagram filter nobody wants.

I drop Hel at a Hotel Bavaria outside Augsburg, figure that will put enough distance between us and New Valhalla for the short term. If I have to stay longer than a day or two, I'll rent some sort of discrete base of operations. For now, the average German hotel chain is going to have to do.

THE 6 and I hit New Valhalla's faux-stone gatehouse—complete with mini-parapets and useless turrets—half an hour after I leave Hotel Bavaria, around three in the afternoon. The gates remain closed as I pull up, the guard (a strapping, blond Bjorn) steps out of his fake fairy tale cottage and moves to the driver's door.

"Business?" he asks, eyeing me with practiced suspicion.

"Don't you want my name first?"

"Fine, what's your name?"

"Loki's the name."

He nods, raises a device that looks like a cross between a .38 and a grocery store pricing gun. "Smile pretty," he says.

I tense, but the thing just buzzes. He goes back to his tiny castle and talks to someone on the phone. A few seconds later a light turns green, the gate rises, and Bjorn waves me through.

BEYOND THE gatehouse and the electrified fence, New Valhalla is a picture postcard brought to life. The gunmetal brick structures and red roofs of the former Varsang Castle make up the property's pinnacle, a stone crown rising in the distance, backlit by the darkening yellows of a falling sun. Rings of trees, white fields sloping upward, seemingly untouched by god or man. The deeper I get into the property, the quieter the scene is, a prayer in pictures rather than words.

At the front doors (ten feet high, mahogany, double), I ring-a-ding-ding. And again. And again, waiting for whatever Odin's current butler's name is—Heinrich? Klaus? Moose? Maus? —to show his soon-to-be-distressed face. As I reach for my fourth ring, the doors open. There's no Maus, just Frigga, her glossy face set to a sub-z glare.

The narrowed, trustless eyes (sky blue and gleaming with pride); the angelic cheekbones and tapered jaw; the frosty lips pursed to spit poison...in her fall, Frigga has remade herself. She's turned herself into someone with real resonance in Germany these days, a woman of the far right. Twin strands of pearls ready to clutch, an iridescent-blue skirt suit (tight, knee-length with a fitted jacket), and four-inch pumps...I mentioned it's three in the afternoon, right? It's enough to make you ask, "Why's she dressed up? Why, Loki? Why?"

I could tell you it's for kicks, some vomit-inducing sex game Odin cooked up—and there are plenty of those—but more likely Frigga's off to chair a meeting of the "Ladies Auxiliary of the International Council on Nationalism" or some other such horse doodle. Oh, it's not called that I'm sure, probably isn't even formal, just some toney club where Frigga meets with Munich's rightist she-lite. They plot, plan, and eat little sandwiches, sip Riesling and dispassionately discuss the coming race war, the final genetic Armageddon they've spent the last century angling for.

The John Birch Society back in the US? The Moral Majority? The Tea Party? Sure, that's what happened in America. But fortunately, the Tea Party was the apex. Fortunately, America realized what sort of terrible road it was beginning to travel down and moved back the other way. In Europe, though, all those workers' fronts and united nationalist something or others just keep getting more popular. All of them are Odin's handiwork, too, every last one. No, I don't have proof. I just know it's true.

Oh, they won't come out and say it, these members of the neo-fascist New World Order—they'll deny and deny until it's too late—but what they really want, what they lust for, is that somehow, someway, someday, they'll get Old Adolf back, somebody like him at the very least. And when that happens, when their new Old Adolf comes along, he'll win, forever and ever, amen.

"Loki, you're still black," Frigga snaps, as though she needs to make her disenchantment or racism more obvious after all these years.

Speaking of disenchantment, Tyr enters the frame; stands looming a few feet away, in the middle of the petrol-black-and-gleaming-gold-tiled front hall, the double staircases snaking towards the second floor; that, given the height of the ceilings, is really where a third floor should be. No surprise from Tyr: that's what Tyr does. He looms—like dark clouds and vultures, like insurance agents at cocktail parties and divorce lawyers at yard sales.

"Guilty as charged, Friggs," I respond with the toothy smile she used to like, maybe even love. Ah, but those were the bad, old days. Yeah, sure Frigga and I had a thing. Odin still doesn't know, of course.

My mother? Oh, come on, I told you I was adopted, a literal babe in a basket. Anyway, the affair was her idea, the lech. Does that still work with women, goddesses I mean? Are they leches; or is there a feminine? Lechess, lecheur, lecha con leche…Point being Frigga is one. A lech, I mean. She practically held me down.

"I wish you wouldn't call me that. You know I hate your stupid nicknames." The intensity of her stare upshifts from snow princess to ice queen in the process.

The stare, you see, is Frigga's "big trick," her *methode de vie et guerre*. Some trick, too: she used to be able to turn people to ice with it back in the day. I mean that literally. We're not talking about the impenetrable death-gaze of some heart surgeon's trophy daughter, some Leticia or Bambi prancing down a triple-buffed, see-your-goodies runway, eyes full of naïve stoicism and teen entitlement. No, no, no: We're talking see, stare, zap. Quick as that, you're solid ice in need of a place to chill, or else.

Me? Oh, no way. No. Fucking. Way. Frigga's stare only ever worked on you guys. Of course, she tried on me, after things fell apart; before, too, to tell the truth. She tried on Surt, Thyrm, Fen, all of them…no luck. She kept trying though, does still; even now that her look has no physical effect on anyone, even you guys. That's the thing with the Asgardians: They're locked in the past, lusting for some mythic, unspoiled dreamworld. No wonder they fell for Hitler.

"I guess I was just surprised. I was expecting Gerhard or Klaus or whichever cryogenically frozen Stormtrooper you've got answering the door these days…"

"That would be Gestalt. Odin sent the mortal servants to their quarters when you arrived," offers Frigga. "One of the Valkyries will show you to Odin's study."

"Which one?"

"Oh, who can tell them apart anymore. Tyr, summon a Valkyrie."

Tyr claps his hands thrice and a Valk jets in. She's centimeters off the ground. But for her speed, it's hard to say whether she's using her wings at all.

I'm still eyeing her, trying to figure out which one she is from the olden days. Is it Synesthesia? Dyspepsia?

"They're all new, by the way. In case you were wondering. We got them here on Earth, after you left," says Frigga, as though in response to my question.

"Follow, me, please," says the Valk.

When she turns to go, I see her wings are mechanical, a framework of gears, levers, and spindles powering their magnificence. I want to shout, "You're a fake Valkyrie!" but I don't. I do what I'm told and follow.

"FERRET, FERRET, ferret," Odin shouts as I enter.

I do a double-take and another—I do a quad-take—but I don't see any ferrets, just what passes for Himself's throne room in New Valhalla, a place of silent reflection and secret communication, a place to scheme, "a study" as they say.

Odin's wearing a smoking jacket—deep red with iridescent Valkyries, and a cornflower blue ascot that matches his lone good eye; a tinted-glass monocle on his bad one, the overall look is Hefner hobo-hipster meets Norse Monopoly Man. All around him, the afternoon air flickers with shadows somehow both reluctant and oppressive.

"Ferret," someone on TV finally replies.

I realize Odin's watching a gameshow on a wall-sized

TV, an American show at that. I forget the name. Something alliterative with a synonym for luck and a sobriquet for money rolled into one big bad Bye, Bye, Miss "American Pie."

"Co-rect," says the shiny-suited, intensely white host, his level of surprise suggesting whatever "ferret" was the answer to was one tough question.

In response, a golden-haired, French-braided model tippetty-taps across the stage, does a snappy little kick-turn, and pushes one of thirty TV's. The screen explodes in a maelstrom of color then segues from monetary prize to typeset question as she struts back the other way.

"Used to have a Valkyrie looked just like her," Odin adds, seemingly to himself, gaze going a tick nostalgic, still apparently unaware I've entered. I can't help thinking this is all a dodge, done for my benefit. He knows how I loved the Valks, how I've missed them. Then, again, he could just be wasted.

"A-hem," I say.

And he turns. "Son," he responds with what appears to be true delight. He moves towards me, practically hovering across the floor. "You came! I can't tell you how good it is to see you. Though a little notice would have been nice."

There's a tear in his eye. Yes, a tear. But I'm not fooled, so don't you be either. I've seen Odin's tears before. I've seen them a thousand times. Even though they look real, they almost never are.

"I didn't want you to know I was coming."

"Hmm. Well, the important thing is you're here." He wraps his arm around my shoulder, pulls me deeper into the room, towards the quartet of dark chocolate leather armchairs set in a half-circle around the ten-foot-wide hearth. The fire's light pours into the room, falls to haze on the chairs' cushions, twinkles in the nail heads that decorate their arms. "There's someone I want you to talk to. Someone who's going to help us change the whole game, help us get home."

"Home?"

He nods, calls, "Ladies," as the doors to the study close and lock behind us. Another set of doors, these in the room's far, northeast corner, creak open, the darkness beyond seeming almost to spill into the lit room.

Two women step from the shadows into the light. They wear black, flowing gowns, these women; dresses of silk and lace that seem to move almost of their own accord. The dresses put off light even in their darkness, seem to shimmy and flounce as the wearers stand still, gazing fiercely. They're serious about something: I just can't tell if it's of the kissing or killing variety. Honestly, the scene leaves me thinking of Stevie Nicks. And Sunshine, of course. They both look exactly like Sunshine, albeit under different color schemes of skin, hair, and gaze. They look like what might have happened if Andy Warhol had been in the cloning business, these Neo-Norns his only subject.

"I'd like you to meet Halflight and Darkness," Odin says.

Nods from both. "Trickster," they offer simultaneously.

"Well, obviously we've met, in the past. But which is which, in the now?" I ask.

"I'm Halflight," says the one with black hair.

"And I'm Darkness," says the one with white hair.

I turn to Odin, "So, she was telling the truth?"

"She?"

"Oh, come on, Odin, I know you know Sunshine has been to see me."

95

He nods. "I know what you've been thinking, Loki. You've been thinking we haven't seen each other in half a century. You've been thinking we haven't spoken in decades. You've been thinking." He pauses. "I'm up to something. It's not true, though, son, not at all. I've made a fresh start and I want you to help us, to work with us. For the greater good." He raises his arms, Jesus taking in an imaginary multitude.

"Help you do what?"

"Ragnarök, what else?"

"Have you forgotten the part where we all die?"

"You don't understand, son. We've had it wrong all these years. And I…well, I have to take a lot of the blame for that."

Halflight and Darkness nod solemnly, knowingly. They nod in knowing solemnity.

"The Norns were right to leave when they did. We were a mess. And what's happened since, well, that's just proven how right they were. But they're back. And we've got a chance, all of us, to make things right, to finally let humanity live without us, completely. See, the way the Norns have been explaining things to me, Ragnarök was never literal. It was always a metaphor, about us leaving humanity with the power to help themselves."

"So, we're not going to die?"

"Oh, no, you're going to die…" Darkness replies.

"…on this world…" adds Halflight.

"But not for good."

"Not…"

"…forever."

"We'll all go back to Valhalla and live there," Odin exclaims. "Just like in the beginning!"

"Happily ever after, eh? You, without any worshippers for

the rest of time? And how is it we're supposed to get all this going? We don't have any powers left to speak of."

"The Norns can give us our powers back," Odin chimes in. "They can re-form The Wheel of Fate."

"You mean that thing you turned into a Hitler statue so you could pass some of your power to Old Adolf?" I turn to the Norns. "He's been meddling constantly since you left. Hitler was just the worst example."

"Even if that's true, you weren't blameless. Were you, Trickster?" asks Halflight.

"What do you mean?"

"You meddled."

"I didn't help Hitler."

"That's not what we've been told," Darkness replies.

"Told by whom? By him?"

Odin lowers his gaze, faintly shakes his head as if too deeply hurt to finish the action. I find myself wishing I had a ham so I could throw it at him.

Halflight: "Not by the All-father. That is all we will say now."

Odin looks up, vindicated.

"Just because some mythical person says something, you're going to assume it's true?"

"Mythical?" Darkness asks.

"You know what I mean."

"We have seen evidence of you influencing human events."

"What evidence?"

"The moving things. The pictures."

"You mean video? Film?"

"That's it."

"I was helping."

"So was I," says Odin.

"You were helping Hitler."

Darkness: "So, you say, Trickster. But maybe you were the one helping Hitler?"

Halflight: "Don't forget we knew you before, in Asgard. You don't have such a good track record, Trickster."

"I played a few tricks. That's my thing, remember?"

The Norns gaze at me, lips pursed, eyes narrowed.

"Fine, if you don't believe me, why am I here?"

Both Norns: "We need your help with Sunshine."

"There it is."

Darkness continues, "She's confused. She thinks you're her only hope. How ludicrous is that?"

I must look hurt because Halflight chimes in, "Which is why she came to see you. Which is also why…"

"What?"

"Sunshine has the statue."

"The Hitler statue? The one from Asgard?"

Odin cuts in, "Can we stop with all the Hitler-this and Hitler-that? Let's just go back to calling it The Wheel of Fate, shall we?"

"Much as I can appreciate why someone who helped Hitler wouldn't want to hear Hitler-this and Hitler-that, I think it's important to stick to the facts. Halflight and Darkness don't seem to understand. Hitler and the Nazis were something you had to experience to fully comprehend."

"Oh, don't misunderstand us," the Norns say as one. "We've read up on this Hitler fella. He was the most dastardly figure in human history."

"And Odin empowered him!"

Darkness: "Or maybe you did."

Halflight: "Or maybe you both did."

"Either way, they're willing to forgive us. All of us," Odin says, spreading his arms as if to take in the entire pantheon.

"Just like that?"

They nod.

"What about all the carnage? The dead Jews? The babies? The wars? Is Sunshine the only one of you who cares about humanity, or good, or truth?"

The Norns glance at each other. They shrug. "Odin has agreed to do everything we ask. As long as he can pass this trial period without meddling in human affairs, Fate will consider him absolved. You will all have your powers restored. And Odin will once again be king of the gods."

"You realize he's behind this Vekk guy, right?"

"That has not been proven!" Odin interjects.

"The one whose image is everywhere? Maybe. But the All-father has agreed to leave the humans to their own devices, let Fate run its course."

I shrug.

"You'll talk to Sunshine then, help convince her?"

"I'll tell her what's been said. As for convincing her, I'll have to give that some thought. I don't trust him," I say, pointing at Odin. "Or you, for that matter," I add, turning to the Norns.

In spite of what seemed a pretty stiff rebuke from yours truly, there's nodding and smiling, even a few stolen glances.

"Alright, ladies, you may return to your lair," says Odin.

The Norns leave me standing there with Odin.

"So?" he asks after they're gone.

"As I told the Neo-Norns, I need time to think. And it

won't do you any good to have me followed. I didn't bring Sunshine with me."

"So, she's back in America?"

"Maybe."

"You left her with the giants?"

"Could be."

"Hel?"

I raise a provocative eyebrow.

"Not the wolf. You didn't leave her with the wolf?"

"How about all of them?"

I leave him standing there, struggling for breath.

"Maybe you should just ask Heimdall?" I call, as I go.

TRAGICOMEDY FOR THE FALLEN, PART 2

AFTER BALDUR and I took up again—after Thor veered back into homicidal homophobe mode—it wasn't long before leaving New Valhalla was the only option that made sense. You should have seen Odin the day I did. The shock on his face. It was like once he lost the magical ability to boot me across time and space, he was clueless as to how to manage family drama. Those dinners while I was at New Valhalla, though. Oh, la, la.

Baldur and I playing footsie under the table. Frigga dropping her napkin so she could cop a little thigh. Thor perpetually shitfaced on cheap lager, crushing aluminum cans against his head, biting holes in them with his teeth—and they say Fen is ill-behaved. Imagine the worst family Thanksgiving you've ever had, multiply it by a thousand, and there you go…

By the time I left, I was so out of sorts I didn't even know where to go. I thought about America at that point. But I was alone. I hadn't even found Fen yet. And the trip just seemed too big. I know, right? It was nothing compared to all those cross-dimensional slingshoots I'd gotten from One-Eye. But imagine the ennui I experienced packing the other night then apply that to international travel in the Fifties. And there was one other little thing I haven't mentioned. No, this wasn't the Sixties yet, but already your reality had a lot to do with vibes.

The minute the war ended there were major anti-communist vibes everywhere. Not without reason, but it was more or less like America and much of the West just replaced the Nazis with the Soviets and called it a day. And I was still in the throes of *Das Kapital* at that point. No, bustling, uber-capitalistic America didn't seem quite right.

I thought about doing some time in the Eastern Bloc, but things were grim over there, perpetually overcast. It really did seem a lot like Nazi Germany at that point. So, what did I do? Well, I headed back to France; the hopeful mantra of, "Liberté, égalité, fraternité" dancing in my black, little heart.

PARIS, EARLY '53. I was on the streets and cold as a dungeon in the bowels of Jotenheim. You'd be surprised how chilly the City of Lights gets in the winter. No wonder the French drink so much. I mean, that's true of all northern Europe, isn't it? It gets cold, people drink. Hell, it's true of the entire world, cold or not, who am I kidding? Anyway, that's what I was doing by that point. Drinking.

My back to a dilapidated wall of sixteenth century provenance—see the crumbling mortar and skewed bricks—a line of hammer and sickle posters pasted above my head like some communist comic book test pattern, I was sporting a ratty red beret, guzzling headache Bordeaux, and gnawing on a crust of stale baguette when I spotted this big, black beast lumbering towards me.

The dude next to me, Martin, must have thought the dog was a dt hallucination, because he split, leaving his street-slick blankie and holey knapsack to their own devices. So, there I was, all alone again, wondering if Odin had sent some sort of spectral hit-hound for me. But as the dog got closer, he started to look more like a wolf, and as he got even closer, he started to look like a wolf I actually knew. Of course, I knew Fen once I could see into his eyes. I'd know those blazing yellow orbs anywhere.

"Fen," I said, as he nuzzled up against me. "You look hungry, boy."

He whimpered.

I hugged him. "Are you cold?"

He looked right into my eyes and nodded. I held out the rest of the baguette which he snapped right up. Fine, I thought, enough living on the streets. I was a provider again. I had souls to care for, one at least.

"How about we go somewhere, Fen?"

He cocked his head to the right.

"Somewhere like, say, America?"

He nodded, sort of, finished wolfing down the bread, and gave me a lick to seal the deal.

After that, I took up petty crime for a while, there in Paris, just long enough to build up my capital, keep me in kippers and Fen in kibble—or was it the other way around? Either way, we never took anything from anyone who couldn't afford to lose it. By we, of course, I mean, me and Fen. The bums I'd been running, or rather, stumbling around with, I had to cut loose...

I picked up some cheap shades at a tourist stall, got myself a white-tipped cane and a cup of pencils, and disguised Fen as a disability dog. We stole wallets and watches, played the odd con of Find the Lady, did all that until we had enough to afford passage to the States. Then we were gone, off to really find the lady, as in Liberty, as in New York City.

THESE DAYS, it's hard to see the American Century as the unmitigated success it seemed once upon a time. Sure, things are still OK in the States. You can still get a Big Mac. You can still find a fried chicken sandwich on every corner and a Starbucks in every strip mall. It's not like some neo-Fascist lunatic has taken over there...But the joyful buzz of peace, prosperity, and unmatched power America felt after the Berlin Wall fell has become a gnawing sense of dissatisfaction, the mother of all hangovers from the nightmare of all drunks.

Yes, America–and more than that the entire West–looked good as the USSR was winding down, fracturing, and finally shattering. With Gorbachev then Yeltsin, the new Russia seemed fertile ground for democracy. But it wasn't. Old habits, maybe it was nothing more than that. Is that one of your history's most distressing lessons, that if you've lived long enough under oppressors—the czar, the politburo, the church, the gods— you're never going to be able to rule yourselves?

From the Middle East to China and now once again even Germany...when things get rough, the impulse is to look for a Big Bad Sugar Daddy to wipe away the tears. Because that's the truth of it. Much as Odin struggles to corrupt your lives and politics, you are the place corruption begins and ends.

Without you, Odin could do nothing. And that's the real lesson of the 20th century, or if not the 20th, then surely the 21st—Hell, maybe even both—not that the American Century and the peace it wrought were illusory, but that the right-left continuum you attributed it to was a lie. You spent so long, gazes fixed at a line on the horizon, that you lost focus. You didn't see the line become a circle. You didn't see you'd become hemmed in, made into cattle, by yourselves.

The Soviets and the Nazis were of like minds, even though they seemed to be ideological opposites. It should be no surprise then that Odin went straight for the Eastern Bloc after he fell. While I was wending my way west, towards what looked like freedom, Odin moved east, first through Germany then Poland, Hungary, and on and on, until finally he came to the USSR.

And I can only imagine that after watching his Nazis fall, Odin must have felt comfort to be amongst authoritarians again, to feel warmth and nostalgia for the duality of the docile and the powerful. Odin still had that small fraction of his powers, the part that seems at once meaningless compared to what we once had and intensely meaningful when comparing us to you, the part that if you think about it too long can convince you not just that you're your own race, but your own species. It can easily convince you that you humans, you…little people…to put it nicely, don't really matter. You might as well be birds or fish or insects.

Do I feel that way? Of course not. At this point, you know me better than that. These days, I'd just as soon be human, not that I'll ever get that chance. Right now, I feel the end, Ragnarök, still coming, try as I have to avoid it. And though I've spent millennia imagining it, gaming out the Big R. in my head, I still can't say what it will be like. The only thing I know for sure is that it will change the world, not just mine, but yours. What will our worlds become? In the end, who can say? Maybe once the Norns knew. Maybe they still do.

6
THING IS

TWO IN the afternoon, I hear the sound and fury of Odin's favorite ditty, "Ride of the Valkyries," come pounding out of my uPhone's tiny, murderously powerful speakers. At first, I consider the idea that I've lost it; y'know, spontaneously started having aural hallucinations. But glancing at the screen shows me Odin smiling back; cues me to the reality that somehow, some way, he's gotten his own ringtone. I pick up.

"Yeah?"

"How are you, son? First night back in the Fatherland agree with you?"

"Not particularly. I'd forgotten every food item here contains onions, potatoes, and cabbage."

"That's nice. Listen, the reason I—"

"I told you. I'll talk to Sunshine, see if I can convince her. If that's it, I need to get ready for my flight." Even as I'm telling Odin this, I realize I'm lying. At this moment, the key thing is to get out of Germany, to get away.

"No, wait…You can't go."

"This is touching, really, Odin. But Sunshine's not going to just hop on a plane and come to Germany."

"That's not what I called about."

"No?"

"There's actually this one teensy thing I forgot to mention last night."

"What?"

"Thing is, I lied when I said I hadn't been meddling."

"Is that all? Well, of course you did. But they didn't seem to care."

"They'll care about this."

"This what?"

"It's about the Bruder woman."

"The German Washington?"

He groans.

"What about her?"

"Well, um, actually, here's the thing." He chuckles, his voice rising an octave as he adds, "We were planning to have her assassinated."

"Assassinated?"

"Right."

"And by 'we' you mean?"

"Y'know, Aesir, Vanir…Thor, Frey, Tyr, Forseti, the whole gang…and these German rightists we've been working with, the, uh, Viking Brotherhood."

"I knew that was you helping Vekk. So, what, everywhere in the world, all these rightist dictators are your thing?"

"Oh, not all, no. I mean, I have a role, a piece. But there are other forces at work, most of them human."

"I can't believe humanity's dumb enough to try this again, after how the 1940s worked out."

"I guess they're dumber than you think."

"Why are you telling me any of this?"

"Because I need you to stop it."

"You started it. You stop it."

"I promised the Norns I wouldn't meddle."

"Just tell them what you did. Confess. Is it even technically meddling if you started it, and you're just stopping it?"

"After everything I said. After finding out I lied to them again, they'd probably leave for another thousand years."

"Would that be the worst thing?"

"Yes," he says, voice going feral, filled with hate, "To be trapped here, without any real power, for another thousand years? Yes, it would."

"You're going to have to find another way to stop it, then, an earthly way. The Norns forbade us all from meddling, remember?"

"That's not exactly true, son. They forbade the gods from meddling. You're not technically a god, though, you're a giant. I mean, technically. Never mind the fact that you never agreed to anything. Technically speaking."

"But I…" I realize he's right on both counts, that he's lawyered the whole thing exceptionally well, no doubt Foresti helped him.

"Son, please, it will be so easy for you, practically nothing, what with your lying and disguise abilities. Who knows, it might even be a little fun? After all, you'd be helping them, wouldn't you? The humans?"

"I don't—"

"Plus, I can help you put together a cover story that's sure to get you through in minimum time. Which is important because, well, like I said, we don't know exactly how, when, or where any of this is going to happen, but it's going to be bad and soon."

"Odin, I just—"

"C'mon, son, this will be like the good old days, when we used to have adventures together, when we had no idea what might happen. You remember, don't you?"

"I do." I say, and I do. There were good times, particularly in the beginning. And of course, I remember them. There've been points, in the deep past, when I actually clung to them. Why is it that we can never forget what we need to forget about our parents? When we want to hate them, we can't forget the good. When we want to love them, we can't forget the bad.

"I need this, Loki. I'll swear on anything you want, to anything you want. Sleipnir, the ravens, Mimir's Head?"

"You're offering to swear on the Head?"

"If I have to."

I realize how serious he is, and that he's got me. The combination of him imploring me and activating deep memories has done what it always seems to. It's left me hoping for his approval, knowing that's exactly what I'm doing, yet still on the verge of agreeing to things I know I shouldn't. I need to get off the phone now.

"This is a big decision, Odin. I'll have to discuss it with my people and get back to you."

"Wait, son, there's just one more thing."

"What?" I barely manage.

"You can't tell the Norn about the assassination. She might tell her sisters."

I WALK into Hel's room ten minutes later. She's on the bed, back to the wall, pillows behind her formed into some sort of ersatz demi-chair, fingers dancing a spritely ballet on the charcoal keyboard of her uThink.

"Alright, Hel, put down the laptop and call up the giants. It's time for a team meeting."

"But that…"

"You know what I mean."

She does what I ask, starts a Zoom, and emails the guys. Then she looks up at me. "Your eyes are red," she says.

"Must have poked myself or something. Just get them, huh?"

A few seconds later, the uThink's screen is filled with life. I see Surtur, Thyrm, and Fen all piled on a bed like some sort of Hallmark video-sleepover card. They're still at Chateau Loki.

"I thought you were going to move her to one of the safehouses?"

"We will if something happens. But everything's fine, and we're almost done with another level."

"*Monsieur von Mayhem*?"

They stare at the camera eye like that's the dumbest thing anyone's ever said to them. Even Fen. It's chastening.

"Wait, has he…Loki, what's wrong with your eyes?" Surt finally asks.

"I just said that a minute ago," says Hel.

"Nothing is wrong. I met the Norns or the Neo-Norns or whatever they are. They want to help Odin, just like Sunshine said."

"Help him how?"

"Give him his powers back. Give all of us our powers back."

"You sure you're ok, Loki?" asks Thyrm.

"Yes, I'm *fucking* okay. Now, fucking concentrate," I yell, glaring at the camera. "The Norns made Odin promise not to meddle in politics."

"Alright?"

"Problem is, he was planning to have Greta Bruder assassinated. The Norns don't know about that. And they can't. If they find out, they may disappear for another thousand years."

"Who cares? I thought you didn't want your powers back, that you wanted to stay here, with the humans."

"That's beside the point. Odin needs me to help him stop the assassination."

"Tell me how your meddling is any different from Odin's?"

"I'm not Asgardian. I'm not technically a god."

"Oh, the Niflheim thing?"

"Exactly."

"He pulled the 'real emotion' bit on you, didn't he?" Hel asks.

"Oh," say the giants as though this explains way too much.

"Fine, yes, he cried, begged, pleaded, reminded me of the old days. Now, are you going to fucking help me or what?"

"Of course," all three say in unison, Fen adds a yip as punctuation.

"For now, I just need you and Fen to keep an eye on Sunshine, make sure nothing happens to her. Speaking of which, have you heard from Heimdall? Or Kurt for that matter?"

"No sign of Kurt. Though Thyrm did spot someone wearing a terrible homeless disguise pushing a shopping cart filled with cans over by his apartment. I guess that could have been Heimdall."

Thyrm nods.

"Yeah, I never really bought the connection between Kurt and Heimdall. Anyone could be H."

"I guess," the giants say in unison.

"Good, now go get Sunshine."

111

The sounds of bedclothes rustling, booted feet thudding, and doors opening.

"Hello," says Sunshine after thirty seconds.

"I met your sisters. It's as you said. They want to help Odin remake The Wheel of Fate. They're willing to do it if he can avoid meddling in the Chancellor's election."

"The one he's probably already meddling in?"

"But if you knew—"

"As I said, I couldn't convince my sisters. They say you guys have to play it out, so we can be sure you've reformed."

"Me?"

"Well, Odin and the rest of them mostly. What happened to your eye?"

"Nothing, got some dirt in it or something."

"If you say so. Is there anything else?"

"Yes, but it's something I can't talk about yet. I need you to stay there with Fen and the giants. Odin's still anxious to get his hands on you. I don't entirely trust him, or your sisters."

"Finally, something we agree on. Not that it's reassuring being stuck here with two lunkheads junked up on a video game."

"I told you they'll move you to one of their safe houses if there are any problems."

"Yeah, about all these…safe houses…if the giants are good now, why do they need safe houses?"

"They are good. But they're also incorrigible, always getting in trouble. You know the type."

"I do."

"Anyway, you'll be fine. Fen's there."

"Fen is a dog."

"Technically, maybe. But if the Elder Eddas teach us anything, it's to never underestimate the Fenris Wolf."

"You made up the Eddas!"

"I mean, technically, maybe. But they're still filled with valuable information."

"Why can't you just tell me what's going on?"

"I promised Odin I wouldn't say anything."

"It wouldn't have anything to do with Greta Bruder, would it?"

"Why do you ask?"

"I can't tell you now. Maybe I'll feel like it later."

I PLAY with my uPhone, leave MSNBC on in the background. I've not even been gone a day but already America seems so relaxing compared to Germany. Even thinking back on last night, when my world still seemed like it was being stirred rather than shaken, things were so much cleaner and clearer in Olde Boston Towne.

Never mind the stress of what I'm going through with Sunshine or being forced to see my family again, there's not the same political agita back in America that there is here. Almost makes you wonder whether that whole "American exceptionalism" thing might not be real after all.

Just kidding: Much as I like, even love, America, American exceptionalism has never made any sense. It's really just a nice version of Hitler's Master Race Theory, a way to make some of you feel better at the cost of making others of you feel worse. You guys, if there are three of you in a room, the only real bet is on how fast two of you will turn on the third.

Speaking of not being right…this Vekk guy, every day he's off on some tirade about the Arabs and the Jews, the disabled, the diseased, the homeless and jobless, the mentally ill, how they're keeping the German people from thriving. If only in his policies and seemingly manic energy level, he resembles nobody more than Old Adolf.

I mean, the guy talks about building a wall around Germany, a hundred-foot-high unscalable wall. Around a country. He talks about it as a jobs program. Talks about using immigrant labor to build it then kicking "them" out when it's done. Talks about taking their children from them, keeping them in cages, and only giving the children back when they finish their work and leave.

No, Vekk doesn't look like Adolf at all, which, in and of itself, seems to be enough for a lot of Germans. He's tall and slender with a deep tan and perfect white-blond hair. He must have a team of people to bleach and tease it on a daily basis. Vekk's hair truly is a work of art. What is it with totalitarians and their appearances?

Hitler with his crazy moustache. Kim with his loopy haircut. Saddam's endless stream of hats, Stalin with his boots, the ayatollahs with their robes, the televangelists with their garish suits. They're all of them trying too hard to stand out. Which should be a dead giveaway. No, I'm not telling you to hate anyone who looks different. I'm telling you that when personal performance artists gain sway over millions, it's time to run the other fucking way.

Oh, Germany, why are you doing this to yourselves and the rest of the world? It hasn't even taken a hundred years and already you're primed for a second darkness, one that with modern technology promises to be far worse than the first. And I have to admit, I think about America a lot these days, even though things are so much better there than here. Because better is relative, isn't it? Better doesn't necessarily mean good.

I think about how America won the Second World War and the Cold War; but now it seems like, actually, she wound up losing both, even if we know that can't be true. Maybe the problem is that war is eternal; that there never really is a beginning or an end, so there can never truly be winners and losers.

The USSR was destroyed by the Cold War, or so we thought. We all remember the Berlin Wall falling. We remember "the peace dividend." Democracy and capitalism, it seemed, were on their way, chugging across Russia, from sea to snowy sea. Democracy never took, though, in Russia or most of the other Rs in the old USSR. For the most part, they fell to a steady stream of worse and worse strongmen, totalitarian communists just waiting for their chances to become former totalitarian communists, faux democrats who would in time become current totalitarian "Something-else-ists." And now they're proliferating, well beyond the former Iron Curtain. France, Turkey, Britain... and, of course, Germany.

Sure, America itself is safe, relatively speaking. In America, unlike so many places, there still really are good people on both sides. President Butterworth and Majority Leader Friendly, argue, sure. But they work together, meet up for a glass of milk at the end of the day, when the dealing's done. Thinking about America, about how unlike Germany it is, makes up my mind for me. I couldn't give up on humanity back in the Thirties and Forties. It's the same now. I love you guys too much to watch you fail.

"YES," ODIN answers when I call. He sounds breathless, as though maybe he leapt across the expanse of his study just to answer the phone.

"Okay, Odin, I'll see what I can find out about this Bruder situation."

"I knew you'd come through, son."

"Did you hear what I said? I'm going to look into it. I'm not promising to help."

"I heard you, son. But we both know once you're in the thick of it, and your juices are flowing, you're going to help. You're all-in already even if you won't say it."

"Don't count on it."

"Fine, have it your way. Now, when can we expect the Norn?"

"Oh, no, this is just about the other thing. Sunshine will have to make up her own mind about you and her sisters."

"Really? Because it would be much easier if you could just grab her and bring her back. She's in America, right? Where is it you live these days, Boston?"

"Nice try. I never said specifically where she was, and let's leave it at that. Now, about these Nazis of yours. Where do they hang out?"

"Neo-Nazis."

"Is there a difference?"

"Sure, one's neo-, one's not."

"Right, so, these Nazis? Where do I find them?"

"It's called Anarchy."

"I'm sorry?"

"It's a sort of roadhouse/clubhouse they have."

"A clubhouse? What are they, perky teenage Nazis who sing and dance?"

"It's a motorcycle gang. That's what they call their base of operations. A clubhouse."

"And what do these Nazi Mouseketeers of yours call themselves?"

"The Viking Brotherhood."

"What's this supposedly fantastic cover?"

"You're an American who calls himself Wrath X. You're former Special Forces dishonorably discharged for being too violent. And you're an expert in demolitions. Which, a little bird tells me, is something they're looking for."

"You finally located Knowledge and Afterthought?"

"No." His voice catches. "I was speaking metaphorically."

"Ah."

"Obviously, you'll have to disguise yourself."

"Goes without saying."

"Yes, but, especially with…"

"Oh, you mean the fact that I'm black?"

"Exactly."

"Is that all?"

"I think so. They're only humans. What's the worst they could do?"

"Well, according to you, they could assassinate one of the two primary candidates for the German Chancellorship for starters, resulting in you and the rest of us being consigned to Earth for the rest of eternity or whatever. Never mind that, if successful, this little assassination of yours would probably help Vekk win, ushering in a new era of darkness for humanity."

"I meant besides that."

THE INTERNET really is amazing, a little like magic if you think about it. The way it connects you all. The way it lets you shoot products, money, and even thoughts all over the place. It's something, I've got to give you that.

Upshot is, thanks to you guys and your Internet, it takes me all of three hours to find a house to rent. It's a villa—that's what they call it, at least—walled and gated, on a lake, all of it far from our current Hotel Bavaria and Odin's looming New Valhalla.

Six bedrooms, pool in the basement, tennis courts, a nice, high, stone wall around the whole thing. And there's a slip, so if we need to, we can escape by lake. Was it owned by a Nazi at some point? I didn't check, but I suppose it would have to have been. Just about everything in Germany was owned by a Nazi at some point.

All of which is to say that you're probably thinking I'm pretty soft, what with Chateau Loki's posh surroundings, my penchants for expensive booze, rental villas, sportscars, and whatnot, I'm living an easy life while you suffer. Which is only partly true. Trust me, I've suffered. Woman, no cry, and all that, but *man*, cry, because I have suffered…

ANOTHER HOUR, and I've signed the paperwork and paid. They tell me I can move in whenever I want. People really are so understanding when you throw money at them. Next to your Internet, money's probably your best trick. Oh, don't let anyone sell you guys short: You've come up with lots of great stuff. And, money, well…it saves you having to carry cooped chickens and bushels of corn around to barter with, saves you having to make change with ears, or legs, or thighs. You guys truly are full of magic. Take it from a guy who knows.

While I'm handling the villa, I have Hel take care of the various vehicles we'll need for the growing list of potential future endeavors, additional surveillance and technical equipment, computers, and the like. By late that night we're ready to make our move over to our temporary Chateau Loki.

We pile in the 6…OK, there are only two of us, so we don't really pile…anyway, we drive around for a few hours to make sure we've completely lost any watchers, minders, and/or other miscreants—Forseti and Tyr spring to mind—then head for the villa.

Once we get there, once we've processed Hel's pleasant, albeit brief, surprise—It's not like she hangs out in a pit, not anymore at least—I send her off to continue her research on everything from Bruder to Vekk, Odin's possible antics to the dubious doings of this Viking Brotherhood. There's something I have to do, and I don't want her throwing me off as she might well try, y'know, just for kicks.

Odin gave me Bruder's contact information. But I've been waiting to contact her, waiting because I wasn't quite sure. Did I think Odin was lying? Well, I'd be lying if I said I didn't at least consider the possibility. And he still could be. Mostly, though, I wanted to get all the details settled and make sure I was at a safe remove before I did anything that might be traced.

"Hello?" says the voice.

"Frau Bruder?" I ask, imagining the youthful fiftysomething on the other end of the phone. Besides her height, which at almost 6' is imposing even for a German woman, Bruder's appearance is, in many ways, the opposite of Vekk's. Her hair is red with copper highlights, short, and always in place in spite of the dearth of attendants and products involved in its maintenance. Unlike the seemingly ever-suited Vekk, she favors the bookish collection of tweed jackets and wool sweaters that have been dubbed, "Bruder Chic," apparel Vekk routinely refers to as "Fake Intellectual," "Anti-German," and/or "Blatantly Marxist."

"Ja."

"You don't know me, but a mutual friend gave me your contact information."

"OK."

"Are you alone?"

"Maybe?"

"Because what I've got to say is for your ears only."

"Who is this?"

"A concerned citizen?"

"How did you get this number?"

"I told you, a mutual friend."

"Who is this mutual friend?"

"Um."

"As I thought. Listen, whoever you are, this is my private line. I have a staff for mundane requests."

"But I'm…"

"Or people who just seem to want to talk."

"I'm neither of those. I'm just not sure exactly how to say what I have to say."

"Just spit it out."

"I think someone may try to kill you."

"You mean like—"

"Yes, as in, an assassination."

The line dies.

TRAGICOMEDY FOR THE FALLEN, PART 3

THE SIXTIES were a trippy time and not just for you guys. The giants and I had migrated from Minnesota to Boston. Chateau Loki was still a few years away, but I had a decent place, down by the harbor. What I didn't have yet was my whole family. I didn't have Hel. I might never have found her on my own either. Took the giants to dig up the Queen of the Dead.

'67 to be exact, the Summer of Love, and the giants had just done a stint at Watsitooco State. No, they didn't need to learn anything, per se. They didn't need to improve their job prospects or master a trade. But they wanted the college experience. And what could I say? Not that saying no would have done any good. So, they headed off to Watsitooco and fell down the rock-and-roll counter-culture hole in short order, taking their junior years off to follow the Airplane.

They bought a VW bus, gave it a psychedelic paint job— lime green, hot pink, sky blue, orange, and yellow water lilies all over—and hit the road. An indeterminate number of tabs of acid later, they were in the Haight when they saw this chick holding court on the corner, armed with an acoustic six-string, some really wacked out philosophy, and a pack of Gauloises. They stopped to take in the show.

During this girl's set, she can't help but notice the giants. I mean, they've always been pretty hard to miss when they set their minds to it. That's the one part of their reality that's stayed constant. Whether they're giants or little people, they really stand out in a crowd, once you lower your field of vision, of course. Call it fate or destiny or whatever you want, but to hear them tell it, they got "this feeling" about "this chick." That's how they put it at least. I asked them to go into specifics, but they went vague, and I realized I really didn't want to know. After the show they headed up to the stage, as it was.

Hel said, "Do I know you guys from somewhere?"

Thyrm said, "I don't think so. But maybe."

Surt asked, "Like, where?"

Hel said, "You want to smoke a joint?"

And the giants said, "You bet."

So off went the three of them to smoke, but before they could light up, Hel narrowed her eyes, leaned in, and said, "It's Surtur and Thyrm, isn't it?"

And Surtur and Thyrm denied up and down because they really had no idea who they were dealing with. For all they knew this was Frigga or Sif, some sort of trap.

How did Hel know them? Man, I have no idea how Hel knew them. What, you think in our world everything makes sense? Please.

Finally, Hel asked, "Did Loki put you up to this?"

To which they replied, "Hel?"

THE THREE of them continued following the Airplane from festival to festival in that ridiculous bus. They met the Stones, the Dead—at least they insisted they had. I asked Mick and Jerry.

There were no memories, but it was a heady time. Rock solid accounts of the 60's were, and are, tough to come by. Eventually, a year after they'd left on their "pilgrimage," I finally heard from the giants. It was the middle of the night when the phone rang.

"Gustav Johansson," asked a voice.

"Err, yes…?"

"This is Officer Blah Blah of the Backward Ass Bullshit PD," or whatever he said. I forget exactly. They were someplace in Iowa or Georgia.

"OK?"

"I have your wards in custody," he continued.

"My wards?"

"Two little guys."

"Little guys, huh?"

"Not yours?"

"No, they're probably mine. Let me talk to them."

"Hey, uh, Gustav?" asked Thyrm.

"Yes, whatever you've told this guy your name is."

"You're never going to guess who we met?"

"I haven't heard from you guys in six weeks. I was getting ready to come after you."

"No, but seriously…you won't believe it."

"Try me."

And he whispered, "Hel."

Sure enough, I was down at the Western Union office wiring bail money within the hour. A day later, the giants returned to Boston, sans VW bus (a long, sad story), but with Hel, a longer, far happier tale.

And it was touching, that first meeting with Hel, surprising too. Seeing her with her physical corporeality more or less static, seeing her *with a face*...it even took Fen a few seconds to get comfortable with it being her. But she had the memories. She had the eyes. This was my daughter, and it could be no one else.

7

MY NONFICTIONAL EXISTENCE

A WORD on magic: Mine, that is.

Even when I had the sort of mountain-chucking, moose-to-mouse-polymorphing sorcerouz-skillz-that-killz—even when I had all that power—Odin had more. Worse, especially for you, he was infinitely more impressed with his magic, and himself for that matter. Odin's pride: They could write books about it. And they should have. But they haven't. Until now...

Instead of accepting the reality of his own flaws, his own *evil*, One-Eye cast me as the fallen angel—that part he accomplished even if he couldn't get the Christians to come along with the rest of it. Sure the Great Integration worked, just not as Odin had hoped.

You're familiar with the Christmas Tree? Mistletoe? Reindeer? Santa Claus? That whole shtick? Yeah, well, turned out—and this is pretty funny if you think about it—that Christianity absorbed us rather than us absorbing them. I say, funny, because, well, it's not real, right? Christianity, Monotheism. I mean, how much sense does that make anyway? One god?

Is there one human? One chipmunk? One brand of peanut butter? No, no, no. So, why should there be one god? Name one other thing that comes in ones and only ones, one thing that is its own beginning and end. You can't because there isn't. The one god is a figment, designed by some of you guys to control others of you guys.

OUR DESTINATION, Hel's and mine and our midnight-blue with a neon-red racing stripe '68 Camaro's is the aforementioned Anarchy, a country tavern in the most faerie-tale-cum-splatter-spunk sense of the word. Before we get there, though, before we start getting to the bottom of whatever Odin was, and/or is, up to, we have to "complete the look" as they say in the image biz.

I snap my fingers, wriggle my nose, and say "Poof."

Hel's visage ages a decade, mine two. And when I say ages, of course, I mean in a human sense, the facsimile of physicality our immortal souls have become, which, of course, we're not really. Still, it can be surprising, even for us.

Hel stops whistling cold. She gives the rear-view a little side-eye, gazes in something like horror at the blonde, spiky hair, purple eyeshadow, and vampiric mascara. Black leather, too. Yes, it's true I've turned Hel into the facsimile of a biker chick, her cover name Satanica Darque. Then again, I've made "me" look far worse, turned myself into Odin's construct, the magical mythical Wrath X.

6'5" in stocking feet, two forty but lean, Wrath is a former SEAL whose hobbies include chewing menacingly on toothpicks, Brazilian jiu-jitsu, and scorpion-milking. He wears mirrored Aviators, a black, Deaths-Head-patterned doo-rag, a goatee so pointy it doubles as a weapon, enough Nazi tats to populate a museum of fascist iconography, and a rotating ensemble of denim, leather, and chains "caked with the dust of the road." And that, dear readers, is the extent of my magic.

I can say, "Poof," and change physical appearances, not just for myself, but others. That's it.

"I've been meaning to mention something," Hel says, still eyeing her appearance in the visor mirror.

"Okay?"

"This Viking Brotherhood, their leadership structure gets sort of murky once you get past this Marc-Fritz guy."

"Murky as in…?"

"Murky as in I'm betting there's actual Asgardian involvement. So…"

"Odin lied to me yet again?"

"Something like that."

"And…who are you thinking is the actual Asgardian in question?"

"Well, with Heimdall back in Boston, Tyr back at New Valhalla, Forseti cloistered with his law books as usual and Frey doing whatever it is Frey does, it can only be—"

"Fucking Thor?"

"Right. Fucking Thor."

IN ADDITION to being a governmental form—or, technically, the complete lack thereof—Anarchy is a spacious, though somewhat dilapidated stone building nearly equidistant between Berlin and New Valhalla. Sort of a bar, sort of a restaurant, sort of a pool hall, it's also more than sort of a hang-out for the Grieste Chapter of the Viking Brotherhood (located in Wikinger-Bruderschaft, to be precise), one of the white supremacist pies into which Odin has apparently stuck his fingers.

Like I said, I've watched from afar for a long time, questioned whether I could see Odin's hand in various putsches and power-grabs, sundry "movements" and other fell trends. Why didn't I do anything, you might fairly ask? But I have. The problem, my dears, is I can't do everything. I mean, I love you guys. I truly do. But even if I theoretically could oppose everything Odin's done and/or doing, which I can't because he's got a lot more resources, Hitler and his aftermath taught me that you have to do it yourselves. You've got to be the ones to change.

For all those years I walked the Earth after Odin booted me from Valhalla that last time, I was helping you guys, doing whatever I could. I was solo, too, always in disguise—a British artillery officer here, a member of the French resistance there— never able to say, "Look, guys, it's me, Loki, here to help." I still helped, of course; did everything I could during the war years.

You'd think that come 1945 everything would have been roses and sunshine. Not, so. Totalitarianism is a tricky beast, one ready to morph from political right to left if need be. Never mind the fact that democracy had to team up with one totalitarian (Stalin) to get rid of the other totalitarians (Hitler, etc.), recent history has only illuminated those problems further. Sometimes, these days, your totalitarians don't even come from right or left. Sometimes, technically, they're not even political, at least not primarily.

Take your ayatollahs and American Dominionists, for example. Not that this should be a surprise either. Your love of gods, your desire to be shown the way, has caused you to create so many of them out of whole cloth; to put your energy, most of it, into the ones that aren't even real.

OVERSEEN BY Grieste Chapter Prez, Marc-Fritz Hoffhaus, Anarchy's where a lot of the local neo-Nazi bottom dogs spend their days, plotting their plots, scheming their schemes, and lamenting the foreigners who've taken over their country as they kill time between relief checks. Marc-Fritz (M-F for short) keeps an eye on things, reports back to Thor, who he, of course, has no idea is Thor, on the noteworthy and the not-so. I guess, in a way, Anarchy's sort of like New Valhalla's farm team.

Though M-F may not be a second stringer himself, he's no rocket scientist. Let's be clear about that. Married his cousin's cousin for starters. Who by the way, also happens to be his great aunt. Yeah, looking at M-F, you can hear the evolutionary clock whining, metallic and shrill, as it's wound back and back and back.

The interesting thing about M-F—besides being something of a Missing Link—is that he's also spent a fair amount of time in the pokey. As a result, he's developed a sense of prison justice and hierarchy, one in which there is a clear delineation of the nobility of various forms of crime. Killer, armed robber, assault-with-intent-er, drug dealer, and counterfeiter though he may be, there are certain activities with which M-F refuses to sully himself, things he absolutely, violently shuns.

M-F's personal sense of honor is especially intense as far as women go, especially beautiful women like…Hel, for instance. Oh, I know what I said about her appearance. And it has changed, not for the better, from an objective point of view. But we all have our tastes, don't we? And when it comes to the Viking Brotherhood's tastes, Hel's current combo of "sorta for sale" and "I'll kick your ass if you try," is a big winner. Better still, there just happens to be a certain miscreant who's been hanging out at Anarchy recently. In addition to her role as Neo-Nazi eye candy, Hel's research skills are unmatched.

This guy—his name is Rolf, but they call him Ralf—this guy, Rolf/Ralf, has a penchant for drugging and raping women, one that bought him a ten-year stay in Uberg Bay.

Now, I'm sure M-F doesn't know about Rolf/Ralf yet. If he did, he already would have gotten rid of him, told him he wasn't welcome at Anarchy, maybe beaten him responseless in the process.

DESPITE NUMEROUS opportunities to drug Hel, Rolf/Ralf never even talks to her. Has he become good? Golly, that would throw a chainsaw into things, wouldn't it? And it does… because, actually, that turns out to be true.

After a couple hours of frustration, we're forced to modify the plan. The new plan being we're going to have to frame Rolf/Ralf. It's the only way. I mean, I'm pretty sure I can work things, so he doesn't actually get hurt too much. I'm good at pulling punches, y'know, kung faux fighting.

Rolf/Ralf has been sitting a few barstools from Hel for a half hour. I get a third beer, keep a steady line of sight. She glances at me. I nod. Hel pops a tab in her drink, heads for the Ladies. Several minutes later she returns, scoots over to a stool next to Rolf/Ralf. Wait. Wait. Wait. And go…

Hel sips her drink, wriggles her nose in distaste. "Hey," she shouts, wheeling on a surprised Rolf/Ralf, "What the fuck?"

In spite of the aural melee that was going on seconds before—the Nazi metal jukebox warring with this convo about meth and that one about football—the bar goes quiet. Hel has, as hoped, become even more the center of attention than she was. I or, rather, Wrath X, saunter over.

"What's wrong, baby?" I say with deep, gravelly menace.

"Fucker tried to dope me, Wrath."

"Actually, it's Rolf," says Rolf/Ralf.

"I was talking to him, asshole. Here, baby, taste this," says Hel, handing the drink to me.

I take a sip. "What the fuck?" I ask, pulling Rolf/Ralf from his stool. "You tryin' to dope my old lady, little man?"

"Um...*what*?"

I throw him across the room. Well, I mean, it's more like a toss than a throw but the guy definitely catches air, lands on his back. I'm on top of him before he can think about getting out of the way. I throw a right cross then another. I hit him with a headbutt then whisper, "Go along."

"Huh?"

I headbutt him again, and Rolf/Ralf seems to get the idea. I pick him up, bring him to his feet, grab him by the throat, so it looks like I'm choking him. I'm not, though.

I won't lie. I've watched my share of televised wrestling. That's the other "sport" I seem unable to do without in America. The giants love it, too. So do Hel and Fen, TBH. Anyway, that's where I learned a few things about faux fighting, kung- and elsewise.

"Listen, little man, your days here are done." I drag him to the door, open it and shove him out onto the icy lot, slam the door self-righteously on my way back inside.

"What the fuck is going on out here?" says a voice I'm guessing must be M-F.

"Rolf/Ralf tried to drug the babe," says some miscellaneous white supremacist pointing at Hel.

"Ah," says M-F, crossing to stand in front of her. "This it?" he says, pointing at the drink.

She nods.

He sips. "Sure enough, that little *sweinhund* tried to dope her. Knew he was no good in spite of what they said."

"What's that?"

"Cut his balls off, pecker too. That douchebag used to rape kids." M-F looks down. "Kids!" he adds, looking up in dismay, an expression that forces me to see M-F as human.

I can't allow myself to get distracted, though. I cross the bar in a hurry. Hel practically leaps into my arms, gives me a big, wet kiss, right on the lips. I mean, yes, obviously it's gross, but sometimes you have to take one for the team.

"Guess you got your reward, huh, dude?" says M-F.

I smile even though I want to say "blech." "Name's Wrath, Wrath X," I say.

"Marc-Fritz," says M-F, reaching out as though to arm wrestle. I return his white man cum soul brother power shake. "Good to see a little chivalry in this day and age, isn't it, boys?"

A roar of approbation goes up from the crowd of chivalrous white supremacists. Part one done.

BACK AT the villa later that night, trying to unwind, watching TV in the great room. I'm feeling good, not bad at the very least. Then I get this weird DM from Hel. Or, should I say, this normal DM from Hel. Because, truth be told, Hel's DMs are normally pretty weird.

"See me," it says.

I walk out of the great room and down the hall. I go to knock on the door to Hel's room, but she shouts, "Come," before I can.

A premonition, you might ask. No, not really: Hel just has exceptional hearing and a heartless sense of humor.

"The giants called," she says as I enter. "They were having a great time playing *Monsieur von Mayhem* with the Norn."

"That's good—"

"I said *were*. Until your buddy Kurt showed up."

"I thought they said they'd take her to location 4 if anything happened."

"They say they were planning to. If things, y'know, got bad."

"Right. So, they're at 4 now?"

"No, they're at 3."

"The church in—"

"Yes. Turns out Heimdall was following Kurt. So, he tracked them all the way to 4."

"Sunshine's still safe?"

"Yes, they got her out in time."

"And Kurt?"

"They were able to subdue and drug him before Heimdall got upstairs."

"So, what, was there some sort of battle?"

"With Heimdall? No, the giants had the doorman call the cops."

"For what?"

"IDK, they probably gave him a couple hundred bucks."

"No, I meant—"

"You know I know what you meant."

"Hmm, that is pretty bad. Not the worst thing I could possibly have imagined, though."

"I don't think I can live up to that, but I'm not done. Kurt knew Heimdall was following him. They're definitely in cahoots. At least that's what the giants are saying."

"And you believe them?"

"Well, they did call me instead of you."

"That doesn't answer my question."

"I know."

I DON'T entirely understand Kurt's part in whatever is happening, but he seems to have one; a part that, if anything, seems to be mushrooming. If he didn't, Sunshine wouldn't have been so evasive about discussing him in the first place, and he wouldn't have shown up unannounced at Chateau Loki in the second.

Sure, he runs this Sexaholics Anonymous thing, that's one bit of it. I mean, I really just started going to that on a lark. I'm not sure it's even a legitimate SexAnon group per se, could be populated with thespians right and left, unemployed actors "working on the craft."

As for the writing workshop where I actually met Kurt, I only wish it were a fake. Yes, I started going to help them out, as I do. Writers, they're sort of like addicts, y'know? They put themselves through all this pain. And, really, they're just looking for love and approval, like any addicts.

Just go to one of these workshops yourself if you're curious. Go and see the sad menagerie of characters that show up. All the poets in heavy eye make-up and odd, over-priced hats, the would-be celebrity novelists in their tight t-shirts tapping away on their uPhones, scanning Amazon for deals on the latest "AI novel-ing software," the future unpaid HuffPo bloggers, come straight from day jobs, still wearing their smart para-corporate attire. All of which is superficial, of course; not to the heart of things.

Which is this: Kurt and I go out for beers sometimes, after the workshops, to laugh and cry, but mostly to laugh. Hell, we've even swapped manuscripts, and you can't get much closer than that as writers. No, I haven't given him the whole sordid thing, my entire *Book of Loki*. Kurt's only mortal, after all. He doesn't have the bandwidth for the sprawling Proustian nightmare of my nonfictional existence.

Actually, calling my life story Proustian seems somehow unfair to Proust. At least he confined himself to a few thousand pages. And he was chronically ill; also, most likely insane. I have no such excuses. Of course, I've had a bit more time on my hands than Marcel. Imagine what sort of monstrosity Proust might have hatched with a few centuries at his disposal. I've been at this fucking thing off and on since the first time Odin booted me from Asgard. Kurt's encouraging me, though. I have to give that to him. Maybe, in a way he's helping me more than I'm helping him. Lately, he's been trying to convince me to go epic.

He says, "Gustav, you're really into this Norse mythology stuff. You should just run with it. Why not make Loki your protagonist?"

"He's evil, isn't he?"

"Good and evil. They're simplistic concepts, aren't they? Anyway, it's not like these characters are real."

"I know, characters, right? Completely made up."

"Yours in particular. Loki, Odin, Thor...give me a fucking break. They're mythological constructs."

"Are you saying that's bad?"

"No, I'm saying it's good. But it's not realistic strictly speaking." I must look hurt because, "Which is fine. Writing doesn't have to be realistic. But you have to let it breathe. You have to let Loki (and Odin and the rest of them) speak. You have to hear them in your mind."

KEEPING DESTINY'S BEAT

BY THE time I arrived at the base of Mount Norn, I was in the middle of a blizzard, and I had my doubts as to who'd started it. Odin himself? The Norns? Fate? Icicles dangling from the tip of my beak, my tail feathers frozen all to Bifrost, I did the only thing that made sense at that point. I turned myself into a mountain goat. Not just any miscellaneous mountain goat, mind you. We're talking magical Asgardian mountain goat. Triple-thick hide, mithril horns, eyes red embers, fur black as betrayal at midnight; I lit off for the top of Mount Norn, as fast as my not-so-little hooves would carry me. By the time I neared the summit, the snow had gotten even worse, the wind circling, screaming as it did, and I was one cashed goat-cicle.

The sky darkening, I paused to get my bearings. Looking down from Mount Norn, I saw out across the white sea of the Asgardian plains to the glint of fair, golden Valhalla, and The Rainbow Bridge kaleidoscopic beyond. I have to tell you I had a premonition then, an image of myself and the end times.

Icy tempests and fiery tsunamis at my back, lightning scouring a preternatural skyscape of pewter and obsidian, I wore armor of lacquered black and gold, the cuirass studded with rubies as big as your fist and deeper crimson than new-let blood. I bore a black-bladed bastard sword that shimmered with scarlet light as I led my giant legions across The Rainbow Bridge by the millions—frost and fire, stone and sea, air and storm. The entirety of Jotenheim emptied for this our last purpose, we marched in time, a great, fell kettle drum keeping destiny's beat.

Soon I came to the pinnacle and my ultimate destination, the mouth of the Cavern of Fate. Which was where I turned myself back into...*myself*...my experience being that goats, magical or otherwise, don't always make the best first impressions. I entered the cavern, calling out as I did...

"Oh, Norns?" I asked.

No reply.

"Here, Norny-Norny-Nornys? Where are you?"

No reply.

"Come out, come out, wherever you are? It's me, Loki."

"Why have you come, Trickster?" came the voice. Well, voices really. This, I'd been told, was how the Norns would first reveal themselves. They would speak in unison—voices icy, gravelly, more than a little freaky. The Norns were big on theatrics back in those days. They still seem pretty big on theatrics if you ask me.

"Odin sent me. He said you wanted to see me."

"Very well, come forth."

I walked until I arrived at the doors of the Norns' Inner Sanctum. Shining like the silvered tip of Odin's spear, covered in glowing runes, I moved to knock but before I could touch the doors, they swung wide. Standing before me were the Sisters Three: Darkness, Halflight, and Sunshine.

They were nothing like I'd pictured. The crone voices, I also learned, were an act of illusion. The Norns were beautiful, on the rare occasions when they wanted to be, all dark-haired and dark-eyed like Odin's ravens themselves. I found myself wondering whether there was a connection.

"There is," they said as one, in the voice that had guided me through their lair.

"Um—"

"You will realize what it is in the fullness of time. For now, we cannot say. What we can say is that the All-Father has deceived you. He has not sent you here seeking wisdom. For simple wisdom will not avail you."

"I knew it."

"The Norse religion is declining. That is why he has recalled you from exile. He needs your help for the religion to thrive. None but you can do this. Now, you must choose one of us to treat with."

"Gosh, I just—"

"You must decide. *Now.*"

They all looked the same, exactly the same. I thought about their names. And I thought Fate had always been pretty literal with us, at least up until then. While Darkness might fit with the role of evil Odin kept trying to stick me with—and picking Halflight seemed like I'd be hedging my bets—Sunshine's was the only name that seemed to promise something positive.

So, I said, "I choose Sunshine." And the other two Norns disappeared, "Poof."

Sunshine became fully corporeal and stepped forward, "Trickster," she said, smiling, "Why did you choose me?"

"Mm, honestly, it was because your name sounded the most promising."

"Well, I suppose that makes as much sense as anything."

"Whither this stuff about Christianity, about Odin needing it?"

"Fate is unhappy with you."

"Me?"

"The religion. You must do better. You must gain more worshippers."

"Then help us."

"That is not our place."

"Why not? You work for us. Odin said—"

"He told you that we work for you?"

"Well, for him."

"Odin's contract is with Fate, not us. We, too, serve Fate."

"So, you don't work for him?"

"Not at all. Which means we see the world as it is, not as Odin wants us to."

There was nothing romantic at that point, not even anything sexual other than noting Sunshine's obvious beauty. For some reason, though, I found myself wanting to kiss her.

"Don't," she said.

"Don't what?"

"You know what. And it's not time."

8
HEL'S WACKY FACTS

MY UPHONE comes alive to the increasingly familiar strains of "Ride of the Valkyries."

"You already gave him his own ringtone?" Hel asks.

"He did it himself."

"That's impressive and yet completely disturbing."

I nod, hit speaker, pick up.

"How'd it go?" Odin asks.

"How'd what go?"

"Don't be coy. Anarchy, the Viking Brotherhood…"

"I'm in."

"All the way in?"

Hel looks away, shakes her head in disgust.

"I'm in, to the extent I'm still going to try to make sure Greta Bruder doesn't get murdered if that's what you mean."

"Splendiferous!" he says, though he sounds skeptical, as though he's holding onto something. "Stupendulous! And when will you be delivering the Norn?"

"No Norn. I told you she'll have to decide for herself when to come back. If ever."

"At least tell me how long it's going to take before she decides. Come on, son, I'm an old man. I can't wait forever."

"I just said…I don't know. A while, I guess. She's still in America."

"Give me a specific location. I'll have someone pick her up, simple as that."

"You mean…someone like…Heimdall?"

Hel rolls her eyes.

I laugh.

"Am I on speaker?" Odin asks. "Who's there?"

"None of your business. Good job ducking the Heimdall question. though."

"Take me off speaker at least."

"And again! Fine," I say, but don't. I mouth 'behave' to Hel. "I do have a question you can answer, though."

"Sure, son, anything."

"You didn't tell me Thor was behind the Viking Brotherhood."

"Gosh, did I forget to mention that? Sorry. Honest mistake, complete oversight."

"What happened to 'no meddling?'"

"There's no meddling and no meddling, right?"

"Not really."

"OK, fine. As long as the Norns don't find out it shouldn't be a problem. Plus having Thor there is going to make it easier for you, so much easier. Plus—"

"You already said, 'Plus.'"

"The *second* plus is there's plenty of room for plausible deniability just in case."

"Wait a second. Why don't you just have Thor take care of all this skullduggerous stuff if he's already involved?"

"Aside from the fact that he's a god and has been forbidden to intervene just like me?"

"Right, besides that?"

"He's not technically in charge."

"Who is?"

"Isn't it obvious?"

WITH WRATH's well dramatized propensity for violence and, still more importantly, Hel's well dramatized propensity for comingling sex and death vibes, we're able to quickly work our way into Marc-Fritz's office at Anarchy.

Snowy rails of meth. Sticky balls of hash. Beer, schnapps, weed, coke, horse, ether, whatever…it's a smorgasbord of mind alteration back there. Fortunately, I'm, well, me, so no matter how much of a pharmacological garbage can M-F sees himself as, I'm beyond his ken, as is Hel. Which means our smorgasbord of mind alteration soon becomes a cornucopia (sorry) of information. Not any of the really good stuff of course. But we get enticing tidbits, tempting crumbs. The next night, M-F has had so much of anything and everything that he gets to talking about Bruder.

"Little Jewess minx. She'll get what's coming to her."

"You sound like you'd do her right here if you could," says Hel.

"Huh?" says M-F.

"She means, 'kill.'"

"Do I?" Hel asks.

"Hell, yes, you do…uh, Satanica. And why not? She's a money-grubber, a socialist."

"But she's not Jewish, is she?" asks Hel.

"She's a show-off, that's for sure," says M-F, not giving two flips about Hel's wacky facts. "Oh, I was in the army. Oh, I was a commander. Oh, I was in the federal police. Oh, I was a commandant. Oh, I was—"

"Yeah?"

"Sure. Anyway, like I said, she'll get hers soon enough. You can count on that. Me and Boris will see to it."

"Boris?"

"The big boss. You'll meet him. Maybe. If you're lucky. If you give me a turn with your old lady," he says, leering at Hel.

To mortal eyes, Hel would appear to be leering back. But she's not. In fact, Hel's leer actually translates to a desire to pull M-F's tongue out through his nose. She could do it, too, technically speaking. But she doesn't. Self-control, that's my Hel. Just like the night before, and the night before that, we stumble out of Anarchy around two in the morning, heads brimming with new leads, phones brimming with missed calls.

Hel tells me she wants to drive home.

"Sure, what the..." I wink, toss her the keys.

Doors open, doors close, and she peels out before I can even get my seatbelt on. Of course, I wear one. No, a car crash wouldn't kill me, but it would still be a giant pain in the tuchus. And I've already got more than enough of those, thanks.

WE'RE HALF-WAY back to the villa when my uPhone buzzes.

"Pull over," I tell Hel, as I put Surtur on video. Thyrm's there with him. Both are smiling, but their eyes are nervous, their pupils retracted, gazes unsteady.

"Listen, Loki," Surtur begins, "we had a problem. Not a big one, just a little one, hardly anything really."

"The Norn got away," Thyrm blurts.

Surtur scowls. "I told you I was gonna tell him."

"You did not."

"I did so."

"Did not!"

143

"Just tell me what happened, OK, whichever one of you want to speak?"

"Anyway," says Surtur, giving a little stink eye to Thyrm as he picks back up, "We were just about finished with level 6, too; fucked the whole thing up."

"Terrible beyond belief," Thyrm adds as commentary.

Surtur continues, "We had gotten the glow worms *and* the Bi-alternate Crown of Grimalda, can you believe that? Then we lost them both because of her, and we couldn't finish the Water Torture Puzzle at the end either. Obviously."

Thyrm nods.

"I meant, what in the entire blessed expanse of Ginnungagap happened with Sunshine?"

Surtur replies, "We ordered pizza, OK? When I opened the front door for the pizza guy, Sunshine said she was heading 'over there' and fled."

"Over where?"

"Europe. I guess."

"You *guess*?"

"Fine, Thyrm checked."

Thyrm nods officiously. "She bought a plane ticket and everything."

"What about Kurt?"

"Oh, he ran right after her. I guess they really are in cahoots."

"Will you guys please stop talking about 'cahoots?'"

"Fine, if you're gonna be that way." Thyrm looks down.

"I thought you had Kurt tied up or something," I say, turning to Surtur.

"We did, but we untied him. So, he could eat. I mean, we're not elves or anything."

"What if he goes to the police now?"

144

"Oh, he won't," Surtur replies. "He's completely in love with Sunshine."

"And who can blame him?" Thrym elbows Surt. "What a babe."

"You guys didn't try anything with her, did you?"

"Try what?"

"Like, sex."

"Oh, no way…we wouldn't do that to you, Loki. Kurt, though, I wouldn't trust him. You know he doesn't even know how to play *Monsieur von Mayhem*."

"Or *DnD*!"

"You guys are being rather cavalier about all this."

"Well, it was just for safekeeping, right? Did you decide what you're doing with Odin? Did you figure out the assassination plot yet? When are you coming home?"

One of the best things about the giants is that they have a completely unrealistic level of faith in me. They are earnestly wondering whether I've already solved everything. All I can say is I must have been much better in my younger days. I mean, this sort of belief is primal, born of the old relationship.

"It's going to be a while still, guys. I've barely started to figure things out."

"But it's been two whole days?"

"Be that as it may."

"Uh-oh. We botched this all to Nastrond, didn't we?"

"No offense, Hel."

She lights a Gauloise, leaves them twisting. Their expressions slowly fall.

"We're sorry," they say in unison.

"I know you are." I smile. "If you guys weren't so frickin' cute who knows what I'd do."

"Oh, I can think of a few things," says Surtur.

"From back on Jotenheim," Thyrm adds.

Both grimace.

"Just, get Sunshine back, huh? And Kurt, too?"

"Sure, sure, don't worry, Loki, we're completely ahead of you, actually already at the airport. Got a flight that lands in London just about the same minute as hers."

"What about Fen?"

"He's with us," I hear them say in unison.

Fen yips.

"Good. Let me know the minute you've got her. And remember…"

"What?"

"You have to walk Fen, y'know, like outside."

Both nod.

"You have to pick up after him, too."

"Seriously?" Thyrm asks.

"Yes. I keep telling you, 'This isn't like the old days. You can't just leave shit in a corner and expect some terrified subordinate to come along and clean it up."

HEL AND I have just cleared the villa's front gates when Kurt calls. I'm getting out of the car and heading for the front door as I answer.

"Gustav? It's Kurt, obviously."

"I wasn't expecting to hear from you after all the trouble you caused over there."

"Over here? Where are you?"

"Germany."

"Oh, so that's why Sabrina—"

x

"I thought you weren't interested in her."

"OK, well, obviously I lied about that. Hell of a lot of good it did me."

"Is she there with you? Let me talk to her."

"She was, but then..."

"Then, what?"

"She ditched me."

"That's...not surprising."

"Hey!"

"I didn't mean it that way, man. But, uh, given the way you sort of...stalked her...and led that crazy Chaim Doll guy right to her, you couldn't really expect her to stick around."

"Chaim Doll? What a strange name."

"You really put my friends out, too."

"The little guys?"

"Right. They're convinced you knew you were leading Chaim Doll to them. They say you're in cahoots."

"Cahoots? What's with all this skullduggerous talk, Gustav? I feel like I've parachuted into some sort of caper. Your friends drugged me, you know?"

"You endangered the whole operation."

"Again, with the lingo? Gustav, they kidnapped me."

"Maybe."

"No, I'm a lawyer. They absolutely *kidnapped* me."

"OK, fine, they kidnapped you. They also probably saved your life. That Chaim Doll guy is extremely dangerous. In a thick-headed, ploddingly vigilant, eternally annoying way."

"What?"

"Never mind. You still haven't answered my question."

"About?"

"Cahoots?"

"With Chaim Doll? This is my first time hearing his name. There have been absolutely no cahoots between the two of us."

"What about Sabrina then?"

"No cahoots there either. She ditched me in Amsterdam, stole my wallet."

"But she left your phone?"

"Yeah, I guess."

"Something about this isn't making sense."

"Honestly, a lot of it isn't making sense to me either."

"OK."

He doesn't say anything, just breathes heavily.

"What? What is it?"

"Actually, I'm stuck with airport security. Sabrina filed a complaint or something before she left."

"Like you said, you're a *lawyer*. Get yourself out."

"Everyone here is speaking Dutch. And I don't understand Dutch."

"Fair enough."

"Look, Gustav, Sabrina seems to really like you. I was thinking maybe you could just get her to drop the complaint."

"I don't know, Kurt."

"I mean…your friends…kidnapped me, dude. They drugged me, tied me up, transported me against my will to multiple locations."

"Fine, I'll see what I can do."

"By which you mean?"

"Yes, I'll get you out."

TRAGICOMEDY FOR THE FALLEN, PART 4

I DIDN'T see the giants again until 1955. I'd been in America a few years by that point. Sure, I'd been wondering about them the whole time, but I had no idea where to even start looking. Fortunately, Fate intervened. Yes, I guess it helps once in a while.

I was pursuing one of my passions back then, which was the demolition derby. Like I told you, during my time in America, I've become more than a little Americanized: football, basketball, bowling, pro wrestling, NASCAR, the demo...yeah, I eat up Americana, what can I say? Anyhoof, I found the giants at the Demo Nationals, that year, in Tundra Lake, Minnesota. They were working as snack vendors.

Back then, in the heavy days of out-and-out little-person discrimination, novelty gigs were the only ones they could get—jobs where their diminution acted as a sort of sight gag. They had too much self-respect to go into the circus of course. Like I said, these guys were kings once upon a time, still are really.

I was standing in line, waiting to buy a beer, just minding my own business. Honestly, I didn't even notice the giants at first. They were the ones who noticed me.

"Trickster!" I heard.

"Mischief maker!" followed.

"Wha?" I asked no one in particular, whirling around once, twice, three times.

"Psst…*here*?" I heard, whirling again.

"No, *down* here." I felt a tug on my pant leg and looked down.

I saw two little guys—one with red hair and jet skin, the other with silver hair and skin so pale it seemed almost blue. Shit, I thought, I'm being harangued by a couple of parti-colored dwarves. I wondered if this was One-Eye's idea of a joke. He's always been comically limited. But thinking of Odin got me thinking of the old days, and I looked back at the one with red hair, the one that had been pulling on my pant leg. I thought back to the first time Odin kicked me out, when I had no place to go, when the giants took me in. I remembered the way Surtur used to sneer when I talked to him, the reassuring grunts, the warm glower of his eyes.

"Surtur? Thyrm? Is that you?"

They nodded, more or less in unison.

"What happened to you guys?"

"Whaddya mean?" said Surtur, feigning offense.

"You're not giants anymore. You're not ugly anymore either," I blurted.

"Ugly?" they asked, chuckling in unison. "What are you implying?"

I knelt to shake their hands, but they hugged me instead. Hugs, I thought. What in Alfheim is this? My giant, murderous subordinates had turned into a couple of pint-sized cuddle bears.

"You guys OK?"

"You mean the hugs?"

"Not to mention I don't see any swords or armor. You were pretty attached to those."

"Disappeared. Poof. One day we're in Jotunheim, all big, mad, and armor clad, next we're in Berlin and the bombs are falling. And they hurt. You were there, Loki. We saw you. How come you didn't recognize us?"

"He was too busy running away."

"Hey, you said it, those bullets hurt. How was I to know they weren't deadly, just painful? You ran too, didn't you?"

"Heck, yes."

"Ran all the way to France."

"On those little legs?"

"Fine. We stole a car."

"A Mercedes," Thyrm added proudly.

"We gave it back, though."

Thyrm nodded earnestly. "With a new set of tires."

"New tires? Hey, wait a second. You guys haven't turned... good, have you?"

"Good?" asked Surtur.

"Why would you even ask a question like that?" asked Thyrm.

"It's insulting."

"Well?"

"Have *you* turned good, Trickster?" Surtur added, lowering his voice, raising one bushy, red eyebrow.

"When do you guys get off work?"

"Eleven or so."

"I'll be back then."

WHEN I picked them up, I thought the guys looked pretty hungry, and I wasn't wrong; so, I took them to midnight breakfast at this diner they were fond of. They could still eat like the giants of old.

Eggs, bacon, ham, sausage, spam, scrapple, pancakes, waffles, French toast, regular toast, English muffins, hash browns, home fries, and gallons of coffee…no fruit, though. If I'd had any doubts about them being the giants, the lack of fiber in their diets would have convinced me.

Thyrm was off searching for the bathroom as Surtur finished his fourth stack of silver dollar pancakes.

"So, what do you think about this McCarthy guy?" he asked.

"The senator?"

He reached for the front page of the paper, flipped it to face me and jabbed a stubby index finger into McCarthy's weak-chinned, sweaty face.

"I think he's a demagogue."

"But the commies, the commies!?"

"They're bad, sure. But McCarthy's no better. He's just the other side of the same coin."

"You think Odin's behind it."

"McCarthy? Wouldn't surprise me. You know I saw him. Saw *them* when they fell. It was after Hitler killed himself. That must have mucked things up somehow, some way, with what they did with The Wheel of Fate."

"Wheel of Fate?"

"The Norns. Their spinning wheel?"

"Norns? You mean those fate broads you never let us meet? That one you fell…in love with…and her sisters?"

"I guess that sounds about right."

"So, this is all their fault."

"More like Odin's fault."

He furrowed his brow. "Well, you seem to have landed on your feet, Loki. No pun intended."

"I've done okay. It's pretty easy to make a buck as a human."

"Maybe for you. But look at us."

"The size?"

"Sure, but not just."

"What, like the hair, couldn't you just dye it?"

"Doesn't work."

"Seriously?"

"Absolutely. So, we're stuck short-assing around with multi-colored hair taking whatever shit jobs society deems appropriate."

"Probably better than the alternative."

"How do you figure?"

"You saw *King Kong*, didn't you? Humans today, they're terrified of anything different, larger than themselves. They might have killed you. Best case, you'd be in the circus."

"Circus? No thanks," he said.

"Hey, man. I didn't mean anything."

"Anyway." He laughed. "The real upside is Faye Wray."

"Touché."

Thyrm returned. "What'd I miss?"

Surtur replied, "We just started talking about circuses."

"Circuses?"

"I wasn't suggesting you work in one. As a matter of fact, I want you guys to come back, work for me."

"Do we even know where the gods are? I mean, it's sorta tough to start Ragnarök without the other side."

"I'm not talking about Ragnarök. I told you. I went good."

"And you were serious?"

"Can't you tell?"

"Meh…I guess," he said, squinting. "I wonder, though, if you're good and all, how'd you get all the money for this?"

"You mean I'm paying?"

Thyrm looked at me, incredulous, dropped an entire forked breakfast sausage in transit from plate to mouth. Syrup splattered onto the newspaper, onto McCarthy's head.

"Of course, I'm paying. I invited you. But that's just the beginning."

"And no Ragnarök?"

"The Norns are gone. We're not even on the Ragnarök clock until they come back."

They nodded.

"And, I mean, would you *ever* come back if you were the Norns? Would you come back to this?"

They shook their heads.

"So, what I'm offering here is I'm willing to start you off as junior partners in Trickster Worldwide."

"What's that?"

"My corporation."

"Oh, yeah?"

"Sure."

"And what is it this corporation does?"

"Currently most of my profits come from trading stocks."

"I thought you said you went straight."

9

CALLING YOURSELF
MEPHISTOPHELES

THE VIKING Brotherhood's sergeant-at-arms, Stuttgart, leads me to a table near the back. He's smoking an Excalibur of some repellent vintage (Russian maybe or Thai) and swilling Jack Daniels Black. His thug or enforcer or bodyguard, Mephistopheles, looms to my left, a golem of constant menace and rare commentary. Which makes sense. If you're going to go around calling yourself Mephistopheles, you should at least look the part, right?

"Immigrants," Stuttgart offers.

"What those fuckers do now?" I query.

"They're destroying the Fatherland, obviously."

"Ah, right." I nod, laugh derisively.

"You're not a Marxist, are you, Wrath?"asks Mephistopheles, speaking for only the second time that day. I guess good old Meph is finally warming up to me. Or maybe I just found his favorite topic.

"A what?"

"A Marxist?" He huffs. "Someone who sucks on the dick of Karl Marx?" He's scowling at me by this point, with what I take for homicidal intent, homicidal interest at the bare minimum. Yeah, I've looked into good old Meph a little, and he doesn't just look menacing.

"Not last time I checked. You are aware he's been dead more than a century?"

"Meaning?"

"Uh."

Stuttgart says, "All right, Meph, give us a minute. I need to talk to Wrath here."

"Things'll get better," I offer Meph, as he exits.

"I doubt it," he grumbles.

"Guy's beside himself," Stuttgart offers, "Bruder's gaining in the polls."

"She's behind by so much. How could it matter? There's no way the Fatherland will elect a woman. I mean, of all things."

He squints at me.

"Not again," I add, "Not after everything we've seen."

"You're right, Wrath. It probably doesn't matter, but we've got a little insurance policy we've been working on."

"Yeah?"

"Oh, yeah. But before we get into that, M-F has a little job for you, a sort of test."

STUTTGART SENDS me north, away from Anarchy, deeper into the countryside. It's near midnight as I pull into the tiny village of Schwarzsee, which means black lake in German. The lake Schwarzsee's on, which is ostensibly nameless, isn't black at all, not even this late at night. In fact, right now, it's pretty white, the top few feet frozen solid, a layer of snow over that, which must make everyone happy round about here, seeing as how for reasons wholesome and unwholesome alike they really do dream of white Christmases.

Speaking of white... I'm apparently doing a little pick-up

for M-F. The address I've been given is #32 on the inaptly named Mittestrasse. Oh, sure, this strasse starts in the mitte, but it doesn't end there. In fact, by the time I've located #32, I'm three miles outside town. I pull the Camaro onto the roadside grass in front of Number 32, park it, lock it—no sense getting the thing stolen. I head past the front yard's obscuring cover of trees, make for the door, and knock three times, as instructed. Wait a few seconds. Three more knocks. Wait. One more. Wait. Whistle.

The door opens. Standing before me is someone who might be described, generically, as "miscellaneous hellion." He's the sort of cat I should be used to simply from being at Anarchy for more than fifteen minutes. And I am, meaning I am used to this sort of cat. He's wearing a bandana, do-rag style, dark glasses, a brown leather vest with no t-shirt, ripped, faded jeans, and moto boots.

"Conrad," he offers.

"Wrath," I say, "Wrath X."

We white-guy soul shake then he steps aside to let me through.

"You want a beer?"

"Sure."

"M-F and Stuttgart sent you?" he asks as he heads for the kitchen.

"Said you knew all about it."

"I do," he says, returning from the refrigerator with a double-barreled shotgun rather than the brews he promised.

"I see."

"Boys," he yells.

Four men burst from what I'll guess is a bedroom, guns

drawn. The first one jacks me in the jaw with the butt of his gun. I'm out. I mean, not really, but I play along, as the others kick me once or twice for good measure.

FIFTEEN MINUTES later, I "wake" in the same room tied to a chair. The five guys that put me down have me encircled, guns pointing at me. I can't help thinking what a pisser it would be if they all opened fire. Sure, they'd hit me, nick me up a bit, but they'd probably kill each other in the process. And even if they didn't, I'd rise like the holy undead which would no doubt, scare each and every one of them to death.

"He's awake," someone says.

My supposed captors step aside for a giant of a man in an exceptionally well-tailored, charcoal blue suit. 6'6", 260, long blond hair, blond beard. Yeah, it's *fucking* Thor. Of course, he's in disguise. But the thing with Thor's disguises is they all read, "Thor." I mean, you have to know how to look, which you guys don't. But I do. See, I taught Thor all about disguises, just like Heimdall and the rest of them.

"So," says Thor, "You're the famous Wrath X?"

"Um, yes, but who are you?"

"I'm Boris."

"Of course, you are."

"You think I'm a joke?"

"Is that a trick question?"

"M-F vouched for you. Said you're ready for some real work. Ready to help us with a big project."

"Oh, yeah?"

"M-F doesn't make the decisions, though."

"OK."

"You checked him?" Thor asks the assembled flunkies. Lots of nodding follows.

"Well at least you weren't wearing a wire."

"Has to be a point in my favor, right?"

"Gonna need to score a few more points, sunshine."

"Sunshine?" I ask.

"Boys?" he replies, winking at me.

The five guys press in on me. They spend the next couple minutes working me over, some with the butts or snubs of their guns, some with fists, elbows, or boots; it's a wild admixture of fighting forms and attempts at improvised violence. The tough part about it is I have to pretend they're really hurting me.

"Oof," I say.

"Ugh," I add.

"Argh," I cry.

"Enough," Thor finally says.

They pull back. Thor steps forward. He kneels, pushes my chin upward, and eyes me. "You don't look much worse for wear." He says, winking again.

Let me tell you, these winks have me uncomfortable to say the least. That hint of conspiracy; that possibility of love or something like it; yeah, the admixture would make me hurl if I was one of you guys. As is, I feel it in my gut, even though I don't come close to tossing my tacos. "Maybe if you had someone other than the girls' volleyball team on it."

"Really?" he says, smiling, winking again. "Well, how about this?" He knocks me right in the kisser with one of those hammer-hands of his.

Fuck. Now, *that* really hurts. Another blow follows and another. Soon, I'm out. Yeah, no lie, I'm not even faking it. I lose consciousness.

When I wake, I'm free and untied, but still sitting in the chair. Thor is slapping my face in a "good-natured" attempt to wake me.

"There he is," he says, adding, "Looks like Sleeping Beauty is finally awake."

"Fuck, man, you can punch."

"Yeah," he responds, "I was taking it easy on you, just remember that."

The truth is, he probably was. Though that doesn't diminish the joy I see in his eyes. Thor has always taken a special interest in making my life difficult.

"Did I pass whatever test that was?"

"For now," he says, pulling me to my feet.

"You did good, Wrath. As a matter of fact," he says, "I've got someone on the line who wants to talk to you."

The number's German, unfamiliar. Like a fool, I bring the thing to my ear.

"Yes?" I ask the phone.

"Herr Wrath?"

"Uh."

"This is Wrath X, is it not?"

"Who dis?"

"Who…Who is this?"

"You called me."

By now, Boris/Thor is totally eye-fucking me, and not in a good way at all.

"Fine, yes, this is Wrath X. Who is this?"

"For now, my identity will remain a secret. But I understand you have been vetted by my associates. And that you possess certain skills that may prove useful to us in the very near future."

"I'm not sure what those skills could possibly be, but I'm sure it's true if you say so."

"You do love the Fatherland, don't you?"

"Of course."

"Good. You will coordinate with the Viking Brotherhood."

The voice hangs up.

Thor/Boris says, "You know who that was, right?"

"No, I have no idea."

"That was the person I work for."

"Gosh, Th-Boris…I have no idea who that could be."

"You couldn't possibly."

"Really?"

"Yeah. It's not who you think, not at all."

"Fine. And what it is your boss wants with me?"

"We're interested in your demolitions training from when you were in special forces in America. Don't worry, Wrath, I told him all about it. And there's a particularly important job we need your help with."

THE MORE time I spend in Germany, the less I sleep. This isn't something new. From the minute I hit the ground in '34 this country has had me at a disadvantage when it comes to sleep. But this time it's different, worse. Maybe after spending so long out of the Ragnarök game, being back in is what's done this to me.

I'm drinking more. The bottles are everywhere in my bedroom—schnapps, bad beer, good beer, wine, whiskey—so many that when the drapes are open sunlight catches every color of the spectrum. I'm smoking more, too. The ashtrays, likewise, litter the place, like rest stops on a highway to lung cancer. Which, fortunately, I can't get so… I'm sure I'd be gaming more if I played games, gambling more if I gambled, shooting heroin more if I shot heroin. I'd be fucking more if there were someone around to fuck. But there's not, so I'm not...

Speaking of which, one thing that hasn't deserted me, especially since I saw them at New Valhalla, is my obsession with the Valks. No, not the robots. The real ones, from the old days. That long, shiny hair, those perfect limbs, and ridiculous cheekbones. The wings, so feathery, so strong...I'm awake...uh, counting...them...the Valks, I mean...by the time Sunshine calls me back. It's five a.m.

"Why are you breathing so heavily?" she asks.

"Breathing?"

"Yes, heavily." She huffs into the phone.

"Never mind that. I suppose you're calling to explain why you ran away from the giants? Maybe ask for my forgiveness?"

"I'm calling to say I dropped the complaint against Kurt. You didn't have to ask."

"You realize we can't have him walking around on his own."

"So, have the giants pick him up."

"Obviously. Seriously though, they're heartbroken at the way you deserted them."

"I bet they didn't even realize I was gone for an hour. You know, they're completely addicted to *Monsieur von Mayhem*. You'd better get those guys under control. You might really need their help before long."

"Is there anything else?"

"There is. I was thinking maybe you should just tell the giants to give up chasing me, join you at that villa in Germany. It's pretty nice from what I can see."

"How do you know about that?"

"I have my ways."

"Does this mean Odin knows?"

"The answer to your question is 'No.'"

"I'm beginning to wonder whether anything you told me was true, whether we're ever going to see you again."

"Oh, you'll see me again. And soon."

"I meant when precisely."

"I know. But I can't say precisely. I have things to take care of."

"What am I supposed to tell Odin? He's all over me about you. And then there's Bruder to worry about."

"Bruder? Oh, you mean the assassination attempt? Yes, I know about it. And you'd better stop it. That's essential."

"Essential to what?"

"I can't say."

"Fine, it doesn't even matter. I haven't been able to get in touch with her."

"Why?"

"Probably because I called her on the number Odin gave me, I started talking about an assassination, and she hung up."

She laughs.

"Hey, you're the one who wanted my help, needed my help. Now, you've got me and mine running around like lunatics, chasing you and trying to do your bidding."

"Don't forget, you're the one who refused to tell me the truth?"

"You already knew the truth."

"Doesn't matter. You still refused."

"I'm hanging up now."

"No, wait, Trickster?"

"What?"

"I've got another number."

"What, for Bruder? Fine, I guess it's worth a try, but I don't imagine it will go any differently."

"It will if you tell her you know me."

"If I tell her I'm the Norse god Loki and I know Sunshine the Norn, that's going to work?"

"Not me, exactly. But I did go to see her before I left Germany."

"Oh?"

"Yeah, as a political consultant named Sabrina van Arsehale."

"OK."

"And let's just say things have worked out for her since then. You've seen the polls, right?"

"She's steadily climbing."

"Exactly."

"And what name am I supposed to give her? What story am I supposed to tell?"

"You're the God of Lies. Come up with something. But don't forget: Stopping that assassination is essential. If it succeeds, we're lost."

"You mean, lost beyond the fact that someone would be dead."

"Exactly."

LIKE FUCKING FATE

EVEN WITH the libertine (hetero-)sexual norms in Asgard, even with Odin continually trying to promote me as the heart of evil, I hadn't ever imagined actually copulating with a Norn. I mean, it seemed, quite literally, or at least quasi-literally, like fucking Fate.

The Norns weren't gods, and they weren't giants. They were something else entirely. And I wasn't sure what would happen. Could we procreate? Who would carry the babies or whatever they wound up being? I remembered Hel and Fen and, especially, Jormungandr. Man, he was a big one! I certainly didn't want to wind up in that situation again. I thought about this for quite a while—days, weeks, years, who knows—until I finally got my answer when, out of the clear blue, Sunshine invited me to dinner.

THERE WAS this secret glade in the Forest of the Norns. You got there by leaving Mount Norn and traveling underground for miles, eventually coming back to Asgard's surface in the middle of a clearing, the surrounding firs and evergreens filled with many-colored lights even though all around it was night. Imagine your neighbor's Christmas lights, but tasteful, and with an infinite budget.

165

"What do you call this place?" I asked.

"The Glade of the Norns."

"Seems appropriate."

"It does, Trickster. Please, sit, relax." She took my hand, led me to a sprawling pile of furs before a fire that almost seemed to whisper at me, offering comfort, maybe even love. Maybe it was nothing more than bio-response: Her pulse and mine, in sync on some level. She let go of my hand and lay back on the furs. She half-smiled, pursed her lips, and patted the space beside her.

I gave her a hard look. "You're not…trying to seduce me, are you?"

"Somebody's full of themselves, aren't they? This is just dinner."

"Oh, I'm sorry…I didn't…'

She narrowed her gaze. "Would that be so wrong?"

"I don't know. It seems like it might be some sort of abuse of power."

"Yours or mine?"

"Yes?"

"C'mon, Trickster, relax. Have a seat."

"Oh, fine," I said, diving onto the pile of furs. I rocked side-to-side a few times, as if I could barely control myself. *Oh, what a fall!* Each time, I drew closer until I was on my side, looking down into the brilliant black of her eyes.

"Wow, you got over that pretty easily, didn't you?"

"I guess. So about…"

"You're wondering what would happen if we…y'know, got involved," she said, lips drawing closer to mine.

I nodded, lips drawing closer to hers.

"You're wondering if one or both of us could get pregnant."

I nodded again.

"Well, I definitely can't. I know that much."

"Why?"

"I don't have the right wiring," she said, batting her eyes. My gaze descended, and I got the point.

"Wait, so you don't have a..." I wondered what I was getting into. Not that it would have been a deal-killer, mind you. But it's always good to have as much background as possible, particularly when it comes to matters of love.

"No, I have that. I just don't have any of the internal bits. I can't procreate, simple as that."

"But what about me? I've been with child before," I said, patting my belly.

"I don't have the wiring for that either."

"So, you're safe?"

"I wouldn't go that far." She gave me a quick kiss, so hard it felt almost like a bite.

I kissed her back for one beat, then another, and another. Finally, we parted. "Are you sure your sisters will be okay with this? The last thing I need is to get Fate mad at me."

"If it wasn't me, it would have been one of them."

"So, what, you're being forced to do this?"

"Not at all. You chose me, remember?"

"OK."

"And you have a part to play."

"You mean in Ragnarök? Honestly, I'm not looking forward to it."

She raised an eyebrow.

"OK, maybe a little."

She laughed. "It really doesn't matter whether you're looking forward to it or not."

"Because it's Fate."

"That's part of it. More so because your current conception of Ragnarök is so very literal. Meaning it won't be like that when it finally happens."

"Won't be like what?"

"Won't be like what you think it will be."

"Don't you think you ought to tell Odin?"

"Oh, we have. He doesn't want to hear it. He's really resistant to change, you know."

"But you were the ones that gave him that story in the first place."

"Were we?"

"Weren't you?"

"You'd have to ask Odin directly. But the truth is, he's made up a lot of what you take as fact."

"Really?"

She nodded, and I kissed her again.

10

A PAIR OF TAILORED BEHEMOTHS

WHEN I wake the sun is at its apex, the room practically bathed in light. But that's not what wakes me. What wakes me is Hel banging on my bedroom door.

"Loki?" she says. *Bang-bang-bang.*

I check my phone: It's one in the afternoon.

"Loki?" *Bang-bang-bang.*

"What?"

"Can I come in?"

"I guess."

The door swings in, and Hel follows. She pulls the ubiquitous Gauloise to her lips and takes a deep drag, cherry going bright yellow-orange-red, a backlit sunset, something like that. She blows a cloud of billowing gray into the air and gives me this sly smile, reminding me of a dragon.

Yes, they're real, but I don't mean the real ones. I mean the ones from those terrible *Hobbit* movies you guys seem to love. I mean, OK, *The Lord of the Rings* movies really were something. Those mass battle scenes…they even gave me chills…but *The Hobbit*? It's a three-hundred-page kid's book they turned into nine hours of movies. What mathematical wizard was in charge of that equation?

I squint at the cloud as it floats through the air and begins to dissipate.

"Don't you think you should get up, get yourself together?" she asks. "We should head back to Anarchy."

"Change in plans. Sunshine called."

"When?"

"A few hours ago."

"And? Have they been in touch?"

"No, I just checked."

"You should call them."

Hel flops into an overstuffed armchair, lolls her head back and just keeps smoking. Stretched out, legs hanging over one side of the chair, she looks effortlessly cool, like she's got all the time in the world at her disposal, like Newman in the Sixties.

Surtur picks up after a couple rings. "There's good news and bad news," he offers before I can say anything.

"Again?"

"It is a classic, Loki, you have to admit."

"What's the good news?"

"We grabbed Kurt, like you asked."

"You didn't drug him again, did you? He really didn't like that."

"Didn't have to. He went along peacefully this time. We did zip-cuff him of course."

"Of course. What's the bad news?"

"Fen had an accident in Charles de Gaulle."

"Number one or number two?"

Hel purses her lips, turns in the direction of the bit of pastel-heavy hotel impressionism hanging on the wall, a painting I've been considering turning wall-ward for the last few days. She clocks it for barely a second, turns back, grimacing in distaste.

"Two. It was awkward."

"I bet. Didn't I remind you to walk him?"

"You did, but it's okay. We used the old service dog dodge. Thyrm is wearing sunglasses and stumbling around. It's totally working."

"You still have to walk him. You know, like, outside."

"Yeah, sure, fine. But the good news is Thyrm thinks he caught sight of the Norn."

"He's wearing sunglasses and stumbling around while holding a large dog on a leash."

"Fen and Kurt saw her, too."

"Fine, where is it Thyrm, Kurt, and Fen think they saw her?"

"London. She was boarding a flight to Amsterdam. So, we got on the next flight to Amsterdam."

"Right?"

"But she got there first and headed for Charles de Gaulle. Supposedly."

"Supposedly?"

"She bought three sets of tickets for flights leaving at the same time: Charles de Gaulle, Zurich, and Reykjavik."

"That was a nifty trick."

"It was, but Hel helped us hack the airlines. Switzerland and Iceland were bogeys."

I turn to Hel. She waves.

"Alright, so where did she go after Paris?"

"Well, she did the multiple tickets trick again, this time with nine. But we figured it out. She went to Prague."

"Then I guess you'd better go to Prague. Now."

I kill the call.

"Well, that sounds like a mess, doesn't it?" says Hel.

"Sometimes I wish I had two of you."

"Only sometimes?"

"Maybe. Yes, I am going back to Anarchy. But you're not."

"Why not?"

"One, I may need to send you after the giants if these cock-ups continue."

"Fine."

"But that's not it."

"What is?"

"What's it is I need you to finish your research on Bruder."

"Such as?"

"For starters, I need to know where she's going to be assassinated before it actually happens."

WITH THE giants chasing Sunshine...and who knows where Heimdall is...but with all that going on, now seems the perfect time to use the number Sunshine gave me to call Bruder. *Perfect time*, you must be thinking, *this sounds like anything but*. By perfect time, of course, I mean I've only been up a little while, and I've already got a headache. Things probably can't get any worse if I call Bruder. Amazingly, she picks up.

"Ja?"

"Frau Bruder?"

"Who is this?"

"My name's Loki, Mr. Loki."

"Ah...Ms. Van Arsehale's associate? She told me you might call?"

"Er...what did she tell you about me?"

"Nothing really, just said you might be in touch."

"When was this?"

"Several weeks ago."

"And did she tell you who I am?"

"Um…she told me your name is Loki. No offense, but that's quite an unusual name."

"True. Did she tell you which Loki I am?"

"Which Loki? How many of you can there be?'

"I… well, there's the Norse god Loki."

"Of course."

"But that's not me."

"I should hope not. So, which Loki are you?"

This stumps me. Have I never, in all these years, tried the, 'I'm Loki but not *that* Loki' dodge?" It seems so obvious, so perfect. "You know what? Never mind. What did she tell you about herself?"

"She said she was a freelance political consultant. Had a little advice for me."

"OK."

"It's worked out well, too, what she said. So, I'll listen. What is it you want?"

"I've uncovered a plot."

"What sort of plot?"

"A plot to assassinate you."

"Wait…your voice sounds…are you the one who called to threaten me before?"

"That's…not right. I was trying to warn you, not threaten you. I was trying to tell you that someone else was going to try it."

"Sounded awfully similar from this end."

"You didn't let me get into the specifics."

"Of you assassinating me?"

"Of the plot against you. I have absolutely no intention of assassinating you. I'm trying to prevent it."

"So, what, you work for the government? Why didn't you say so before?"

"I don't work for any government."

"So, you're part of some sort of secret agent NGO that goes around foiling assassinations?"

"Fine, sure, if you want to think of it that way."

"It's not how I want to think about anything."

"Look, Sabrina got me involved in this just like you."

"The strategist? She sounded almost as insane as you. But she did give me some good advice."

"Did she tell you anything else?"

"Just that you'd call again."

"Listen, is there some way we can meet? I've got solid evidence, details, this thing is imminent. The Viking Brother-..."

"So, you're a member of the Viking Brotherhood?"

"I've infiltrated them."

She pauses. "Fine, what are these supposed specifics?"

"Method, perpetrators. I'm still working on time and place, OK? But we need to meet."

"You realize I have actual security, right?"

"You have a traitor in your midst. A sleeper agent."

"Who?"

"I'll tell you that when we meet."

"I don't know."

"We'll go along with any security protocols you want. Double- and triple-checks, pat-downs, whatever. But I have to speak to you alone."

"Because of the traitor?"

"Yes."

She agrees.

I PUNCH the brakes as the first in a trio of blonde mommies nudges her stroller out in front of the 6. The smiles on their faces make the mommies seem bemused—maybe at me and my expensive, now-halted car; maybe at the sky of smoky slate that roils above, seems to threaten rain; maybe at their own situations, the life of the stay-at-home German mom.

It's a little after four pm as we finally nose off Berlin's new blacktop—sequesters and shutdowns be damned, in Germany there's always money for cosmetic improvements to the scenery—into the parking garage we've been destined for since we left the villa, a special level of the garage to be exact.

Apparently, there's a level below the lowest official level of the garage and another one below that. Is this a German thing? You know, the way there are no thirteenth floors in skyscrapers in America. Which isn't an American thing, per se. It's really a human, developed world thing. This extra-levels-to-parking-garages, though, I've never heard of it. I mean, it's weird, right? Unexpected, to say the least.

Anyway, they are there, these extra levels just like Bruder says, the second guarded by a barricade of black SUV's, their lights aligned to shine in our faces on approach. We motor slowly towards them then hear over a bullhorn, "Stop. Cut the engine."

I'm sure I'm getting busted by the cops, but I do it anyway. Hel, ever the cool one, pulls out a Gauloise. She lights up, cranks the music, waits.

A pair of tailored behemoths emerge from the lights beyond. In jet black three-piece suits with matching ties; gleaming, impeccably shaved heads; and insectine shades: they advance on the 6. Behemoth #1 comes to my side, briefly shines a flashlight in my face. Angling the beam through the 6, when he finally gets to Hel, he simply nods his head, and points us towards the blazing headlights.

"Get out," says Behemoth #1.

"Go," adds Behemoth #2 before we're even out of the car.

We do, and we do. Once we've walked a few feet, I hear my car door shut. I turn, see Behemoth #1 behind the wheel, Behemoth #2 shotgun. #1 peels out and heads back the way we came.

If I were human, I'd probably fear for my life at this point. Which makes me wonder, as the door from double-secret to regular-secret slams shut, what this German Washington is up to.

The phalanx of headlights dies. I can see one woman standing there. No trick. Yes, of course, it's Bruder, though not alone. I realize the three SUVs behind her are filled with people, people with guns trained on Hel and me. She motions for us to follow her out of earshot, though definitely not out of eye-shot/shot-shot. We walk to the other side of the lot.

"So, why am I meeting you?" she offers, by way of greeting.

"Isn't that a question you should have asked yourself before this?"

"Probably. Except there are twelve highly trained people with guns in those cars over there."

"Plus, the gorillas who just took our car. You must feel pretty safe."

She nods.

"Here's where I throw a wrench in that."

"My men already frisked you, ja?"

"Ja. I'm not going to hurt you. No worries there."

She seems to relax, hauls out a cigarette. "Okay, I don't have all day for this *shize*. Now what's going on?"

Hel lights her up, eliciting a double-take of thanks/apparent interest from Frau Bruder.

"Get right to the point, eh? Alright, fair enough. You know how I told you my name was Loki?"

"Ja?"

"And how I said it was 'like the Norse god, but, obviously, not the Norse god?'"

"Ja?"

"That was a lie."

"Your name's not Loki."

"Oh, no, my name's Loki."

"So, what you're saying…"

"Yes…"

Bruder's eyes widen, her gaze jumps to Hel then back and back. She looks like she can't decide whether I'm insane, she's in grave danger, or both. Then I see her gaze catch and she starts laughing. "I'll admit, you had me there for a sekunde. It's been some couple of weeks."

Hel and I nod. It has.

"You seemed so serious. 'Ooh, I'm Loki, The Trickster, God of Evil, Mischief Maker!'"

I turn to Hel. "She doesn't believe me."

"Guess not."

"Fine. Just remember, General Bruder, I didn't want to do this."

Bruder chuckles, shrugs. "Hey, man, knock yourself sideways or whatever it is you Americans say these days."

"Poof," I say, changing into Wrath X.

Bruder closes her eyes almost instantly. Unfortunately for her I'm still there when she opens one then the other; still there, looking big, bad, and not at all like her new not-quite-pal, Loki. Bruder shakes her head several times. She closes her eyes, brings her hands to her face then runs them up her forehead and through her neat blonde hair.

"If you're hoping this'll turn into an episode of *Scooby Doo*, you're pretty fucking well rout of ruck, Raggy."

Bruder opens her eyes and grimaces. Have I underestimated her? Is she going to break? Does the fact that she's not American mean she doesn't even get my Scooby Doo reference?

"Poof," I say, changing back into myself.

Bruder looks like she's going to vomit. I step out of the way, just in case.

"And this lovely lady," I say.

She returns her gaze to Hel, apparently completely recovered. "Aphrodite, she must be Aphrodite," she whispers, eyes a little misty.

Hel laughs.

"Oh, for fuck's sake. You realize you're mixing mythologies, right, chica?"

"Sorry. Who…?"

"It would be Freya. And don't even get me started on Freya."

"OK."

"I'm Hel," says Hel proudly.

"You mean like the Devil? The Norse Devil, like in the movie??"

"Movie? You mean that *Thor: Ragnarök* shite?" She sneers when she says Thor's name, looks like she wants to spit. I'm so proud of my little girl.

"Actually, that's Pops over there." Hel hooks a thumb at me.

"Oh, right."

"And I suppose that political consultant, that Sabrina van Arsehale, she's a Valkyrie or something?"

"There aren't any Valkyries anymore, not real ones anyway."

"Why's that?"

"They disappeared when Hitler fell."

"When what?"

"Hitler. The gods were helping him. You didn't think he could pull off all that shit on his own, did you?"

"So, you helped Hitler?"

"Not me, Odin."

"So, if you're gods and you were helping him..."

"They."

"If *they* were helping him, how did Hitler lose?"

"Okay, fair enough."

She raises an eyebrow.

"Easily explained."

"Waiting."

"First off, we're not omnipotent."

"Okay."

"Second off, he killed himself."

"You're saying if he hadn't killed himself Germany would have won the war."

"Maybe. Though it's true we were really kicking their asses by that point."

"We?"

"I was working with the resistance. I mean, I would never be involved with Hitler…or this new guy, this Vekk. Odin, on the other hand."

"But you're the evil one?"

"Actually, that's not true. They're the evil ones. I'm here to help."

"But the mythology?"

"Think about what you just said."

"So, you're good?"

"You could say that."

"What about the mischief and lies, the darkness and disguise?"

I wink. "Obviously, that still holds."

"Okay."

"Which brings us back to you and this assassination."

"I agree."

"Agree to what?"

"To let you help me."

"Excellent."

"There's just one thing."

"What?"

"That traitor you said I had in my midst."

"Yes."

"Who is it?"

"Actually, we're still working on that."

I ASSUME ASGARD DECADES

THE CHRISTIANS weren't the only fake religion we looked at taking over. I mean, I really did try to help Odin. I suggested he do a merger with the other polytheistic Proto-Indo-European faiths; you know, like the Slavs and the Celts. I suggested teaming up with the Druids and Hindus, even the Muslims. But Odin was set on the Christians, convinced he could really work with the Jesus construct, that he'd be able to absorb JC's followers just like that. One, two, three million...

A few weeks or hours or centuries after that fateful dinner with Sunshine, Odin went to see the Norns, again. He just set out one morning, looking apocalyptically grim, definitionally Odinic...He took the eight-legged horse and the birds. He took a whole legion of Valkyries, the magical boar, Mimir's head... He took the whole kit and caboodle. Left me in charge, too.

He came back a few minutes or decades or centuries later, I forget, with a similarly grim expression on his face. It didn't take long for him to elaborate. That was one of Odin's good qualities back then. He'd tell you what he was thinking. Oh, sure, he'd say it as though he were dispensing the wisdom of the ages to a troglodyte; but you still got the dope.

"Blast those Norns. They gave me an ultimatum."

"Or what?"

"Right. That's what an ultimatum is."

"I mean, what are they threatening to do?"

"They're leaving."

"They can't do that. Don't you have a cosmic contract or something?"

"I do but..."

"But what?"

"There are minimum worship levels I have to maintain. And if I don't..."

"Why didn't you say anything about this before?"

"It wasn't an issue before."

"But why is it...oh, the Christians?" I nodded knowingly. You know, as if I knew? And I did, to tell you the truth. I'd been watching the Christians for some time at that point. I knew they'd be trouble eventually.

There was just something about the way their beliefs mushroomed, first one of them, then a family then a village. Which was understandable since they'd waited so long, since they'd been able to extract the best parts of just about every religion that had come before—a savior here, a father god there, a virgin birth, an amorphous spirit, an apocalypse...they had it all. I just hadn't expected them to take over so soon.

"Yes, the Christians...and it's your fault."

"My fault?"

"You were the last one to visit them, weren't you?"

"I have never spoken to a Christian in my life."

"I meant last time I threw you out."

"Nope, never spoken to a one of them. Swear on Jotunheim's Worldstone."

Odin grunted.

I continued, "I mean look at me and tell me I'd have any

luck. Tell me I'm what a Christian wants to see. They'd be liable to label me Satan or something."

"Well, obviously, you're adept at changing shapes, Loki. But I meant the Norns, numbskull; that you went to see them."

"You said you meant the Christians."

"Did not! Anyway, it's not like I'm unaware what you've been up to with them, those secret, midnight meetings of yours, especially with the third one, Sunshine."

"My 'secret' whats?"

"Enough. I am the All-Father, and I'll have none of your lies. I know you've been boinking that Norn on and off for centuries."

"You make it sound so mechanical."

"Well, isn't it?"

"I love Sunshine."

"The way I love Frigga?"

"Uh, no…"

Odin seemed pleased.

"What's this ultimatum anyway?"

"I already explained that."

"I mean, 'How long do you have?' Like a demi-millennium?"

He started shaking his head.

"A couple centuries? That hardly seems reasonable."

He kept shaking his head, finally opened his eye. "A couple decades."

"Earth decades or Asgard decades?"

"I assume Asgard decades. I didn't check. I was flustered."

"Don't you think you'd better?"

"Why does it matter? We're doomed either way." He looked down sadly, dramatically, a smoked, salted, and cured pork bootay if ever there was one.

"What's this 'we' stuff? You're the one with worshippers."

He fixed his one good eye on me. Then the lid began to droop, and I was sure I saw a tear forming. More likely he was just trying to pull on my heartstrings. Or maybe my logic strings. He was pulling some sort of strings.

"The truth, Loki, is that as the head of a patriarchal polytheism, if I go down, I'm taking all of you with me. That's how it works. You've seen what's happened with enough of these phony polytheisms to know the truth. Remember the Greeks?"

"Ha, yeah, Zeus," I said chuckling. "Mr. Lightning Bolt!"

Odin leaned forward, cradled his face in his hands. "Oh, what's the use?"

"Don't get all emotional, Pops? I'll help you out."

He looked up, eyes dry as the Mojave, smiled for a second before shifting back to imperious. "Let's get to work then."

That was the way it was for long stretches at a time. I was on top, the councilor in chief, the consigliere in mob parlance. Something always happened, though, to screw things up. That something, more often than not, was Thor.

11

AS FOR KURT

BACK AT the villa, I glom the remote, and fall forward onto the couch as the TV comes on. I watch real American ESPN (in German), try to sink back into the Americana that's become more comforting than I could have imagined. It doesn't work.

Everything in the room, everything everywhere is in German. I mean, I understand it all, naturally. If you can speak it, I can understand it. But watching American television with German voices just feels phony, wrong.

Eventually, Hel shuffles out wearing her jammies. White flannel with decorative pink death's heads—they're sharp, a nice combo of comfy-looking and supernaturally daunting. It's two a.m.

"They're in Prague," she says, leaves that hanging in the air as she takes a drag off her Gauloise. She exhales a long trail of smoke. "They found her."

"Really?"

"Yeah, then she disappeared."

"They lost her again?"

"No, I mean, she literally disappeared. As in, magic."

"Like, 'Poof?'"

"Yeah, like, 'Poof.'"

"No wonder she's been so many steps ahead of them."

"They insist this is the first time she's employed magic. Well, first time they can be sure of."

"I thought she was down to parlor tricks like the rest of us. What about Heimdall?"

"They say they think they may have seen him earlier that day dressed as an animal control officer. They can't be sure, though."

"That's…pretty specific. What aren't they sure of?"

"Jurisdiction. Fen yipped. He was definitely an animal control officer."

"Alright, they're officially done chasing her. We're going to need them here."

"That's what I told them. They want to know what to do with Kurt."

"In what sense?"

"I guess he's giving them trouble, always complaining. Wants to eat, wants to piss, wants to go home."

"Those seem like reasonable requests."

"Yeah, well. They're talking about beating him, torturing him, seeing if they can extract any additional information about Heimdall."

"He's my friend."

"Is he? They say the more they're around him, the worse he gets. Boring, annoying. Honestly…they sorta sound like they want to kill him."

"Kill him? Wow."

"So, what do I tell them?"

"Is this a real question?"

"Is that a real question?"

"Tell them it was a valiant effort. But you're obviously not going to catch up with Sunshine if she's using magic. You know, really stroke their egos."

"And Kurt?"

"I mean. Bring him with."

"And…"

"Unharmed. I guess drug him if they have to. Sometimes I really wonder about you guys."

"You should, Loki, especially them."

"And make sure you tell them: no drinking in transit."

"Yeah, like they're gonna go along with that."

"And make sure you buy the tickets and meet them at the airport, wherever it is."

"Anything else, commandant?"

"Yes, leave me alone so I can revel in my bilingual football highlights."

HEL DOES as I ask, which always surprises me on some level. She lets me be then leaves around midnight, taking the 6 to get the giants, Fen, and Kurt at Tegel, leaves me watching football highlights just as I'd asked. She's not gone more than an hour before my uPhone buzzes. I brace mentally, hit speaker.

"Yah?"

"Herr Loki?" comes a voice.

"Err."

"This is Loki, is it not?"

"You called me."

"Funny, it sounds an awful lot like your voice."

"How would you know whose voice this sounds like?"

"I spoke to you just a few days ago. Oh, but you weren't quite yourself, were you? You were telling everyone your name was Wrath X."

"Wait, is this the voice from the phone?"

"Phone?"

"I mean the voice *on* the phone Th-Boris handed me."

"Now you're getting it. But you can drop the act. I know Boris is Thor."

"If you say so. I still have no idea who you are."

"I'm Reinhold Vekk."

"Assuming you really are Reinhold Vekk, why would you be calling me?"

"Because Odin has been lying to you all along."

"He's been lying to me my entire life."

"The Norn's lying, too."

"Norn?"

"Yes, Norn. You know, the Norse Fates? The one called Sunshine has been to see me?"

"I didn't—"

"Before she left Germany. Though she wasn't calling herself Sunshine. She said she was a political consultant named Sabrina van Arsehale."

"And how do you even know it was her?"

"I know because Odin told me."

"Fine, voice on the phone, what are all these supposed lies I've been told."

"Well, for starters, you have no idea why he wants to stop Bruder's assassination."

"Because he has to."

"Yes, but why?"

"Because the Norns told him to."

"But that's not all of it."

"What is all of it?"

"He wants her alive because he realized he needs her for something."

"For what?"

"Why don't you ask your buddy the Norn?"

"I'm tired of these riddles. I'm hanging up."

"Wait."

"What?"

"Try making Bruder disappear, after you save her."

"Look, dude, I can't do that sort of magic anymore."

"I mean, hide her. It'll be a good trick. And it'll show you just what Odin's been lying about."

I FALL asleep around two a.m., staring at Facebook, still waiting for the giants to show. By the time I wake, it's a quarter to five, my impromptu alarm the mélange of post-industrial metal, tinny bips, and loopy boops that is Monsieur von Mayhem. I can tell it's coming from the great room. Based on that, the loam of sativa smoke, and sweet staleness of spilled beer, I know the giants are here.

I walk into the great room, see Fen on the couch, head on upside down, lips quivering with peaceful, rhythmic, (thus, loud as all fuck), snoring. The guys are on the floor in front of him, elbows on the ground, controllers in hand, lower legs sticking up in the air, bouncing to the beat of *M von M*.

"Loki," they say, without turning. I see their intent faces in the glare of the screen and the great room's wide windows, black and shiny with reflected light. They're still on level six. Still.

"You guys actually brought your PlayStation?"

"Nah. Couldn't take a chance losing all our history."

"We bought one in the duty free."

"And you're already up to 6?"

"Dude," says Surt.

"What?" I ask.

"The cloud," answers Thyrm.

"What?"

"We're saving to the cloud."

"While we're here."

"Oh."

Hel wanders into the living room, rubbing her eyes like a tired toddler. Just like Fen, she was never a kid before, back when we were gods. Now she is, once in a while at least. Yeah, I know what I said, and I really was a baby once, not that my memory is terribly clear. But Hel wasn't. Ever.

One day I was fucking this giantess Angrboda—more like being fucked, to be honest; *way* more like being fucked—we finish and a couple minutes later out pops Hel. Followed by Fen and Jormungandr. They went about their business right away: Fen chasing Tyr, Jormungandr patrolling the deep, Hel descending to the Underworld—Who knew it even existed?— taking over just like that.

How she did it, I have no idea. Point being, especially when Hel wakes, she looks more like a child than I've ever seen her and it's touching, y'know, in a way I can't fully describe, a way that makes me feel like a Hoo whose heart has grown a size or two. People say children's books don't get to you, but they do. At least they get to me.

"JFC, will you keep it the fuck down out here? We have a busy day ahead." She turns to me. "They're wasted, aren't they?"

"Probably?"

No reply.

"You guys wasted?" I ask.

"Define wasted," says Thyrm, as Surtur sets down his controller and wobbles to his feet.

"That's it, guys, showers and sleep."

"But...it's the end."

"You've been saying that for a year."

Both giants, "Meh."

"And where is Kurt?"

"I'll never get back to sleep. I might as well show you," says Hel, as the giants head off for their room.

"THEY DRUGGED him," she says pointing at Kurt once we're downstairs, the door to his erstwhile quarters wide open.

"Yeah, obviously. You think we can wake him up?"

"Probably. If they told the truth about what they gave him and when." She steps into the room, bends down, touches his cheek.

Kurt's only response is to snore more loudly. Hel starts patting his cheek, harder and harder. He begins moving his hands and mumbling. "No more hornets, no more."

"We don't have all day," I say in response to her raised eyebrow.

Hel hauls off and smacks Kurt's face, leaving a red handprint on the right side. He starts, rises to his hands and knees like a fighter trying to beat the count. He's already wearing a confused glare when he looks up and sees Hel.

"Hello!?" he asks, expression softening. Then he sees me and goes back to glaring. "Gustav, finally...I was dreaming. This really hot goth chick was about to kill me."

"Sounds more like a premonition," says Hel.

191

"Anyway, you're awake. Go get him some coffee, will you, uh, Becky? We need to talk."

Hel leaves for the kitchen.

"Who is that?"

"Oh, that's my daughter Becky. She's under-age so don't get any ideas."

I quiz Kurt about how much he knows. Whether it has to do with grogginess from the drugs still in his system, I can't be entirely clear, but he doesn't seem to know much. I convince myself he won't pose a threat as long as we keep him under house arrest e.g. kidnapped. Which, OK, fair enough, that's not what you might call being "good," but he already basically agreed to overlook that as long as we rescued him in Amsterdam.

THE BIFROST CONVENTIONS

ONCE THERE were to be great herds of reindeer all over Asgard, roaming free, just chilling; y'know running, leaping, playing games (butt-sniff and antler-clash are the biggies), eating (grass, obvis), mostly making more reindeer. You should have seen them go at it, those Asgardian reindeer. Honestly, they were beautiful, majestic.

Sometimes I'd find a good spot, sit, and watch them for hours, not the fucking necessarily, mostly the running around and eating parts. Was I working on my disguises even then? Sure, I was. *I'm always working on my disguises.* And it's true: Many's the time I've done a few hours as a reindeer. But that wasn't it, not entirely.

I mean, my love of reindeer disguises descended from their beauty, not some self-serving desire to increase my ability at subterfuge. Odin, on the other hand, while he may 'appreciate' reindeer, even admire them, he is a father god who loves nothing more than to hunt. All of them do. And not just my brothers. Freya, Sif, Frigga…they're killers, killers all of them.

All you have to do is read the Eddas to get it. Hunting's the source for many a tale, some comic, many more tragic. Me? Oh, no, not anymore. I used to go with them, sure. It was a requirement. And I took a fair amount of abuse for all the missing I did. Especially from Thor. Which is, like so much about Thor, extra-laughable.

I mean, the dude "hunts" with a sentient, flying, magical hammer. Talk about an unfair advantage. I don't know what he's so proud of. No doubt he gets it from Odin: You should hear the conversations Odin has with Gungnir when no one's around. I've seen it get sexual more than once. Not a pretty sight.

Anyway, back to the giants, we were out on a hunt one day. Odin and the rest of them were on the trail and I was lagging, lollygagging as usual, doing my best to throw them off their game.

"Oh," I might say, "Isn't this tree impressive."

"Ooh," I might offer, "Will you get a load of that bird?"

As usual, they weren't listening. They were just so balls-out for blood that they could have cared less about me, the trees, or the birds, so death-driven they didn't even notice the giants off to the right, disguised as trees. They were good disguises, too; don't get me wrong.

Was that my fault? Probably, technically. I mean, I didn't do the actual disguises but I'd given the giants more than a few subterfuge lessons over the years. Anything they know about disguises, mischief, lying, and any number of other things, you can pretty well trace back to me if you want to get technical about it.

I didn't know it was the giants, at first, but I did realize something was off. So, I circled around to try to figure out who it was and see what was going on. I got close enough to realize one of them was Thyrm. I whistled to get his attention.

"Trickster," he said.

"What are you doing here? You know you're not allowed on Asgard."

"What, you mean The Bifrost Conventions? Oh, that's hardly worth more than the magical, golden parchment it's written on."

"I'm not talking about some piece of paper. I'm talking about Fate."

"Ooh, Fate," said Thyrm, "Big word, that."

"You didn't just shit-talk Fate, did you?"

He meh-ed. "We have a plan. Trust us, you'll be glad we did this."

"Did what? And why?"

"The why is because things have to move along, the what is this." He moved out of concealment, and I saw just how good the disguise had been. He'd been holding a spear the whole time, the end so sharp it practically made me cry. He smiled with a malevolence that I have to admit was both terrifying and endearing.

"You can't make Fate happen, Thyrm. We've been over this. Surtur, you're not actually going along with this, are you?"

"It's destiny."

"That's just another word for Fate! Why are you doing this? Have you been talking to the head again?"

"Not the head."

"Then what? Was it the Norns?"

"The who?"

"I forgot. You can't see them."

"If you say so." They both shrugged.

"So, who?"

"Steinfaltz," Surtur said.

"Who the hell is Steinfaltz?"

"He's a shaman back on Jotenheim."

"A stone giant," said Thyrm, nodding gravely. "And you know how smart those guys are."

"Never heard of him."

"He's new. But he's all the talk in the caves and villages."

"That's it? You're throwing out Fate's cosmic plan over some stone giant huckster?"

"We were bored. We decided to give him a try."

"And what he said made a lot of sense."

"Can we talk about this, guys?"

"No," said Thyrm, emphatically. I was…taken aback. "We may be your henchcreatrues, Loki. But you know we pursue autonomous agendae on occasion. We have our own motivations, beyond your will or that of Fate."

"I know, but…"

"You'll be glad we did this."

Thyrm reared back and let fly.

I shouted, "No, stop!" in Giantish. And just like that I was an accessory. Back in the old days, back on Asgard, speaking Giantish was basically like speaking Arabic in Berlin today, a big no-no.

Anyway, I saw them coming towards us: Thor, Frey, Freya, Baldur, the whole wretched gang. And I began to hear the cries of, "Loki. It's Loki. Somebody get Loki."

What could I do? I turned myself into a tree and ran after the giants, who'd already set to booking. But no matter how good your disguise is, once someone's seen it's just a disguise, it's not really much of one, you know? Also, we were running trees, so…

We were apprehended within minutes, brought before a bleeding, bellowing Odin. I had to hand it to the old guy. I wouldn't have been bearing up as well. Because, sure enough, his eye was mangled beyond description, spear still lodged in the socket.

You might ask, "Weren't there doctors, or spells at least? Maybe both? Couldn't something have been done?"

Problem was that was the story Odin had been told by the Norns, not to mention Mimir's Head. Sure, it was something he rejected, battled against, something he refused to believe. Who wants to admit, "Yeah, I guess I'm gonna lose my eye someday?"

Sure, you fight against the stories you're told, struggle to convince yourself they'll never come true. But when they start to, you get that spooky feeling, that out of body, oh-shit-this-is-really-happening sort of vibe, and you're back to being Rosemary Woodhouse staring into the eyes of ultimate evil.

A couple weeks later, after a throne room show trial, I was launched towards Midgard for the first of many times. I won't even get into what they did to the giants. It wasn't pretty. Honestly, I tried to warn them. I did my best. They're stubborn, though. Never would admit it was a mistake. Not even today. They still talk about it like it's their crowning achievement.

Odin's eye? Yeah, it's weird how he still only has one, even after he fell, even after he changed. I'd have to say, of all of us, he's probably changed the least, but for, possibly Thor, and maybe Baldur. I mean, this is random, guys, not the product of some Amazon algo. We've all changed, in mysterious ways.

12

UNLIKE THE EVIL GENIUSES

YOU'D THINK with all the do-it-yourself skullfuckery that goes into having an "ideology" terrorists would get a little more creative when they pursue their raisons d'etre; y'know, autonomously deciding when, where, and how to end other people's lives. But they don't.

Unlike the evil geniuses brought to us by the Bash McGoverns and Dingo Morrisons of the literary world, once RL bad guys get an idea rattling around in their noggins, they're a lot like kids, unable to let it go no matter fucking what. Think about all the hijacked airliners and embassy attacks, the hotel takeovers and subway bombings. These days, in Germany, it's Christmas markets...

Greta Bruder will be in Greater Berlin tonight, the toney borough of Spandau to be exact, opening one of *das kapital*'s newest, flashiest Christmas markets. While she's there, Bruder will do what German politicians do. She'll wring a few mitts and knock back a couple pilsners, smooch some babies and mow some strudel. Then, as night comes, Bruder will do her real thing; she'll act out her very own raison d'etre.

Bruder will stand on the red, baked brick steps of grand old Hoffstadt Church, the sole surviving section of the now-ruined Hoffstadt Castle…She'll stand there and give eight minutes of stump to a well-manicured throng of supporters, a crowd that in spite of her staff's best efforts—or, possibly, because of them—hasn't been manicured quite well enough.

OUTSIDE, THE age-faded paint, rust-eaten metal, and cracked brickwork of Wulfgarten, a scummy, slummy, largely deserted industrial zone a half hour from Spandau. Inside, Stuttgart, Mephistopheles, and I stand in a defunct Stadtbus terminal, waiting for M-F.

They're already well into it when Stuttgart says, "But White Pride. Gin Leichtenstieger, who can play the guitar like that? The twelve strings, eighteen?" He raises his eyebrows, adds, "Twenty-four," as though he's just completed a titanic mathematical proof.

Mephistopheles replies, "The quad, sure. But with Leichtenstieger, there's no speed with that one, no power. White Pride, man, they just fucking need more amps, more energy. Now, you take People's Front, that's some true aggression, some fucking musical mayhem."

The place is unkempt, definitionally, the dust on the floors an inch thick when we arrive and find the twin panel trucks, in a smaller garage beyond; waiting, dust undisturbed around them, as if they fell from the sky and have been waiting there a thousand years.

The ceilings are high in the main terminal and relentlessly industrial, crisscrossed with pipework, ductwork, and skeletal metal supports, the sort of spindly ceiling structure these places always seem to have, as though in preparation for a forgotten drop ceiling or something like that. In spite of all that, you can still see the hope beyond the incompletion and decay, the hope that existed here, in that time after the war, when it was a place of commerce and dreams, of transit from one symbol of renewal to another.

I'm on the verge of screaming for Stuttgart and Mephistopheles to shut the fuck up when M-F saunters in, completing our quartet of would-be assassins. Shades, shaved head, and full beard, bleached, patched jeans under riding leathers, he looks completely conspicuous; like he should have a sign hanging over his head that says, "Was zum Teufel mache ich hier?"

"Where's your outfit?" I ask, nodding in the direction of my compatriots.

We're wearing fluorescent orange jumpers, ready to pretend at being environmental testers or some such shit. Stuttgart and Mephistopheles have been talking about Nazi metal for an hour, first in the truck on the way over, now standing around, smoking these foul, sweet, cheap German cigars. The smoke they put off smells sulfurous and it's black. I mean, seriously, black. Like pitch, like coal. Back and forth, they go, forth and back, the conversation growing ever more obscure as the minutes crawl by, the black smoke builds, and I scan for ventilation.

M-F unbuttons his shirt's second button, flashes orange jumpsuit, launches right into giving orders. "New guy, you'll drive the truck. Our helper will seal the entrance, Stuttgart and Mephistopheles will take out the exit, and I'll leave the present. Not in that order, obviously."

I chuckle, get some stink-eye, and look down.

Stuttgart speaks up, "We had it planned, though, already, M-F. You were going to give me the honor of leaving the device."

"You're disagreeing with me?" asks M-F.

"'Course not, it's just, we need a little time to reconfigure this."

"What's to reconfigure? I just told you how it's gonna work."

Mephistopheles nods crisply, good Nazi that he is. There's no heel click or "*sieg heil*" but with that sort of energetic chin-bounce let's just call them implied.

"Any other problems?" M-F asks. "Maybe you, new guy?"

"No problems, M-F. If there's one thing Wrath X loves to do, it's drive."

"And kill traitors to the Fatherland, am I right?"

THE VB wanted to use sarin at first, but they couldn't find a legitimate seller. After that, they thought they had a line on neurophysalgia but when the Austrian Islamist Front found out they were dealing with Nazis on the neuro-, second-rate, transnational Nazis to boot, the deal got killed faster than you can say "peace be upon him" in pidgin German.

Which caused the VB to fall back on good old mustard gas, care of someone's World-War-I-reenactment-nutter of an oh-pa who apparently had a stockpile of unexploded WWI-era canisters laying around, in addition to the odd spiked helmet, riding crop, and Cthuluuan gas mask. Then oh-pa kicked, the federal police found the stash, and that fell through, too.

Which was when they decided to use plain water, a plan that seemed, to them at least, almost elegant. And maybe it was. Worse still, maybe it is. Because on the other side of an old, secret tunnel, about ten feet down from where we'll connect, there's a water main, one that hasn't serviced the church for decades, one that's nonetheless still functional.

THE SKY is twilight blue by the time we get to the drug store in Vitasbund, which is adjacent to Spandau, in a weird sense, one of its suburbs. Eight tenths of a mile from the Christmas market, there's a DrugMarkt that has been closed for renovations for a month now. M-F gets out of the truck, opens the high chain-link gate on the back of the impromptu equipment yard, the one I learn has itself been closed, at M-F's order, left teeming with equipment, for a week solid.

He shuts the gate behind us, gets back in, and I drive the rest of the way to the loading dock, where Stuttgart and Mephistopheles are already waiting in the other truck.

In through the loading dock—a quick jimmy with a cheap crowbar, and there we are. We unload the equipment, gear up, and move through the deserted store, down concrete steps to the basement and sub-basement beyond.

The sub-basement abuts the old tunnel, something dating from the Middle Ages, or maybe even earlier, something not even the Nazis, or the Allies for that matter, managed to destroy. This far below ground, this far from the world's present tense action, the equipment is completely muffled.

Working with jackhammers and light charges, we're through the wall and into the old tunnel, the one that runs east-west. Twenty minutes of moving west and we come to the point we've been looking for. It's been marked with an orange swastika. Beyond that wall lies a shorter, newer, tunnel, one that leads back to a hewn-stone staircase ending in a secret door, beneath the High Prelate's Sanctuary in Hoffstadt Church.

THE SURROUNDING square decked in crimson, gold, and hunter green, accented with silvered tinsel and lights varied in color and intensity (some blinking, some strobing, some stolid as stars), cheer and cheer's common twin, the sweet, stinging scent of booze, pervade the crowd of thousands, many here for the speech alone.

"And hear my words, there will be a new Germany. Not a fatherland for a special, holy few, but a motherland for all; a beacon of love and hope for every race and color, creed and religion!"

Applause.

I'm in the getaway panel truck. I'm waiting, watching the clock, as I know M-F, Stuttgart, and Mephistopheles have already left their charges, surreptitiously defused by me. I guess I really am a bit of a demolitions expert. Who knew?

"From Syria to Uruguay, Bangladesh to Azerbaijan, Germany will be a mother to immigrants the world over, a mother with a heart big enough to take in the whole world!"

Applause.

Roped-off in their special area, gazing up at the steps fronting the red, baked-brick facade of Hoffstadt Church, hijabs and skull caps are integrated completely with the red and white Cat-in-the-Hat toppers that are so common with Bruder's younger supporters. This is Greta Bruder's Germany, the promise of it, and it's sort of the opposite of what Odin intended with the Great Integration. I mean, the Great Integration—and I helped with this, so I really do know—was a power grab, pure and simple, an attempt to coopt Christianity to our own ends. So you can probably imagine the confused feelings of success and sorrow Odin must have seeing something like a Christmas market, knowing how it got here. And it's true, I do feel sorry for him on some level. I mean, he is my father. How could I not?

As for Bruder, in addition to having her outfitted in surprisingly sleek scuba gear just in case the water gets to her before we can, the plan, my plan, is for the giants to get to the one point where the old tube tunnel hits the one beneath Hoffstadt Church. As long as they do, the water from the final explosion will pass harmlessly down into the abandoned tube tunnel. Bruder will be safe, Odin will be in the clear, and everyone will be happy, everyone except the VB.

I watch the rest of the speech. I've read the whole thing, and I know there's barely a minute left before she closes, leaves the stage, and heads towards that old tunnel. I call Hel.

"Yes?"

"Is Bruder with anyone?"

"The Chief of Staff."

"You think she's the mole."

"Probably not. She's almost certainly going to drown with Bruder."

"Bruder's not going to drown."

"Exactly. But Helga doesn't know that."

"So, it's the High Prelate then, the old dude, Klausenschmictal."

"Wait, that's not supposed…"

I hear an explosion; thundering, vibrating, it's followed by several lesser though still potent charges. The truck, the phone, the me, we all shake as the blast comes in stereo…through the phone and the air. The line dies. That's when I see the police cars coming in the rearview, silent as the Valks, and realize Hel's words won't matter, and that they never could have.

Once the cops are within fifty yards, sirens start whirring and wailing and I begin honking the horn like a mad man, the signal that we're fucked. Stuttgart and Mephistopheles take off in the opposite direction from the cops.

M-F is not so lucky. As the cops haul me out of the truck, I catch a glimpse of him being frog-marched towards me. One of the German cops gives me a baton to the ribs. I barely feel it but yowl, double-over, and fall to the ground. Pretty soon, I'm zip-cuffed and in the back of a paddy wagon. And as we speed away, through the darkened, neon-inflected Berlin streets, as shadows seem to press in on all sides, I think about how everything went according to plan up until the blasts came. We were just a few seconds from perfection, and I wonder if Greta Bruder and any number of other people are still alive.

TRAGICOMEDY FOR THE FALLEN, PART 5

CENTURIES PASSED. I did my thing. You know, walked the earth in disguise. Most of the time I just pretended to be one of you--a nutty minstrel, a spunky outlaw, a nameless drifter--but we're talking about a lot of years here. Sooner or later, I was bound to take a spin as just about everything under the sun.

Trees and shrubs, fruits and vegetables, inanimate objects, animals, forces of nature, ghosts, concepts…Other than you, the animals were the biggest hoot. How much nuance is there to being a wine glass, a fishing pole, or a Kierkegaardian dilemma, anyways? Animals, on the other hand…well, they're like you guys, just a bit simpler. They think and feel; they *experience* the world, each in their own way.

October 19th, 1932. I was experiencing the world as an animal, a North American black bear, as a matter of fact, standing in the middle of a stream somewhere in the Big Empty, stuffing the tail end of a trout into my maw.

I remember being intensely, addictively into that fish. You wouldn't believe how bears feel about seafood. Honestly, it's something like how you guys feel about street drugs after you've been at them a couple years.

Unlike you and drugs—they really are the last thing you guys are designed to handle, what with all your doubts and insecurities—bears are well outfitted for fishing (claws, jaws, teeth). Seafood's healthy, too, broadly speaking—high protein, low fat, omega 3's—so there's that to be said for bears and their obsession, too.

That fish was formidable, at least twenty pounds, but I was making quick work of it, powerful teeth slashing through flesh, breaking down those pin bones with ease. I remember daydreaming about Keynesian theory that day as I ate.

The world economy had already been in the shitter for a few years by that point...Black Friday, Great Depression, all that. Honestly, I hate to say it; but things felt a little like today. And just like today, I was doing my part; trying to help you guys sort things out. Odin, of course, was doing his part; trying to make things worse.

"Psst, Loki," said a voice. The speaker sounded familiar, but it had been so long since I'd heard from Odin, it didn't even occur to me that it could be him. I looked around, up and down, side to side, couldn't see a soul. I was on the verge of putting it down to some sort of trout-frenzied delirium when he continued.

"I'm having a party," said the voice. There was something about the way he said "party"—guttural, Germanic, like a party was the last place he really wanted to be. That was when I knew.

"Odin?" I asked, speaking in a fish-garbled ursine drawl. Slow and rumbling, my speech surprised even me. Well, it's not like you turn yourself into a bear when you're looking for conversation, is it?

"Guilty as charged," said Odin, a large, spectral head appearing in the air above me. Bearded and grim, craggy-faced, functionally cycloptic and blue-eyed (the one I could see); the image was...*Odinic*.

"Fancy meeting you here in the middle of the woods. How long's it been; two, three centuries since our last tête-à-tête?"

He smiled blankly, probably unable to remember the meeting in question. No surprise, the last time I'd spoken to Odin had been during the Renaissance. Back then, he'd get in touch just to yell at me. You know, show up in a drunken stupor, complaining about this infraction or that misdeed. Most of the time he'd just bitch about the Norns leaving and the Great Integration failing, how the whole mess was my fault.

"So you're having a party? What's it to me?"

He grinned. "I want you to come. What do you say, son?"

"What do I say to you showing up out of the blue after all these years?"

"No, what do you say to the party?"

I stared. So did he. Odin's really good at deceit when he wants to be. Hell, he could even convince me of stuff sometimes back then. He held my gaze, used that eye of his; the expression of fatherly concern, the deep need for filial love that's bound to elicit sympathy.

"Is this a trick?" I asked, pausing to consider.

"That's some question coming from you."

"Well?"

"No, it's not a trick. We've been without your company far too long, Loki. The party's for you, to welcome you back."

"Really?"

"Of course. Plus, I have a few friends I want you to meet."

"Who?" I asked, sirens going off; not, it turned out, loudly enough.

"That's a surprise."

"Gee, Odin, I don't know."

"Thor misses you."

"Oh, please."

"Asks where his brother is all the time. Freya, Frey, Heimdall, Sif, Tyr, Baldur, the Valkyries…they're all waiting."

"The Valks? Really?"

"Of course."

"What about the whole thing with the Norns?"

"Forgiven and forgotten."

"There's nothing to forgive."

"Have it your way. It's still forgotten."

"Things haven't worked out with the Christians, have they?"

He scowled.

"I told you they wouldn't, not after the way the Great Integration went."

He sneered, finally responded. "Time to scale back the whole Ragnarök angle, make it a little more nebulous…like it used to be. May even have to go spiritualist."

"Crystals?"

"Pagan. Druidic, maybe? I don't know."

"Trees?"

"Not just. Shrubs, and grasses, too. Plus, the pagan stuff and the spiritualism."

"You really think a combo can work?"

"Why not?"

"Seems like they're drifting further away from you guys."

"What's this 'you guys' stuff?"

"I guess I don't really feel very Asgardian anymore."

"I'm telling you. These friends I want you to meet. Could be a real game changer."

"You're sure this doesn't have anything to do with Ragnarök?"

"Not even a little bit."

13

A SORT OF BEMUSED CONCERN

IN BOOKING, Marc-Fritz is next to me scowling like he knows better, like it's all my fault. But he always glares like this, even when he's smiling, even when he seems happy, has from the second I met him. For a tough—even a German neo-Nazi tough—I guess the glare is just a tool, one of your things.

"What the fuck happened?" he whispers.

"Gosh, I don't know, M-F. Just doing what you asked. Drive the truck, honk if…you know."

"You were supposed to start honking *before* the cops were on us."

"I didn't have time."

He furrows his brow in thought.

"Not to say anything against anyone…"

"Don't say it," M-F replies.

"I just said I wasn't—"

"I'm fully aware of the fact that two of us got away, and two of us didn't."

"Hard to believe Stuttgart was involved."

"Right."

"So, what?"

"We need to get out fast, that's what. Figure out who sold us out, make this happen before it's too late."

"So, you think Bruder's alive?"

"You don't?"

"I'm really not sure. There was a big explosion and the cops showed up. She could be dead for all we know."

"True. I guess there's still hope."

THE COPS don't even think about throwing us in the veal pen. No, we're bad news bears, and we're hustled off to a secure wing, stuffed into the same cell for some ungodly and what-would-be-terrifying-if-I-weren't-me reason. Because M-F still has that homicidal stare fixed in place, that all-I-need-to-find-is-something-to-kill expression both Thor and Odin cultivate. He doesn't speak, just lays on the cot, scowling at the ceiling, trying to work things out.

An hour later, he sits up suddenly. "I've got it," he exclaims, completely interrupting the TV show about a 19th century typhoid outbreak I was only half-watching but really starting to get into. So weird how that works, isn't it? There are just so many things unexplained about you and us. It's almost enough to make you think none of us are gods, or even were, not really. Like I said, we're not omniscient, omnipresent, or omni-anything.

"Typhoid?" I ask.

He rolls his eyes, looks at me with intellectual dismissal, rather than brute aggression for the first time since we got pinched.

"The answer," he says, with the cryptic tease of an over-ling who's just had a revelation he refuses to share with a little guy.

"What is it?"

"We need to get out of here quickly."

"Okay, but how?" I ask.

"I… I don't know," he offers, "maybe you could create a diversion, and I could escape."

"That's not very detailed."

"Hey, I'm just the ideas guy," he says tapping his temple. "But I guess if I were to do your job for you…"

"Yeah?"

"I'd say you distract the guard, then you get her to turn around, then you grab her baton and hit her on the back of the head with it. Then I get her keys and escape."

"But I'd still be stuck. And I'd be the obvious person who helped you escape."

"But I'd be free."

I must seem unconvinced because he adds, "You could do it again later."

I squint back. "How much time have you spent in jail?"

"A lot. Why?"

"To start with, you're overestimating my—well, basically anyone's—diversionary skills."

"Eh," he grunts, lies back, and eventually goes back to eye-fucking the ceiling. I turn to the wall, watch the typhoid show via side-eye until the guard, Marta, shows up and tells me my lawyer is here.

"Really? What about *my* lawyer?" M-F cuts in.

"No, just him," says Marta.

Marta ushers me into a private room where I'm cuffed to a table and made to sign several more forms. What, you think Wrath X isn't real, that he can't sign stuff? You probably thought Loki Niflheim wasn't real either, right? Or Gustav…Oh, no-no-no-no…Wrath X has a social security number, credit cards, all that shit. His info's probably plastered all over the Dark Web, just like yours. He also, apparently, has a lawyer, though even I/he wasn't aware of that.

JACOB MACHTMEISTER arrives in a traditionally barristerial gray suit. With closely-clipped blond hair, horn rimmed glasses, and the sort of smile that would make a wolf nervous, Machmeister carries a briefcase that's big, black, and practically bursting... with what, it's not clear. Papers? Secrets? Schemes? Weapons?

Once he sits down across from me, he raises his index finger to his lips in the universal symbol for "shut the fuck up."

"You may leave," he says to Marta.

"Now, Herr X," Machmeister offers as the door closes.

I laugh because I think he's being funny.

He stares back at me like like there's a live raccoon crawling out of my mouth. "You'll be here for about forty-five minutes then you'll be released."

"Do I get to…"

He holds his finger up again. "That's it."

"OK?"

"Oh, there's just one more thing. You have a call," he says, producing a uPhone.

"Yes?" I answer.

"Trickster! I just wanted to congratulate you." It's Sunshine.

"Where are you?"

"Asgard. Valhalla to be exact."

"How'd you manage?"

"I know. It shouldn't work, but it does. Technology, right?"

"And what are you doing there?"

"As if you didn't know."

213

"I really don't."

"I had to pick something up. I'll tell you all about it when I see you."

"Oh, when's that?"

"Shouldn't be long now."

"Hold on."

"What?"

"I still don't know what happened to Bruder."

"True."

"I'M GETTING out," I tell M-F.

He growls for a second then adds, "Well, isn't that perfect?" Man, I don't even want to tell you what that growl meant in lupine. Fen would be offended, maybe more than offended…

I stare at him absently, try to fill my eyes with the sort of lack of intelligence he'll buy. In other words, I copy M-F's own expression. That's the great thing about these white supremacists—and it's just another way they remind me of Odin and Thor—they're so arrogant, so self-absorbed, that if you spit their reflections back at them, they have no way of seeing what it is you're up to.

"So, what happened to Bruder?"

"I have no idea."

"You don't even know if she's alive?"

"That's right. I don't even."

"What about your lawyer?"

"He just handed me a phone. Said there was some mysterious benefactor on the line."

"It wasn't Boris, was it?"

"No, it definitely wasn't Boris."

"Who was it then?"

"I have no idea."

"But you're getting out?"

"I know, it's crazy. Is there someone I can get in touch with for you?"

"I guess you could at least do that," he says and gives the digits of the lawyer I just met.

THERE ARE a lot of sentences I could start with "I'd be lying if…" Is that only because I'm me? Maybe. But I bet you could do it, too.

I'd be lying if I told you I'd never been sad. Boy, would I be lying there. I've spent whole human centuries as an un-bucked-up buttercup. I'd be lying if I told you I'd never been in love either. That, of course, you already know. TBH, the whole conjectural lying/not lying gambit is a pretty nifty opening when you think about it: intriguing, playful, truthful in an ironic way…

And so, I'd be lying if I told you I'd never been picked up from jail in a limo. However, I'd absolutely be telling the truth if I told you I'd never been picked up from jail in a limo following an assassination attempt. Which is what happens.

Mercedes, of course. This is Germany. And in Germany, does anyone else make limos? I'm not talking about those suburban defense enviro-wrecking homunculi all the politicians favor these days, with their three or four or sixteen rows of seats. I'm talking about a legit limo, the kind of monstrous metallic centipede you can host an orgy inside. That thing.

Black with blacked windows—windows so black I can't even see myself in their reflections—it's waiting out front after

I'm released, idling in the weak, fall sunshine. The afternoon shadows seem almost to grow as I approach.

Across the street, a church clock strikes the half-hour, sending a flock of birds whirling into the cloudless sky. For an instant, they go serpentine, winding into the shape of a whip, or a question mark, before they crack, or interrogate, or whatever, off in the direction of the Sun. The scene makes me shudder, even though it shouldn't.

This is Berlin and for some reason it's different in the daylight, different for me. You'd think it would be better, what with all the evil the Nazis did under cover of darkness, but it's not. Maybe it's about the day the gods fell. Maybe that's what the sunlight brings home for me.

Sure, I act like it's cool, like it's what the gods deserved. And both those things are true. But there was also real loss to their fall, the knowledge that the world had lost a fundamental part of itself.

THE LIMO door opens as I approach. It's Odin, of course, alone, inside, smiling, not just with his mouth but with his eye. I won't lie. That's a good sign.

An eye-smile from Odin is the tip-top smile he possesses, the veritable Faberge egg of Odin's expressions. It's like he's already thanking me for what I've done, and it makes me feel whole in a way I've rarely ever felt, proud and clean and perfect in a way. But only for a split-second. Because I still don't know what happened to Bruder, which means even if Odin doesn't realize it, his smile's actually a lie.

I duck my head inside the limo, see Heimdall's surly, bearded visage in the rearview, scowling at me from the driver's seat, and decide to step back. I decide, in fact, to get the fuck out of there as soon as possible. Odin sees us lock eyes, raises the divider, and grins.

"You kids, I swear. Still unable to play nicely together after however many thousand years."

"And you like it that way, don't you?"

He smirks. "Listen, son, what I want to say is…well, I don't know how to thank you. You did it. Played your part perfectly. The human 'authorities' think it was nothing but nonsense from a bunch of incompetent Nazis."

"Which is, more or less, exactly what it was."

Odin's speech catches for a second, as though me calling his Nazis incompetent cut him off.

"The entire family owes you a great debt," he says, recovering, extending his hand.

I take it, shake like a good dog.

"Aren't you going to get in?"

I nod at where Heimdall was before the divider went up.

Odin purses his lips like I'm being silly. "Maybe there's somewhere we can take you? Perhaps to get the Norn now that you've saved Bruder?"

"That's just it, Odin. I'm not sure she made it."

"You're not what?"

"No, you heard me. I've been in jail. Y'know, no contact with the outside world. Well, except for one phone call. And it wasn't from Bruder."

"So, that's how you got out?"

"I thought you got me out."

"I would have."

"Then, what are you doing here?"

"Well, I mean, I am here to get you out, but obviously you don't need me for that anymore."

"If you're aching to get someone out, M-F's still stuck."

"Oh, I can't get him out. That would be too obvious." He pauses, as though assessing the truth of his last statement. "Listen, Loki, you really need to get in the limo. We need to sort all this out."

"I'm not getting in there, but I will sort it out, on my own. There's just one other thing I need to mention."

"What thing?"

"She escaped."

"So, you were joking? Bruder's fine?"

"I meant Sunshine. I really don't know about Bruder."

"Sunshine? How did…how did you manage to fuck this up so thoroughly?"

"If you're unhappy with the results I guess you should have taken care of it yourself. I just got out of jail, remember? I was there on your behalf; yet you, apparently, didn't get me out. I'm really not in the mood for any of this."

"The mood!?" He stares at me gape-mouthed. Slowly, the reaction builds. Whatever form he takes, Odin's eye has this weird quality when he gets angry, a sort of deep, internal darkness, even though it looks shiny, steely blue. Even though a few seconds ago it was smiling. Now, it's decidedly not. In fact, it might as well not be sunny at all outside, because the darkness in Odin's gaze is all I can see.

"Right. The mood."

"This escape?" he asks, recovering his composure.

"Yeah?"

"When?"

"A couple days ago."

"And you're just telling me?"

"Ultimately, it's her decision. I can't make her come. I told you it was up to her from the start."

"Do you at least have some of your…creatures…out there looking for her?"

"My creatures have been busy thwarting that assassination plot you cooked up."

"Which you're not even sure you thwarted."

I shrug.

He smiles, nods his head. "Whoa, you almost got me there. That was a good one, kiddo."

"It's not a trick."

"It has to be. Come on, tell the truth, son. What are you playing at?"

"Nothing. I was just trying to help you."

"Why don't you close the door then? We can go back to Valhalla, plan strategy, have a real family reunion."

"You know, I think I'll just walk, Odin. But don't worry, I'll be in touch."

He opens his mouth to speak as I shut the door. I turn and walk the opposite direction down the one-way street. Once I find a drugstore, I browse men's hair care for a tick, waiting for enough privacy to turn myself into a little Arab kid. Fifteen minutes later, the aforementioned kid strolls past Odin's parked limo. He and Heimdall are standing in front of the car, eyes locked in angry confusion.

THE ANSWER THAT DOESN'T EXIST

I KNOW how the story goes: Thor was there from the beginning—
or a wink and a nod after the beginning—at any rate, long before
me. But it's not true. I was there waiting when Thor showed up.
How old was I? Oh, who knows precisely? But one minute he
wasn't there, the next he was, full-blown, all grown, and ready
to crack skulls. No, there was no birthing, no babe in a basket,
none of the pageantry of my own, touching Loki-tivity.

"A God of Thunder?" I asked, once I got a good look at him,
all musclebound, self-satisfied, and goldie-locks-ed. "Isn't that
sort of a silly thing to have a god for?"

Odin smirked. "May seem silly to you, Loki, but they're
seafaring people. The cycles of wind and rain mean a lot to
them. And then there's…"

"What?"

"Tell him, Dad," said Thor.

"Tell me what?"

"We need help with war."

"You want to expand war?" I'd been after Odin for centuries
to cut back on war. I even tried to get him to shift Freya; y'know,
bring her under my authority. Goddess of quiet, I thought,
goddess of the night maybe.

"What can I say, they like fighting down there."

"But there's you, Tyr, Freya, the Valkyries…How about a

little more peace? I know: why don't you make him the God of Peace?"

Thor scowled at me for the first time, and I knew it was on, on like cosmo-apocalyptic Donkey Kong until the end of time. It's odd, though, thinking back, that first memory of Thor brings a tear to my eye and not only for the trouble he'd cause. Not even for the dirt in that first look he ever gave me. Maybe I even cared about Thor once, or more than once. Maybe when I realized how Odin would use us, set us against each other, maybe I even loved him? Maybe I still do? But maybe I hate him, too.

That's how it is though, right? With everything really, love and hate, good and evil, pain and pleasure. Nothing is ever pure and perfect. Nothing is ever clean.

"It won't be war exactly, more like the battle/combat angle and berserk fury, that sort of stuff."

"Hear that?" said Thor, turning to Tyr. "I'm gonna be a god of war, too!"

Tyr grumbled. I mean, can you blame him? After everything he'd put up with—losing his hand and all that—Odin up and brings in like the fifth new guy to do the same job. Talk about forced obsolescence, talk about layering, talk about a workman's comp injury gone awry.

With time, though, it would become clear Thor was there to do the same job as more than one of us. Oh, yes, he had grand designs did Thor. He was born with them; the greatest, his desire to be Odin's heir. Those desires placed in his heart by Odin himself.

Is that what started it? The fraternal hatred, I mean. The realization that he was special, Odin's chosen? Who knows, but he's always treated me like a little brother, even though I'm older. Was it his strength? His innate aggressiveness? Or was it the way Odin and Frigga began to treat him like the princeling, me like the stepchild?

Sure, they'd loved me once–at least Odin had–I was the babe in the basket before they had another and another and another… And it hurt when I realized they could love others, that I wasn't special in that way. But what really hurt was when Thor came along, and I realized they didn't love me, not like him. I started to wonder whether they loved me at all, and the answer I came to was that they didn't. And they never had.

GIVEN ALL this, you'd think Thor would have stayed out of my way. Not so, not so at all. He was, and still is, particularly adept at intricating himself into events in which he has no place. When Odin and I were working on something, for example, when we were working on The Great Integration.

"But he's weak," Thor was talking to Odin about Jesus. We were in the middle of gaming out The Great Integration, sitting around the table in the Hall of Counsel, staring down at a map of Midgard. We had all the religions spread out, like a game of Risk, each one with pieces representing worshippers and influence. Yeah, sure, Islam was the hot thing right then, the religion with sizzle, but we were never going to be big in the desert world. It wasn't a cultural fit. Christianity on the other hand had, somehow, someway, proliferated into the lands where our worshippers already lived. It seemed perfect. "You don't want to be weak, do you?"

"I wouldn't be weak. This is superficial, about integrating the two religions so we can goose our number of worshippers, start to siphon off some of the Christians. Get the Norns off my back."

"We're talking long game, Thor." This was me.

He replied, "Haven't you always told us perception is everything? Maybe if we merge, you really will get weaker."

That logic stopped Odin for a second. Losing power has never been a prospect he's found remotely appealing.

Thor, of course barreled ahead. "Maybe this Jesus guy will become real. It's not like we know everything. He was real once, for a little while. Who knows what might happen if you start acting like him?"

I piped up, "OK, Thor, this is really not helpful. We have no reason to believe the god of some phony religion will become real just because humans believe in him."

"What if that's what happened with us?" He asked. "Is it, Dad, is that what happened with us?"

"Absolutely not," Odin replied, "I had to wait for worshippers until they'd evolved into full humans. I waited, and I waited.

The Neanderthals, the Cro-Magnons, they were useless when it came to imagining themselves as deities, bunch of sun, sky, and animal humpers. I couldn't get through to them at all. Trust me, I tried. Sky signs, apparitions, all sorts of wondrous bullshit."

"Maybe you should go ask the Head? Or the Norns?" I offered.

Thor cut in, "Norns? They haven't done a thing for us in centuries. Jews, Christians, Muslims. All those lies from all those bogus religions, and they do nothing."

"Hey, Thor, careful what you say about the Norns."

"Shut up, Loki. Just because you're fucking Sunshine, never mind sneaking off and doing her sisters once in a while when no one's looking, you think they're special. But show me what they've done. Show me what Fate has done for us!"

"Thor, shush," said Odin. "Do you want Fate to hear you?"

"Bah, Fate!"

Odin and I looked at each other. His eyes were as big as mine. "Seriously, Thor, shut up!" We both said.

And Thor did. He always—well, usually—did what Odin told him. And he still does.

I bet a lot of you have had the sort of sibling who always complains about and/or tries to control events—and gets their way more often than not as a result. In addition to all his flexing and fighting and hair-tossing, that's Thor.

And Thor may not have succeeded then and there, but he'd planted a seed that would grow into their downfall. So, yes, I blame Odin for what happened. Why wouldn't I? He did it. But that's where you guys are wrong in the way you look at things.

You're always searching for the alexandrine masterstroke, the one variable that explains many, if not everything in the Universe. Why do you think you've wound up following so many nonexistent gods and kooky demagogues? You're looking for the Universe to give you something it simply can't. You're looking for *the* answer that doesn't exist.

14

A STATUE OF YOU

PAST THE retinal entry scan, through the creaking outer gate, through the front door scans (another retinal, followed by a fingerprint) and keypad, and I enter to the metallic, aural blur of bips and boops that is *Monsieur von Mayhem*'s theme music. There's a loamy sativa smell in the air and the attendant purple haze lingers, tinging the air in the front foyer the color of lavender and lies.

Hel is sitting in the dining room avidly scanning her laptop. Lo and behold, Greta Bruder is there, too, avidly scanning Hel. The guys are on the floor in the great room, the source of the aforementioned sound and smoke. Fen lounges on the couch, wearing his massive noggin upside-down. He snores quietly— yeah, I know; it doesn't make sense—cycles his legs from time to time. Probably dreaming about chasing Tyr.

"Guys," I call, and they nod, eyes never leaving the screen. "I'm home," I say, raising my voice so they'll get the point.

Fen shakes himself awake, flipping his head right-way then left-way and back. He looks sorta like he's doing a doggie double-take, jumps down, saunters over for a pat.

"Game off. Full concentration."

The giants set down their controllers, though the game keeps bipping and beeping as they join us in the dining room, grumbling to each other on the way. I catch Bruder eyeing Hel again. Which is when I catch the fact that Hel is also eyeing Bruder.

Bruder turns to me. "Finally, some information." She rises, walks over to me. I'm surprised by her moxie at this point, makes me wonder whether she's lost her mind, which would be the obvious, and probably appropriate, human reaction to everything that's happened to her.

"What information is that?"

"For starters, you can tell me why we're all here?"

"That's…sort of a broad question. Can you be more specific?"

"I'm not just hanging out with Norse gods out of the blue, am I?"

"You can quit calling us 'the Norse gods.' We're *the* gods."

"Fine, as you say. But you guys still haven't explained anything to me, other than the fact that I was about to be assassinated. I mean, bravo on that, y'know, helping me out and all. But this…" Her hand sweeps nonchalantly in the direction of the great room.

"I'm still not following?"

"Like, what's this about. It must be important. Is it climate change; nuclear war; an impending asteroid strike? Are we going to stop the apocalypse or something? That, what is it you guys call it, Ragnarök?" She chuckles, shakes her head. But when she looks back at me, her gaze is lit, burning blue. I'm 99/100 she's lost her mind.

"The assassination wasn't enough for you?"

"Actually, no, it's…"

"Hold on. Where's Kurt?"

226

Surtur replies, "Did you know there's a room downstairs."

"There are a bunch of them. Laundry room? Wine Cellar? Sauna?"

"No, but behind the wine cellar there's another room."

"There is?"

"Yeah, it's sort of…"

Thyrm cuts in, "Well, it's kind of like a dungeon, a cell at least. There's this secret wall then there's…"

"A room…," Surtur adds.

"Maybe from the war. Maybe they hid people back there from the Nazis. How'd you guys find it?"

"We just sort of did. You know we've always been good at stuff like that, Loki."

"And that's where Kurt is?"

Thrym nods. "Exactly. We had to leave him someplace when we were in Berlin, someplace that would be convenient for Fen to guard."

Fen grumbles a little, though it might just be indigestion.

"He's getting air, isn't he?"

"Yes," Surtur replies.

"Probably," Thyrm corrects.

"Probably?" I ask.

"There was a vent."

"I think."

"You were OK with this?" I ask, turning to Hel.

"They were adamant. He's definitely getting air. I made sure of that. And we gave him a pad of paper and a pen. He said he needed something to do. He's really like a child, you know?"

"Who is Kurt?" Bruder asks.

Surtur offers this, "Loki's supposed friend."

"Supposed? Is this another one of your Viking Brotherhood guys?"

"No, not that sort of friend. He's American."

"Oh," Bruder replies, as though that explains a lot and none of it good.

"Let's just, can we get him out, bring him up here?"

Surtur and Thyrm head downstairs, bickering about whose fault it is they have to go get Kurt.

AFTER A couple minutes, the guys return dragging a bedraggled Kurt. Each giant with a hand, Kurt's face is both ashen and dirty, his expression one of hopelessness gone to anger.

"Hey, buddy, how's it going?" I ask Kurt.

He winces. "Gustav, they locked me in a dungeon."

"Secret chamber technically," says Thyrm.

"I did just have them get you out of the secret chamber." I turn to the rest of the group. "Nobody told him what was going on?"

"What?" he asks. "What is 'going on?'"

"Exactly," I add.

Everyone shakes their heads except Kurt.

Bruder says, "I didn't realize there was another normal person here."

"You're Greta Bruder," says Kurt.

"And you must be Kurt? Finally, someone who knows less about what's going on than me."

"That's true," I say, "Kurt definitely knows less than you. I guess the only thing to do now is rectify that. Somebody get him a seat and a drink."

Surtur and Thyrm stare at each other.

"Surtur, get him a seat, Thyrm, get him a drink. Actually, make that a bottle and not that Jägermeister crap you guys love."

Surtur pulls out a chair for Kurt, motions for him to sit. Thyrm returns with a shot glass and a bottle of scotch.

"You want me to shoot scotch?" Kurt asks. "Are you fucking nuts?"

"Get him some water, Thyrm."

Kurt sits shaking his head as Thyrm returns with his water.

"Seriously, you're gonna need that drink so just do me a favor and take it."

"Fine." He does. "Satisfied?"

I pause, give him a few seconds for the booze to do its work. "Kurt, my name's not Gustav."

"Yeah?"

"It's Loki."

"Sure, it is."

"This is Hel," I say, pointing to Hel. "And you've already met Surtur and Thyrm. Oh, and Fen, or should I say, the Fenris Wolf." Fen looks up, grumbles. He jumps down, saunters off for a more amenable place to nap.

By this point, Bruder is gazing intently at Kurt. Man, is she a killer. She's looking at him like she's wondering, maybe hoping, he's about to lose his mind before her eyes. No wonder she got into politics.

Kurt looks back at her. "But you're still Greta Bruder?"

"Yes," she says.

"The German Washington?"

"That's what the press calls me. I'm just Greta Bruder."

He nods. "OK, I'm still not getting the big reveal, Gustav or Loki or whatever you name is."

"Here it comes," says Bruder.

I reply, "Loki's a pretty unusual name. Don't you think, Kurt?"

"I guess. But you've got people walking around with names like 12345, Apple, Fake Apple, and Nonsense these days. It's hardly that strange."

"But y'know, like the Loki from my book?"

"People have been named after mythological constructs in the past. Jesus, how many Jesuses are there in Mexico?"

"The pronunciation is different, but I take your point."

"So, no, not that strange."

"Oh, it's going to get stranger in a hurry," says Hel.

Bruder smiles. Hel winks back.

"Kurt," I say, "When I tell you my name's Loki, that's because I am *the* Loki."

"What, like the dude from the comic books? Gustav, is this about your novel again. Man, I told you it's good. Go with that epic stuff, all the weirdness and magic. But you don't have to bring it into the real world, man. You don't have to start pretending the characters are physically real in order to sell them. I mean, this isn't supposed to be nonfiction, is it?"

"It always comes to this," says Hel.

"Every time," says Thyrm.

Surtur nods ruefully.

"Fine, you asked for it. Poof," I say and turn myself into a woman.

Kurt does a Scooby Doo double-take and grabs for the Scotch, takes a quick swig.

"Poof," I say again and turn myself into Wrath X.

He grabs for the bottle again, this time closing his eyes and taking a longer pull.

When he opens them, I say, "Poof," and turn myself back into Gustav.

"How'd you do that?"

Bruder responds, "Because, you dummkopf, he's the god Loki."

Kurt shakes his head in obvious disbelief. I look to Hel, Surtur, Thyrm, and Bruder. They each shrug in turn. When I look back at Kurt, he's still shaking his head.

"Kurt, buddy."

He won't even meet my gaze.

"Put him back in the…"

"Dungeon?"

"I guess. And station Fen outside."

"Tie him up, too? Gag him?" the giants ask as one.

"There are no windows, right? No one can hear?"

"Right."

"Nah, just lock him up, give him his pen and paper. So, he can sketch or write poetry or whatever."

"Wait," Kurt says as the giants near him. "So, this basically boils down to me either believing you are the god Loki or you guys tying me up?"

"It's probably not an either/or at this point, buddy. But, yeah, believing and not believing are your only choices."

"So, what, you want me to swear fealty to you or something? Are we gonna do a pact?"

Hel laughs.

"I'm not that kind of god."

"There are different kinds of gods?"

"Well, there are the *real ones* aka us. Then there are all the others aka the unreal ones aka not us."

"You're saying all the other ones are fake. Jesus? Allah? Yahweh? Zeus? Vishnu?"

"Obviously."

"All fake?"

That's when the doorbell chimes, and the intercom cuts on. "Hey," I hear Sunshine say, "Are you gonna let a girl in or what?"

SUNSHINE TROMPS into the front hall, dusting the snow from her shoulders and shaking it from her hair, which is golden, now, and even longer. She's wearing big, round, black shades; a long, tan shearling coat; and knee-high boots that are deep navy but somehow work.

The guys are practically on top of her the second the door shuts. I mean, to the extent they can be on top of her at half her size. Neither of them seems angry, though, for the way she ditched them, made them chase her halfway across Europe, then stone-cold disappeared. They relieve her of her bags, blushing and tittering like a couple of rodeo clowns whose long-lost Queen of Barrel Racing has just returned.

Who knew she could have this much effect on them in such a short time? Certainly not me. I'd wonder about them at this point, the way they're acting, the fact that they could have let her get away, theoretically at least. I'd wonder that if we didn't have so much history, if Hel weren't here and wholly unimpressed. She's glaring at Sunshine, eyes burning black and deathly, still Daddy's little girl.

Sunshine meets Hel's gaze then quickly turns away, to me. The look she's wearing, halfway between a smile and a sneer—that and her clothes—make me think of Jagger in the Seventies. But not just of Mick. Sunshine also has me thinking of the women he'd be seen with—the flowing tresses and flawless make-up, the endless cigarettes and impossible physiques, the earthly pantheon of models and actresses that seemed drawn to him and still do, tbh; she has me thinking of how Mick and his women all sort of look(ed) the same. But that was the Brits in the Seventies, puzzling over their last hurrah at relevance, lingering in the neo-Romantic afterglow of the Beatles and James Bond. Sure, those British rock stars may not have been the first gender-twisters— I mean, hello! —but they were certainly some of the best. Jagger, Freddie...*Bowie*...yes, they were all wasted constantly, but I'll tell you this truly, on my word of honor as a narrator, it's hard to create without a little external help, a little chemical inspiration, if you will. I know, you think artists drink too much and smoke too much, snort too much and shoot too much. And they do. *We* do. Thing is, you would, too, if you really *saw* reality.

"Trickster." Sunshine hustles over to give me a big, cheeky hug and smooch, leaving the giants basking in her afterglow, flushed, smiling. "And Frau Bruder, what a surprise!"

"Fraulein," says Bruder, eyes going a little too wide.

Oh, Jesus, it's clear now. Apparently, Bruder's as much of a sex hound as most other politicians. First it was the aide, then it was the Hel, now it's the this. I mean, what is it with these people? Is politics the default state for people who can't get laid?

"And my old buddy, Kurt."

"Sabrina?" he asks, gaze newly enlivened.

"New color," she says, giving her hair a light shake. "You dig?"

"You left me in Amsterdam," Kurt adds plaintively.

"I know, baby, I'm sorry. I had places to be, places you couldn't."

"Places I couldn't what?"

"Be."

"So, you're which one?" asks Bruder.

"Which one what?"

"Which goddess?"

"Actually, I'm a Norn. My name is Sunshine."

"The fate chicks?" Kurt asks. "Like from the book?"

"Book?" asks Bruder.

"Yeah," I say, "I've been writing a book. Kurt's a writer, too. He's been looking it over for me."

"You're a writer?" Bruder asks.

Kurt replies, "Is that so hard to believe? I've just been informed, among other things, that he's Loki, she's a 'Norn,' and you're Greta Bruder."

"Fine," Sunshine says, "You're exactly right. My sisters and I…are the fate chicks."

"And your name isn't Sabrina?"

"Nope."

"Why is everyone's name changing?" Kurt asks.

I can't help but laugh.

Kurt points at Hel. "But she's not one of your sisters?"

I respond, "As I already said, she is Hel."

"As in the Queen of the Dead?" asks Kurt.

"Right."

"So don't fuck with me, Mr. Tax Attorney," Hel says, blowing several perfect smoke rings in succession.

Sunshine grins. "This is heartwarming. Didn't I tell you things would work out, Trickster. It's practically like I never left."

"You haven't seen the news, Sunshine," says Hel.

"No, she has, she called to congratulate us while I was locked up."

"You're behind, too, Loki," Hel responds. She picks up her uThink, walks over and flips it so the screen's facing me and Sunshine.

And there I am, along with the rest of my erstwhile tribe, the Viking Brotherhood. The banner reads, "Neo-Nazi Assassination Attempt Thwarted. Perpetrators Sought."

"Oh, right, of course! The *assassination.*" Sunshine exclaims brightly, saying "assassination" as if her team just scored the winning run.

"Attempt."

She chuckles. "Attempt. Right, of course. I suppose that wasn't the important part anyway."

"What was?"

"That the gang's all here, of course."

"Gang?" I ask.

"Team," she corrects herself.

"How about 'mythos?'" asks Hel.

"Well, Death...normally, you'd need both sides to make up a mythos," Sunshine replies.

"The other side's right down the way," I respond.

"Indeed," Sunshine says, "Which is why I'm here. I'm going to Valhalla."

"Why would you do that after all that stuff about not trusting Odin or your sisters? After all the hoops you've made me...made *us*...jump through?"

"But, first, before I answer that, why don't we open my bag and see what's inside?"

She motions to Surtur who kneels to unzip the suede duffel.

"Is that gold?" Bruder asks, squinting. "Did you rob the Bundesbank or something?"

Sunshine reaches down and pulls the thing eye-level. She looks like she's about to give an Oscar acceptance speech. Except…

"That's Adolf Hitler." Bruder says.

"Right," I reply.

"So that's how they did it?" Hel says.

"But not for long," Sunshine replies. "If the gods are going to get their powers back the way Odin wants…"

"The Wheel will have to be remade," I finish.

"Wait, Wheel, what?" Kurt asks.

"That statue," I say, turning to him and Bruder. "Was once The Wheel of Fate."

"What in the fuck is The Wheel of Fate?" asks Bruder.

"It was what the Norns used," I say, pointing to Sunshine, "To govern Fate."

Sunshine replies, "Govern isn't accurate. Destiny is in charge. We're merely its interpreters, handmaidens, if you will."

"Point is, the Norns left. They deserted the gods."

"Why?" asks Kurt.

"Oh, the gods deserved it, make no mistake," I answer.

Sunshine smiles.

"But without them around, Odin had no one to control him. He took possession of The Wheel."

"OK," Bruder adds, not at all convincingly.

"And, well, when Hitler showed up—" I add.

"Yes?" Bruder asks.

"Odin saw his chance."

"Chance to do what?" Kurt adds, well past confusion.

"To be worshipped again."

Bruder asks, "You mean, all that crazy 'Thul Society' stuff, that was real?"

"Don't be ludicrous."

Bruder squints at me.

"I mean, obviously, the Thul Society was real. And their evil was real. But all the supernatural stuff…"

Bruder replies, "And that's the reason we're here?"

"It's not the only reason," Sunshine says, batting her lashes.

"JFC…" says Hel and sits back down.

"Right, though. First and foremost, I'm here to talk strategy of course. How to convince my sisters. Not that your involvement with the Viking Brotherhood's going to make that any the easier, Loki. Obviously, we'll need Frau Bruder to plead your case to them directly."

"My case?"

"Right. My sisters think you were behind the assassination plot."

"It was Odin! He set me up."

"That's not the way they'll see it. Unless we can convince them…well, they're ready to go along with Odin's plan to remake The Wheel."

"And how do they do that?" Kurt asks.

"By turning it into a statue of you," says Sunshine, pointing at Greta Bruder.

TRAGICOMEDY FOR THE FALLEN, PART 6

THE TIME I spent living with Odin and the rest of them, back in the late-40s, back when your postmodern world was still oh-so-young…that was *Ozzie and Harriet* time, even before *Ozzie and Harriet* came along. And not just in America.

With big, clunky TV's and bigger, clunkier cars, human space flight still barely comprehensible and the simplest computers taking up entire city blocks, the 60s felt long off. In America, yes; but even more in Germany. Thinking back on it, the transition from the end of war to the height of the 60s still seems almost unfathomable.

For his part, Odin took those post-war years as a time to build himself a fortune, to create an earthly identity as a fierce capitalist and little-d democrat. And he succeeded. The money poured into post-war Germany, from America mostly. Odin sopped up what he could, used the accumulated capital to short stocks and option commodities, to make, as you guys like to say, a *fucking killing*.

And in spite of his PR, he cared little for distinctions like right and left. Before the world became re-polarized into tribes of free and un-free, Odin was happy to work with either bloc. East or west, it didn't matter. Anything he could do to make a few deutschmarks he did.

So, Odin acquired any number of companies both legitimate and shadowy and he built his estate, New Valhalla. He settled in to stay on Earth, reestablishing his family unit as best he could. Sure, there weren't any Valkyries left, but he had his memories—boy, did he have his memories—and they were, turns out, enough to work with.

EVENTUALLY, ODIN ran me down in a flophouse in Hamburg. I was trying my hand at being a degenerate artist, armchair leftist, and hobbyist drunk. And, I have to say, I wasn't half-bad at any of them. He broke into my garret around two in the afternoon one October day. I was sleeping, pretty soundly as I remember.

"Loki," he yelled, stepping over the door he'd just knocked in.

"Eh?" I wiped the sleep from my eyes, scanned for some mode of escape. Nothing. Odin looked different but it was obviously him. He was wearing a bejeweled, metal patch over his left eye, a monocle covering his right. "What happened to your eye? Last time I saw you, you had two."

"One of them didn't work. It was pointless, superficial to keep wearing it."

"So, you plucked it out and replaced it with a Fabergé eyepatch?"

"It's Cartier Especial Reserve, actually. I didn't pluck it out though." He raised the patch, and there it was. I guess he'd gotten a better look at me by then as well. And a pretty serious look I have to add. I've never been big on pajamas. "You're still black," he added.

"I'm what?"

"A darkie."

I reached for the sheet, looked down at myself. "Eek. You're right. Whatever will I do?"

"I was just saying. Don't you find it…difficult…to look like that here?"

"Here where?"

"Here Germany?"

"The Allies won, Odin. Germany's like the rest of the West now."

"Only part of it is." He scanned the room, from hot plate to bookcase, easel to desk, gaze latching onto my weathered copy of *Das Kapital*. "And you're in the wrong part, apparently," he said, "You're a Marxist."

"Surprised?"

"Unfortunately, no."

"Don't get too excited. I'm just trying it out."

"Be that as it may, I want you to come home with me, son."

"You discovered a way back to Asgard already?"

"Not that home. We're stuck here, on Midgard, for the time being. But I've got a place outside Munich, an estate. We're calling it New Valhalla."

"Novel."

"It's all we have now, son. We made some good memories at Valhalla, didn't we, back in the old days?"

"Maybe a few. I don't know."

"Sure. Remember when I used to get the Head to tell you stories?"

"Not really."

"Well, it happened. Or all the time I spent teaching you to rule?"

"That, I remember…but only until Thor came along."

"Oh, don't be silly. The smart king never gets himself boxed in. With you and Thor both around, the Nine Worlds always have a spare, in case whatever happens to me happens to one of you."

"But nothing's going to happen to you, not until the end."

"True but beside the point. We need to all be together now, Loki, now that we're stuck here, on this fucking Midgard."

"You forget you kept tossing me here for being "bad." I'm used to it. I sort of love it in fact."

"Good. Then maybe you can help the rest of us learn to love it."

"Why would I?"

"We've seen the error of our ways. All of us have."

"Really?"

"Sure. I'm not helping them anymore. Not one bit."

"By them, you mean the Nazis?"

He nodded solemnly.

"Pretty convenient, seeing as how they lost."

"Please, son," he said, getting down on his knees, clasping his hands. "A guy just wants his children around him at a time like this."

"And everyone else feels the same way?"

"Everyone."

"Even Thor?"

"Especially Thor. He's anxious to see you."

"I don't…"

Odin crawled forward. He was kneeling next to the bed now, looking up at me. There was a tear in his eye. And then it fell, rolling down his cheek into his beard.

I thought back on the giants and what they had done to him. I thought back to him bleeding and screaming, so many centuries before. And in spite of everything he'd done to me, in spite of how unfair it had all been, I agreed to go along. I just couldn't seem to take the old man crying. That's one thing I've never been able to do.

so, I fell for the "real emotion" bit, again. No, I'm not proud of it, nor am I of all the other times. But you try being an orphaned baby left on the steps of Valhalla. You try being raised as the chosen one only to have that status yanked when Thor comes Bam-Bam-Bam-ing along. You try it and see how you feel.

Bitter? Yes, of course, I feel that. I *am* that. But I also feel a deep longing, a need for the All-Father's, *my father's*, love and acceptance that I can't forget, no matter how much time passes, no matter what I do. And I wonder sometimes whether it's all beyond my control. I wonder whether emotions can constitute fate, or whether memory can? What about the things we do because of those memories and emotions? Can they be our fate?

The question, as Greek good old boy, Heraclitus, suggests, is whether character is destiny? While this may be true in a functional sense, in that character determines outcome; that's a rather shallow interpretation of destiny. Character seems definitionally within our control. Destiny on the other hand, Fate…is well beyond our control, both yours and mine.

At any rate, Odin and I left the decrepit little garret I'd later come to miss, got in his expensive car, a Benz, of course, and drove south, our goal the ranging forests and snowy hills of what had become New Valhalla.

Once we got there, it seemed briefly like things might be

different, like they might actually work out. And maybe there were even a few of them, the Asgardians I mean, who'd actually given up on the Nazis, who wanted to make a clean start. But Odin wasn't one of them. It was just that I couldn't see it at first.

15

TO LET FATE MAKE YOU A LIAR

I STILL haven't slept with her. And you might be asking yourself, because you can't ask me, "Why, Loki, why?" You might also be asking yourself, once you've thought about it a tick, "How many times did you do the do in all those centuries together on Asgard?" True enough, and I was close to it this afternoon. Then we both fell asleep.

What, you think that doesn't happen to us? I mean, it did, sometimes even back in the day. But now, earthbound, even sex can routinely seem like more trouble than it's worth. And I hear you also, you're full of questions, my dears, "You've been telling us you love it here. You've been telling us you never want to leave." And that's all true. What's also true is that heartbreak never leaves you, not even after eight hundred years.

Staring out at the back yard, from my bedroom's panoramic window, surveying the snowy hill that runs down to the lakeshore and the dock. The shadows seem to lengthen as I watch. But even if I couldn't see night coming, I'd be able to feel it. Ever since I got back to the villa, events haven't done what they normally do when you're released from jail. They haven't gotten better. My uPhone vibrates. It's Odin.

"I was just meaning to call you. Why am I all over the TV?"

"I was going to ask you the same thing."

"You didn't set me up, did you?"

"Possibly."

"What does that mean?"

"It means, 'Where is the Norn?'"

"I'm surprised you don't know the answer to that yourself."

"Well, I don't."

"Given the admitted possibility that you set me up, and the late hour at which you call, I'll have to say goodbye."

"It's five in the afternoon."

"I'm still on American time."

"No, wait. I didn't set you up, son. It was the Norns. They made me do it."

"And by the Norns you mean?"

"Fine. I mean two-thirds of the Norns. Why else would I keep asking about the one you're withholding from me?"

"OK, assume I believe you. Which is still doubtful. Why would they do that?"

"They say they need us to be our true selves. They say you have to be evil, no matter what it takes."

"What if I'm not? What if I never was."

"Then, we have to make you evil."

"How do you make someone evil?"

"OK, poor choice of words. We had to give you enough material to hang yourself with."

"That doesn't sound much better."

"It really doesn't—"

"And did I?"

"The jury's out. Once we have the third Norn. And the statue. The *real* statue. And Bruder. They'll be ready to decide. And we can all go home."

"But you don't have any of those things."

"Right. You do."

"Which is why this call is ending now."

I wonder then if I should just make a run for it, with Bruder, Sunshine, and the statue. The only part that might work is the statue. Bruder will never desert her country; Sunshine would never accept constantly being on the run as an adequate conclusion; and it wouldn't really be a conclusion at all, simply the delay of one.

I'm still turning it over when Sunshine walks into the room, fresh out of the shower, a towel wrapped around her head like a turban. Bright, cornflower blue, it sets off her eyes perfectly, turns the dazzling into the otherworldly. And it strikes me funny the impact you have on us, the powerful impact you have; that a towel manufactured from cheap materials, in some veal pen, can change things even for us. You really do have so much power, you just don't realize it.

"Odin called. He was fishing."

"Did he catch anything?"

"He denied setting me up. Or, more precisely, he blamed it on your sisters. He said they wanted me to be evil, that I had to be evil. That was the only way."

"And what did you say?"

"I hung up."

She smiles and gives me a quick golf clap. "I'm impressed."

"Thanks. Nice towels, by the way."

"They really do match this form's eyes, don't they?" she says. Raising her hands to her head, she gives the turban a little shake on both sides. It falls and she starts drying her hair vigorously. As she does, she looks at me and smiles. She knows she's shaking in all the right places; knows I'm watching those places shake.

"They do."

"Are you still being a good little Trickster? Going to kick me out of your bed this time, too. Now, that I look like one of your Valks."

"Oh, is that why you came back looking like this?"

"Maybe."

"You don't have the costume. Or the wings."

"I could just pop over to New Valhalla and pick up a costume, be back in a jiff."

"Don't do that."

"You could disguise me?"

"It wouldn't be the same. Honestly, you'll always be more beautiful than they could ever be. They have no personalities. With me and the Valks it's psychological, probably even psychiatric."

"I know." She finishes drying her hair, tosses the towel onto the back of a chair, then starts moving across the space between us.

I move forward, too. We meet in the middle of the room, chests touching.

"So," she says, "What's it gonna be, Trickster?"

"What's what gonna be?"

"Do you…"

"Do I…"

"Do you…want a reading or what?"

I catch my breath. "Sure, why not?"

"Good." She steps back, strips the towel from her middle, and flings it at me.

The towels lands on my head, so that it covers one side of my face. She stands there, letting me take her in for a few seconds.

She walks away, calling, "After I get dressed."

And I watch her go. Until she closes the door. She doesn't shut it though or lock it. I consider following her into the bathroom. Yes, I really do give it a thought. And something tells me it would work. But I don't do it, and I'm not sure why.

SUNSHINE RETURNS wearing those tastefully tight, ridiculously sexy jeans of hers, the ones she showed up in at the SA meeting, and a Minnesota Vikings sweatshirt.

"I had no idea you were a football fan."

"A what?"

"The guys with helmets?"

"I'm still not following you."

"With, y'know, the horns on the sides of their helmets."

"Warriors?"

"No, like your shirt. The Minnesota Vikings are an American football team."

"Oh, gosh, I thought I was just celebrating our culture with this."

"Really?"

"I was sort of surprised there were so many Vikings in Minnesota, whatever that is."

"OK."

"Plus, I guess I just liked the color."

"The jewel tones really do complement your form's complexion, especially now that you've dyed your hair."

"Aw, thanks, Trickster, that's really sweet of you."

"So…"

"Oh, right, the reading? Hop up on the bed."

"OK."

We sit cross-legged on the bed, staring at each other. Sunshine holds her hands out, palms-upward.

"Give me your paws," she says.

"Fore- or back-?"

"Just the two in front, thanks."

I do. And it feels delicious, exciting. All these recent stolen kisses and aborted couplings, all the eight centuries without seeing her still have me spinning. I look into her eyes, and I almost want to dissolve into her gaze, to become one with it, the simple hope that I can become closer to her.

"You've found the three women. I'm not seeing them anymore."

"I think I'm holding hands with one of them now."

She opens one eye. "You're saying you think the others are Bruder and Hel, not my sisters?"

"I'm...I didn't...I don't know. It's your vision."

"True. OK, so I see a great, deep forest. I see snow. And a park and..."

"Wait, what?"

"That's it, it's over." She lets my hands fall.

I open my eyes. She's smiling.

"Gosh," I say, "that was a little like séance interruptus."

"So, I got you all hot and bothered metaphysically?"

"I think so."

"What about physically?" she asks, putting a hand on my knee. "Do you finally trust me again?"

"Well," I say, leaning in myself. "I think I might be able to trust you again, now that so much has worked out. We've got you, Bruder, and the statue..."

"And Kurt, don't forget Kurt."

"You're not going to invite him in now, are you?"

"Do you want me to?"

"Umm."

She raises an eyebrow. "Is that a 'no' or a 'yes?'"

"It's definitely a 'no.' I just don't see Kurt in that way."

"Pity," she says, laughing. She swoops in for the softest imaginable kiss. I feel like it's happening and not happening all at once. I kiss her back as my hands fall to her waist. She's not wearing a shirt beneath her hoodie. Kissing still, and as my hands move up, I realize she's not wearing a bra either.

"Well, isn't this a pleasant surprise," I say, palming one of her nipples then beginning slowly to slide skin against skin.

The rough, the smooth, the rough, the smooth. Back and forth, faster and farther. A few more seconds and I begin to push at the shoulders of the hoodie. She raises her arms, wriggles free as I pull it off her. She lies back and I'm on top of her. Hands, fingertips, lips. She's writhing as I ease down between her legs, say a little wordless hello. Then I'm parting her lips, revealing the sweetest, the pinkest and tenderest, of flesh, and my tongue moves round and round, until it's inside her. Which is when the real fun begins.

THE NEWS evolves that night, before us, on TV. Bruder has been in touch with her people so there's not a bust-down-the-doors, federal-police-in-riot-gear search going on. I wouldn't say we relax, but we do pretend for a few hours at least.

Sunshine and I pretend to be in love again, physically at least. Hel and Bruder pretend they're not into each other. The giants and Fen pretend to keep an eye on Kurt. He tried to escape! Twice! The only one, I assume, that's not pretending to be something is Kurt himself. I haven't asked him, but I'd guess he's feeling real fear and confusion. Odin's not pretending either. He's calling every twenty minutes, texting every five. I've had to change sim chips twelve times.

"You promised me an answer," he says.

I play his messages for Sunshine, and we laugh at them but we both know this remote mockery of Odin can't continue indefinitely. I avoid the actual discussion as long as possible.

"I'm going. It's the only way," she says.

"You're not taking her with you?"

"Her meaning Bruder?"

"Right."

"Yes, I am. She has to help me explain what happened with you and the Viking Brotherhood."

"Take me instead. I'll explain."

"That won't work. They're convinced now."

"Of my guilt?"

"And your evil. But I'm going to leave the statue with you. That way, it can't be remade, no matter what happens."

"What about Ragnarök?"

"That's always the question, isn't it, Loki?"

"I guess."

"Well, that's not even for us to say. Fate will make a decision when the time is right."

"So…wait…you guys have been lying to us all along?"

"Not lying exactly. We just don't know precisely when Fate will choose, though we do know what's generally going to happen."

"Which is?"

"It's what you've been told, the myths."

"So that is Fate, that's been it all along."

"Yes and no. It's what you've been told, just not in the way you think."

I WAKE in bed, hours later. Without looking at the clock, I can tell dawn is approaching. I turn to Sunshine, realize she's awake too, awake and avidly staring at me.

"Why did you come here?" I ask.

"Don't you know?"

"Well, I could say, Fate. But I know that's not really why."

"That doesn't make sense and yet it does."

"So?"

"Well, I needed Bruder of course."

"I knew it. Used again."

"And I needed to see you. That was Fate, too."

"You mean, we're fated to be together. Is that what you're telling me? That this was ordained at the dawn of time?"

"OK, get a hold of yourself, Trickster."

"I think I'd rather get a hold of you," I say, reaching for her.

She rolls her eyes but smiles and reaches for my hand. Guiding the two us to a recline, she presses her mouth to mine. Electricity, just like before, but this time there are no clothes and it feels like magic, real magic, I mean, no poof involved.

We settle into a rhythm, writhing against each other, on and on until I catch the light of a sunrise at the edge of the drapes. Sunshine sees it, too, and we finish for the last time. Yeah, it was only three hours, but that was some of the best sex I've had as a man. I won't bore you with the rest of my escapades. Oh, heck, maybe I should. But I won't. Not now at least.

"You're leaving in the morning, aren't you?" I ask.

"It's already morning."

"The later morning?"

"Something like that."

"So, this is the last time?"

"For what?"

"To see each other."

"No way."

"I was thinking about the last time you left."

"On Asgard?"

"You said you were telling me the truth then."

"And I'm telling you the truth now."

"But you didn't really, did you?"

"How do you mean?"

"You said you'd be back, eventually. But you didn't tell me any of the stuff in the middle."

"Stuff in the middle?"

"The ever-declining worship. The way Odin would have to watch all these phony religions flourish and what that would do to him. What it would lead him to do."

"I didn't know. I don't know everything. Or anything really. There's what I want, and there's what Fate decrees. They're not always the same. In fact, they almost never are."

"So about coming back to me?"

"You mean now."

"I mean in the future."

"I want to."

"But you're not promising again. You're not going to let Fate make you a liar?"

"I am promising again. I spent eight hundred years wanting to come back to you. But it wasn't the right time."

"What if it had never been the right time?"

"Then, you're right, Fate would have made me a liar."

TRAGICOMEDY FOR THE FALLEN, PART 7

THE DAY Odin got that last big idea he was feeling especially nostalgic for the Norns. They'd been gone centuries by that point. Still, once a year, he'd make the pilgrimage to Mount Norn, dragging his sons along. Imagine going on a fishing trip with your old man and your brothers, but you hate to fish, all your brothers hate you, and even the old man isn't really your biggest fan...

So, there we were in the cave I'd once learned the truth in, the cave that still seemed to hold images of Sunshine and her sisters, the way they'd been then, once upon a time. Three gray-robed sisters, faces hidden by shadow, speaking their proverbs.

As usual, Thor was walking around slack-jawed, kicking at the floor, and looking bored. You know how it is when you take your seven-year-old to look at cars, right? Well, that was Thor, once a year. More than once—quite often actually—but you get the idea. Not that Heimdall and Tyr were much better. Hell, even Baldur was annoying me. He wouldn't stop mincing about the drafts in the caves, about what the cold was doing to his hair.

So, the others are off doing whatever whenever and I wind up alone with Odin in the Cavern of Fate. There's that big golden Wheel of Fate right next to us. He's just staring at it, and he starts sobbing.

"They'll be back eventually," I offered, trying to comfort him.

"But I want them back now."

"Of course. But can you blame them for leaving, I mean, really, can you?"

"Yes?"

"No, you can't. Our time dominating Midgard is over. Time to satisfy yourself with the other eight worlds. Maybe take up a hobby or two."

"A hobby?"

"Philately?"

"That sounds dirty."

"It's stamp collecting. You just–"

He passed a hand through the air, little arcs of magenta flames shooting this way and that. That was how Odin cleared his throat back when he could really do magic. I mean, he cleared his throat, too. But he also did this. "No, Loki. Something must be done."

"What's to do?" I asked, dodging an errant arc. "They're not coming back until the end. That's what they said."

"I'm not talking about them, not exactly."

"What then?"

"I'm talking about The Wheel. I'm talking about taking it back to Valhalla for starters."

"Are you serious? Look how big it is. Who knows how much it even weighs?"

"Thor!" he bellowed.

And there was Thor, flexing, tossing his flowing hair to and fro, ever ready to kick ass. "This one do something again?"

he asked, putting fist to palm, and grinding, the way he's done at me, and to me, more than once.

"No, it's The Wheel. I want you to carry it back to Valhalla."

"The Wheel of Fate? You're actually going to let me touch it?"

"Obviously."

He reached for the thing, started petting it like it was a dog or something.

I shook my head, turned to Odin.

"I didn't tell you to fuck it, son. Just carry it back to Valhalla, eh?"

"No problem," he said, stepping to the thing and lifting it with one hand. Actually, if memory serves, it was a pinky.

BACK AT Valhalla, Odin left the thing there in the middle of the throne room for weeks, months. Who knows how many times I heard someone ask, "What's that?"

I mean, it was a conversation starter, obviously. But it just sat there gathering dust and starting conversations, until One-Eye called us all together in The Hall of Counsel.

"I've come to a decision," he said, "I'm going to use The Wheel of Fate."

I asked, "To do what?"

"To help the Führer."

"Odin, I don't know why you keep at this. He's obviously not going anywhere. And if he does get anywhere it's going to be a terrible place."

"Nonsense. We can remake The Wheel, use it to help the Führer realize his vision."

"Remake The Wheel into what?"

"Remake it into a statue of the Führer."

"But you can't. Nobody can do anything with it other than the Norns."

That was when he pulled out his trump. "Not true. An appropriate sacrifice will allow me to manipulate its magic."

"That would have to be a pretty big sacrifice. You don't mean me, do you?"

"I couldn't."

"That's good to hear."

"I mean, I literally can't. You've got to survive until the Norns gets back, period."

"Touching. So what?"

"I've been considering sacrificing my magic boar."

"You love Gullinbursti. As much as you love anything."

He locked eyes with me. "Something has to be done. And you're saying you refuse to help us, aren't you?"

"Well, yes. But what I'm also saying is, 'What happens to Fate if you remake The Wheel?'"

"Nothing, I guess. I don't really know."

"Or care!" Thor added.

Odin continued, "The Norns will figure it out when they come back. If they come back."

"You're doubting that."

"It's been eight hundred years."

"But we're immortal."

"It's a long time for humanity. And that's all I'm worried about right now."

"But…"

"The All-Father has spoken," he said, banging the shaft of his spear on the floor of the throne room. *Kranng.*

"But…"

"The All-Father has spoken," said Thor.

"The All-Father has spoken," said Tyr.

"The All-Father has spoken," said Heimdall.

And all the rest of them chimed in like good little Aesir and Vanir. The Valkyries, too. Even the ravens were cawing. Sleipnir neighing. Even Gullinbursti was…snorting…little did he suspect.

I left, headed for the citadel I kept on Asgard in those days, the original Chateau Loki, if you will. I needed to think. Unfortunately, I wouldn't have long to do it. Odin and the rest of them were at work on The Wheel by nightfall.

16

GODDESS OF THE NIGHT

MY SLEEP's fitful, the transit between wakefulness and dreams blurred, gauzy. Asleep, I dream of being awake, of not letting Sunshine go to Valhalla. Awake, I consider a litany of second-guesses about agreeing she could. It's almost like sleep and dreams have become the same, or two sides of the same coin at least. As though my existence has become a sort of dreamy demi-Hell governed by Ambien, postmodern goddess of the night.

Every time I wake, sure this is my last and only chance to save Sunshine, I see her in bed beside me, a fact reassuring enough that by my final take-off for dreamland I've convinced myself everything is going to be okay, that when we wake for good in the morning I'll tell Sunshine to stay put, play it safe.

Hours later, when I finally do wake, I see Sunshine isn't there, but I can smell food cooking, breakfast to be precise. I can practically see the giants bumbling around the kitchen like a couple of lovesick kids, making a "big breakfast" to impress her. Oh, sure, they're hell in the kitchen, no lie. But the thought leaves me happy enough that I fall back asleep, wake up moments later, the air still thick with the smell of charred meats, just like Valhalla in the old days.

I rise, give Fen a "click-click" so he follows. He comes, eyes bright, tail wagging. We wander towards the kitchen as the smell of the giants' cooking grows: the buttery sizzle of frying eggs and the smoky bite of French roast, the rosemary-sage sausage and garlic pepper potatoes. I make out the sounds of clanking pots, good-natured bickering, and intermittent crooning from a pair of baritones whose best work is done in silence.

"Where is everyone?" I ask as I enter.

"Don't you remember?" Thrym replies.

Surtur adds, "You told Sunshine and Bruder to go to Valhalla."

"The way I remember it, I told them we'd decide in the morning."

"Well, I guess that's not how they heard it."

"And no one thought to wake me?"

"They were adamant."

"What about Hel?"

"No, she didn't say anything either."

"I mean, 'Where is she?'"

Surt replies, "She said she had to go somewhere."

Thyrm cuts in, "Juice, Loki?"

"She went after Sunshine and Bruder, didn't she?"

"It's possible. She just said she had to go somewhere."

Surtur adds, "She'll be back. She said."

So much for thinking Hel has herself together. Then it hits me. I go back into the bedroom and look under the bed. The statue is gone.

SUNSHINE HAS a new greeting on her phone, "If you're looking for Sunshine, she's not here. If you're looking for Halflight or Darkness they're not here either. But wherever we three are, even though it's not here, we're all together."

I call Hel. She picks up. "Where are you?" I ask. "Did you take the statue?"

"Yes, we did."

"We?"

"Greta, the Norn, and I. We're at Valhalla."

"It's Greta now?"

"I couldn't let her just walk into this alone."

"What this? They were supposed to be going there to talk, leaving the statue behind to be safe."

"Well, that was really the Norn's idea. She said she made a promise."

"She's not answering her phone."

"She won't."

"Why not?"

"She threw it in the lake before we left for Valhalla. She said you'd understand."

"You can tell her I don't."

I hang up. I guess I shout or scream or possibly even howl like an Alfheimian banshee because the guys run in, followed by Fen.

"Loki?" they ask.

"We're going to New Valhalla."

"What about breakfast?"

"Haven't you already eaten?"

"Sure, but we could always…"

"Now."

I fill the guys in on the way, not that I should have to, but I do. I tell them what I think is going on, which to be honest, doesn't make much sense. I mean, I really have no idea. Has Sunshine turned? Has Bruder lost her mind? Has Hel gone suicidal? Or maybe Sunshine doesn't have the statue at all. Maybe she left it behind and Hel took it, went somewhere to hide it. Or…

Ah, the women in my life…what can I say? Five miles from New Valhalla, I pull off the road, park the 6.

"You guys go back to the villa until I call."

Fen looks at me like he wants to come.

"You too, buddy."

"What about Kurt? What if he gets away?"

"A. Don't let him. And B. Don't let him. And, C. It's not like he could screw things up worse than they already are, is it?"

They shrug.

Fen turns to look at them and squints.

"So, we definitely shouldn't…"

"Ki-…"

"Right, you definitely shouldn't *kill* him. Now, go."

I FOLLOW an old snowmobile trail into the forest. Yes, it may be old, but not unused. There's been coming and going, who can say by what or why; but based on GPS I'll follow this until I hit a stream then bang a left and follow the stream to its terminus, somewhere on the grounds of New Valhalla.

I get to the stream and turn left as the last sallow rays of day filter down through the net of spruce and pine, beech and oak. Maybe I'm distracted—maybe it's the noise from the stream—but I hear voices closer than comfortable, one clear, near; the other distant, staticky.

I see one of Odin's idiot guards heading towards me, and I know I have to hide. I look to the stream. It looks chilly and, well, wet. I look up at the trees, and the pale, electric blue of the sky—cloudless, birdless. That settles it. I disguise myself as a deer, make to saunter off in the other direction, but the guard sees me.

"Hey, du, reh?" he asks.

I pretend I can't hear him, pensively nibble a tuft of grass, shake my ears as though oblivious, then keep walking. That's when he pulls out his Luger. I hear him release the safety, and I know he's just gonna shoot me for some godawful reason, some primal deer hatred or what the fuck ever. I don't have time to wait around. I don't have time to turn back into myself and reason with him. How would that go anyway? Yeah, I'm Loki, now I want you to forget you ever saw me sneaking onto Valhalla. I'm not Count Dracula, for whoever's sake.

No, the only thing I have time to do is flip a one-eighty and sprint back towards him, weaving in case he takes a shot. And he does. He tries, that is. But I'm picking up speed by then, and I leap towards him. I take the guard in the chest with my forehooves. He falls to the ground, *klonks* his head on a rock. I can only imagine the sort of story he'll have when he wakes up.

"I was assaulted by a deer. He's loose on the grounds. Red alert, red alert."

I turn into the guard I just assaulted, steal his clothes, and move towards the main house. No, I don't *need* to steal his clothes. Of course not. I could replicate them. But stealing his duds has the added bonus of complicating his story further, of leaving him waking up an hour or two from now, in the middle of the woods with no clothes on and some whack-ass story about a deer attack. Also, it takes less energy, at least for me.

ONCE I'M inside New Valhalla, I meander around as the idiot

guardsmen until I find the staircase I'm looking for, guarded by one of the fake Valks. I dissolve into the shadows and slip past.

I find Darkness and Halflight in a vast natural cavern, in the lowest of the subbasements. You could probably call this Odin's dungeon if you wanted. No doubt, some have. Not these Norns, though. They seem happy, animated. They're talking, whispering actually. But the acoustics are so good I can hear everything.

"So, how long do you think?" asks Darkness.

Halflight replies, "Couple...I don't know...two, three..."

There's a little golden statue of Hitler between them. *The little golden statue of Hitler, the one Sunshine or Hel or whoever took?*

Darkness responds, "Days, tops?"

"As long as Loki doesn't find out."

"You think she has that handled?"

"She better, because we certainly don't."

"Speak for yourself."

"Oh, you think you can pull off an apocalypse single-handed?"

"Of course not. The gods are our only hope."

I cough. *Time to move things along*

"Eh, what's this? Come out, show yourself," says Halflight.

Do I run? Do I turn back into myself? Do I turn back into myself and run?

Darkness follows up with this: "You know you're not supposed to be down here? Either it's come out and show yourself..."

I step into the light.

"Is that?"

"A guard?"

"Yes, my ladies," I respond, eyes drawn to the statue.

I realize this is my chance, maybe my only chance to explain. Or maybe to just grab the statue and run. Those are my choices. So, I decide to turn back into myself. I decide to go with explication rather than thievery. Poof.

"Trickster!" Halflight shouts.

"Yes."

"Returning to the scene of the crime?"

"No crime. I'm here to explain."

"Explain what, that you did exactly what we told you not to?"

"That was Odin."

"No, it was you. We saw it on the-what-do-you-call-them… the picture box thing."

"TV?"

"The Internet?"

"Odin wanted me to do it, to stop the assassination he'd already put in play. He set me up."

"That's extremely far-fetched."

"It's true?"

"Should we believe him, Darkness?"

"Absolutely not," says Sunshine, stepping from the shadows. "You remember what he was like, so long ago. Turning us against each other. Making us his playthings."

"Sunshine, what…"

"Save it, Trickster, I knew you'd try to sneak in here, lie, steal, whatever, pit us against each other. When you've always been the source, the veritable…font…of evil."

"Font…"

"Of evil, yeah!"

"What about last night?"

266

"It was fun, but now it's done."

"So, this was payback…for, what, something I did ten, fifteen, twenty centuries ago? I knew it."

"Knew what?"

"This was all about jealousy. That's why you left, and that's why you came back."

"You are as thick-headed as Odin. You think the entire pantheon moves on your whims. You think we're not independent agents, that we can't come and go of our own accord."

"Fine…But you came to me. You put all this in motion."

"Did I?"

"Did you what?"

"Did I come to you?"

"Of course…"

"So, you hadn't been secretly planning to have your… minions…assassinate Bruder? So that you and Vekk could usher in a new era of darkness?"

"Wait, what?"

A door slams behind me. I turn to see Odin, flanked by Thor, Heimdall, Tyr, and Forseti. Fucking Forseti.

"What is this?"

"Your incarceration, one you'll not be getting out of until we're all back on Asgard. And then, only…*maybe.*"

"Prison? For what?"

"For doing what the Norns warned us not to do. Take him away, boys."

A COUPLE hours later, I hear Odin's drunken Santa Claus laughter booming down the hall, followed by his ever-commanding

267

voice, and the various "yessirs" that come in response. Sunshine is with him.

"Let me guess, you've come to gloat?"

"Nope," she says.

"To cheer me up?"

"Nope," he echoes her.

"To explain?"

"Exactly," says Sunshine.

"Well…"

Odin replies, "There's going to be a trial. Tomorrow."

"A trial for what?"

"You, of course. This is the comeuppance for your ultimate evil, son."

"My what?"

"While the Norns were gone you were a busy little guy, weren't you? You stole The Wheel of Fate and melted it down to help that horrible Hitler fella."

"I what?"

"No sense lying, son. You helped him and when he killed himself, we lost all but the barest shred of our power. And fell to Earth. If the Fate-blessed Norns hadn't come back, we'd be consigned to spend the rest of eternity…here…on this shithole of a planet."

"I didn't help Hitler, Odin. You did."

He laughs. "But you're on film for everyone to see helping these neo-Nazis try to kill Frau Bruder, trying to corrupt their politics?"

I turn to Sunshine. "I know you don't believe this."

She smiles and says, "Maybe, maybe not."

Odin nods. "Get some sleep, son. You'll need your energy."

KNOWING YOU'RE REAL

AFTER THE Norns left, I was really missing Sunshine. Hell, I was even missing her sisters. Yeah, I know they were…daunting—still are—but you live with someone for that long and you're bound to miss them when they go.

I guess, in a sense, the whole mythos is like a family, y'know? There's a special solidarity that goes with knowing you're real even though hardly anyone else believes it, and the ones who do are considered and/or may really be insane. I mean, it's a little like being a writer.

They have to keep telling themselves they're good, that they'll make it. In spite of what usually amounts to great evidence to the contrary. Yeah, sure, I write. But it's a hobby for me. As a vocation, I wouldn't wish it on anyone, not even Odin or Thor, not that Thor would be capable of more than a few sentences in a row…

Obviously, Sunshine's company was the real loss. And no number of Valks, elf-maidens, giantesses, or human women could salve the pain. I was without companionship. I was looking for a friend. Which was when Baldur and I started playing chess.

"Hey, Loki," he said, winking.

"Yes, Baldur?"

"I got a new…Ragnarök chess set. Wanna *play*?" he said, winking again.

"We are talking about a chess set as in a board, chess pieces, that sort of thing?"

"What else would we be talking about?"

Sure, I knew he was gay. And, yes, I'd dabbled, away from the eyes of most of the rest of the mythos. But y'know, I'd always liked Baldur and been, let's say, a bit of a libertine. I mean, I basically let it fly, did whatever with whomever. I was the force of evil. It wasn't like Odin expected much. But Baldur. Beautiful Baldur with his flowing hair and golden voice. Yeah, Baldur had to sneak around. He had to skulk. I gave him a few pointers on that.

"Sure, let's do it."

So, we played, and we played. And he gave me his ear, listened to my troubles. Sure, Baldur had always been on the sympathetic side, in spite of the fact that everyone was sure I was going to kill him one day to usher in Ragnarök. He didn't hold it against me. I guess you'd have to say that maybe, possibly, deep down, Baldur is…good.

One thing leads to another and pretty soon we're spending way too much time together—playing golf, double-dating Valkyries, sneaking off to the forest, doing who knows what? It was nice to have a brother even though, obviously, he was more of a Brazzers type stepbrother than a real one. Anyway, Thor found out. He followed us out into the forest one day. I was surprised he actually had it in him to track us down. And, man, did he get an eye full. Rage overwhelmed him and he hit the glade swinging Mjolnir left and right, taking down scads of trees with every swing. It was all I could do to get out of that glade alive. Baldur wasn't so lucky.

Odin and Frigga were distraught obviously. Then, of course,

when they found out what Baldur and I had been getting up to, not that they were unaware deep down, they went well beyond distraught. They summoned Hel, Goddess of the Underworld, Divine Lady of Death, desperate to get their baby boy back.

"A violation of Fate," Odin said.

"A crime against nature," Frigga added.

"Can't trust the queers," Thor said. "I always knew Loki would do that. I mean, who didn't?"

"Thor, leave," Odin said. He knew what had really happened. Thor protested, of course, but then he left, kicking the floor as he went. Who knows, probably off to commit another hate crime.

Now, you'd think Hel would have been the right...entity... to call at a time like this; that her time as goddess of death would have given her more of a taste for law. I mean, one second, you're alive, the next you're not. That's death. And that was Hel, back then.

Problem was, back in the day, she was a stickler for all manner of legalese: her view of the law as black and white as the two sides of her face. The death of Baldur? That was all Thor. Not bringing him back, though. Hello...that was all Hel, every last bit of it. You should have heard the way they pleaded with her.

To which, Hel said, "OK, if Dead Baldur's as great as you say, All-Father, get every creature in the Nine Worlds to cry over his death. If you do that, I'll let you take him back to Valhalla."

Seeing an opening, Odin and Frigga made everything in the universe cry—squirrels and vultures, fish and deer, monkeys and foxes...all of them were going boo-hoo-hoo. But try as they might, there was this one giantess who wouldn't budge; one petite twelve-footer they couldn't get to shed a tear, hard as they tried and threatened and bribed. She disappeared, too, that very day. Honestly, funny thing is I just…I can't even remember her name. It's so weird. But rules are rules, and Hel said no.

She said, more precisely, "Dead Baldur, take a fucking seat, you'll be here a while."

She said, "Dead Baldur, you might as well get used to the unrelenting cold of my fearsome presence."

She said, "Just kidding, Dead Baldur, Ragnarök's right around the bend. Once the fire giants hit Bifrost, thing's will be warm before you know it!"

Fine, I made the last one up, but we all thought it was true back when. Odin, Thor, Baldur…all of us thought that once Baldur was dead, that would be it. Honestly, it seemed sort of funny how serious Hel was taking the eternity of death thing what with the Big R. just down the way. But that was Hel.

Judgmental? Hell, yes, she was. Unforgiving. Malevolent. And she was glorious, the apple of my formerly evil little eye. Now, not so. The judgmental, evil part, I mean. Hel is still my kid, and I love her to pieces. But a true last stop, do-not-pass-go-do-not-get-two-hundred-dollars justiciar of the un-living, the girl is not…

17

YOU AND ME

SIX IN the morning when the buzzer goes off and my cell door slides open. Thor, Heimdall, and Tyr—or, as I like to call them, The Assholes Three—enter. They surround me, then grab a hold of me. Yes, all three of them at the same time. An arm to Heimdall and Tyr each; Thor with a fistful of the back of my hair (and scalp): Honestly, it's like an out of body—or outer body as that one dude on Facebook called it—experience. I feel like a Thanksgiving turkey at the kids' table. I feel like I'm back in Valhalla, it's dinner time, and I'm the main course.

They sing as we walk, or march or whatever, the Assholes Three, as they're want to do…and it's Tolkienian, this happy bluster of theirs, like it's 1914 and they're foot soldiers marching off to the latest War to End All Wars, except they're not really soldiers. They're more like generals or officers, MP's at least, marching someone else off to war. We wind our way through the, what…? The bowels of Odin's domain? His internal caverns, his subdermal catacombs? His dungeon? Right, that's it, his dungeon.

I think of playing D&D with Hel and the guys back when it was big, you know, in the pen and paper days. Now, you might as well just play videogames, right? Not that we don't have a little game every so often. I've got this high-level fighter I play called Thud. Let's just say he's big and blond and strong, based on someone I know but can't quite place…

The more I look around down here, the more it reminds me of Valhalla in the old days, the dungeons there and this whole trial and punishment thing. It's a place I've been before, many, many times. There was a time, actually several, when punishing me was the main source of entertainment at Valhalla.

Blamed for everything, no matter who did it. No one else could do any wrong except Loki. God of Evil, Mischief, and Strife. God of Murder, Betrayal, and The Night. God of Fire and Assassination. God of Giants and Betrayal. Did I mention Betrayal? Given how many times Odin and the rest of my family have betrayed me, that's a laugh, isn't it?

Yes, of course, I did some bad things, but the reaction was completely out of bounds. I could count on the Norns, though, back then at least. They never let any romantic entanglements color the work. Now, I can't help but feel that's exactly what's happened. It's like maybe I was a bad boyfriend years ago, and I'm paying the price now. The end of the line, on The Assholes Three Express, comes at the doors to Odin's den, or study, or whatever it is. Heimdall and Tyr turn to me. Thor gives the back of my head a powerful shake.

"Wake up, princess," he says. "Time to pay."

"For?"

"Being you!"

And the doors open.

THE ENTIRE study has been reconfigured. There's a throne, just like the one from Valhalla. Odin's sitting on it, of course. He's flanked by the wolves on his left and the boar on his right, a raven settled on either shoulder of his golden throne. They're robots, though, Odin's animals, just like the Valks—the odd joint visible, the eyes without the spark of life. I wonder whether there's a fake Sleipnir somewhere?

Odin's wearing his armor and helm. The helm has some sort of jeweled eyepiece for his bad one. Did he steal that from Anthony Hopkins in the movies? Oh, who knows, right? He's holding a replica of Gungnir. I mean, I assume it's a replica. I assume they all are, every last thing he's wearing. It's not like any of this could be the genuine article, right? Or is it? If Sunshine could carry the statue, could she carry other things? I can't say I know precisely what her powers are at this point. I just know she's got more than the rest of us. Her sisters must, too.

She sits off to the side with her sisters does my Sunshine. Their chairs are smaller than Odin's great throne, but definitely grander than the ones the audience, for want of a better word, are using. If the deal hadn't been obvious before this, it is now. Whether through benign implicity or willful complicity, Odin's scheme has worked. He's got the Norns on his side, ready to serve as jury to his judge. I look around for my executioner... because, who wouldn't at a time like this?

There are two tables for the two opposing "legal" camps. I see Forseti there, behind the one on the right. He turns to me with an expression I can't read, face so placid he looks like he's taken an anti-expression pill. I decide to give him a big wink to throw him off. Odin notices and scowls. So does Forseti. His cheeks begin to blush. He looks down, away. Thor grunts in response, gives the hank of hair and attendant scalp, a hearty shake.

On the left, it's...it's Hel. At least I don't have to worry about where she's gone anymore. Does this mean she's in on it; that I've been betrayed not only by my father but by the Norns and even my own children? I can't bring myself to accept this last part. To be cast aside by my actual blood. Man, that would hurt.

The Assholes Three shove me through the doorway, Thor giving me a final size-eighteen boot to the ass. I fall, slip, and slide across the shiny marble floor, getting a snoot-full of chlorine bleach and fresh floor wax as I do. I'm tragicomic, I guess, or maybe just comic. Because everyone's laughing at me by that point.

Everyone's laughing at the dopey trickster doing his sad, silly, stupid trickster tricks. It's funny, don't you think, how Odin managed to get everyone to hate me and deride me, belittle me, but how he somehow also got them to buy me as a source of fell power, the force of infinite evil? The truth is: That happens a lot more in reality than you'd like to admit. It's not the strong that are held up to ridicule. It's the weak. The ones that can't defend themselves. The loners, the outcasts.

A couple Robo-valks wind up kneeling to collect me. I can almost hear their hydraulic legs wheezing as they bend down. They haul me to my feet. The laughter dies as I'm given over to what passes for the justice system, here at Valhalla. The Robo-valks walk me the rest of the way to my table. Hel is there waiting for me.

"So, you're defending me?" I ask.

The Valks point at my seat, the implication they'll shove me down if I don't go. So, what do I do? Cause a disturbance? Make a break? No, I fucking sit.

"Seems so," she replies.

"You're sure?"

"Yes, of course. What do you think?"

"Well, you just sort of disappeared, didn't you, yesterday morning? Along with Sunshine…and Bruder…and the statue…"

"I had my reasons."

"Care to share?"

"Not yet. Suffice it to say this has to do with me, too, at this point."

"I'm touched."

"You know what I mean. If Odin takes you down now, it's a loss for all of us. Never mind the dishonesty of the whole thing. Honestly, I never understood why you were so keen on tricks. I mean, little practical jokes, ok...but stuff like this, the grand, Machiavellian mind fucks. They were always better at it than you were."

"You really think so?"

"Of course, why do you think you always wind up losing?"

"Because they have more power?"

"Well, yes, I guess that could be it, too. Point being: What part of it ever feels good for anyone. Even Odin," she says, motioning towards Himself.

"He's always been completely transactional. If anything explains...*everything*...it's that."

"Exactly!"

"Exactly what?"

"Odin's transactional style of leadership. We'll get to it. All in good time."

"Boy, you're really putting this together, huh?"

"Well, I don't want to scare you, but this may be it."

"It, what?"

"It, Ragnarök. It was always a metaphor, right? Even if we don't get our power back, even if we don't re-ascend, this could be the actual end."

"No, it can't."

"Why not?"

"The giants aren't here. Fen isn't."

"I called them. They'll be here."

"Wait, why?"

"IDK, just sorta seemed like the thing to do."

"Well, there's still Jormungandr."

"True, we haven't seen him in a while, have we?"

"Are you trying to make me feel better?"

"Not especially."

"Thanks."

"Well, look at our lives and tell me a little fatalism hasn't been earned at this point."

Hel has me thinking. She has me thinking maybe this is the end. I mean the real end, the end end, the end of the end, the last and final end and I'm thinking…I'm thinking I'd be grateful for death in a way, if that's what's coming.

I've been alive so long. Yes, I can still imagine a million things to do with my time and myself. But I can also comprehend that I was never really immortal, not even when I was a god. This was never going to be endless. And it would be nice to finally be free of Odin's schemes, eternally free of being "the force of evil." It would be nice to finally sleep or simply not be. And maybe I even do get a little sleep, right then and there. Maybe I nod off for a few seconds, go into a trance because I'm shaken awake by a horn blast from out of the metaphorical blue.

"Ow-oooo-ga…"

Heimdall, of course. He's treating this like it's Ragnarök, but then he treats everything like Ragnarök. Dude lives for it, just like all of them. But what about me? Did I, once? Y'know, live for the end? Sure, I did. For a long time.

But I was tired of being a god long before they joined me here on Earth. Tired of the feeling that we were no better than you guys, that we were Fate's playthings, like you were ours. And the realization that Fate was someone or something's plaything, too; that everyone is someone's toy. And the game is death. The end.

"HEAR YE, hear ye..." says Heimdall, putting down the horn, "All rise for the case of Fate versus Loki Niflheim, the most heroically good and honorable, great, noble, and just Odin Allfather presiding. For the defense, Hel, Mother of Pain and Goddess of Death, Disease, and Pestilence. For the prosecution, Forseti the Just."

I cough.

Odin bangs Gungnir on the floor several times. "Silence," he demands. "The Prosecutor will call his first witness."

Forseti beams up at Daddy. "The Prosecution calls...this video from a few days ago."

Over the next fifteen minutes Forseti narrates a comprehensive video record of my recent crimes. There's footage of me at Anarchy, though it's not me. It's Wrath X. There's footage of Wrath X. at the Christmas Market, footage of him behind the wheel of the truck, then trying to run, then being carted away. But the most damning footage is the stuff of me just hours earlier in the villa changing back and forth from Wrath to myself, again and again. Who recorded that? Sunshine? Hel? Bruder? Kurt?

"The Prosecutor is done, Allfather."

We get a brief recess, at which Hel scares the crap out of me. Not so much with what she says but with what she doesn't.

I finally ask, "You do have a defense, right?"

"Absolutely. Don't you remember how good I was with the law back in the old days."

"I do. But the question remains."

"Phh. I'll call Sunshine then Odin then Bruder then you. We'll get you off in two shakes of Sleipnir's tail, no problem."

"Wait, have you seen Sleipnir?"

"It was a figure of speech."

I keep trying to catch Sunshine's eye. No luck, then we're back in session.

"Does the defense have any witnesses?" Odin asks.

Hel replies, "Does the defense have any witnesses? Oh, you bet it does, Grampy. The defense calls Sunshine the Norn."

I'm staring at Sunshine when she finally catches my gaze. She moves to stand, but before she takes a step Odin says, "Denied."

Hel: "De- what?"

Odin: "De-nied."

"I was expecting that," she says under her breath. "All right, then, I call Odin Allfather."

"All right, then...also denied," he replies.

"I was more or less expecting that, too," Hel says, again under her breath.

"No offense, but this isn't going that well."

"Anything else?" Odin asks.

Hel smiles. "I call Greta Bruder."

Odin catches on this one. In his throat I mean. I see him turn to the Norns. I see Sunshine wink at him and fucking smile. Wink and fucking smile.

"Fine," says Odin, "the defense calls Greta Bruder."

BRUDER'S TESTIMONY doesn't help. She seems, in fact, mysteriously unable to prove anything that would be remotely beneficial. When Hel says, "No more questions," I'm convinced it can't get any worse.

Odin replies, "Prosecution, anything else?"

And Forseti comes up with this beauty. "No questions, your honor. But I would like to show a final exhibit if the court would indulge me."

Odin nods.

And Forseti cues the footage of me changing back and forth between myself and Wrath X. All context removed, it's just a montage of me looking like a cartoon villain changing costumes. Except, apparently, I'm not a cartoon villain. I'm a real one.

Hel objects. "That is not how it happened."

"Oh?" asks Odin.

"I was there. That video has been edited. Heavily..."

Forseti chimes in, "So, defense counsel is saying she was involved with the crime in question?"

"I was..."

"Take her," says Odin. "And him. Keep them apart." And he turns to the Norns, Sunshine, it seems, specifically. "Evil like theirs cannot be allowed to flourish."

And she smiles. Sunshine just smiles.

LATER, ODIN and I are alone in his inner sanctum, Himself lording the situation over me. I've failed, as I always do. I mean, I suppose I should have seen that coming. *You* definitely should have seen that coming. I never get it right. Ever. I guess that part is true and will be forever; until there's no more forever.

Betrayed, lied to and about, cast out, that's been my life and there's no reason that should change. What's going to happen to me? Well, I suppose maybe the dripping poison thing. That hasn't gone down yet. I can only hope that was metaphorical or that you just made it up out of whole cloth. Honestly, though, I feel worse about what's happened to you guys.

Odin and the others are going to get their power back then they're going to do what they've always done: Help whoever will swear fealty to them. So, they'll help this Vekk guy. And now that the Norns are on their side, now that Sunshine has betrayed me, what else could happen?

"Son, I have a surprise for you," he says.

"What? You're going to have me executed?"

"Of course not. You're my boy."

"Your supposed Hitler-loving boy?"

"Couldn't be helped."

"So, what? What's the surprise? You're going to execute Hel?"

"Of course not, I'm her grampy."

"OK, enough with the 'of course nots.' What is it?"

"We're going to remake the statue. The Norns have agreed to go along."

"But…"

"And so has Greta Bruder."

"Why would she agree to that?"

"You'd have to ask her. Not that you'll be able to."

"What happened to free will?"

"Yeah, funny how the Norns gave us a pass on that, seeing how everything else went. You know, with Hitler betraying you and turning evil, tricking us and all that?"

All I can do is nod as he waves me away, a squad of Robo-valks leading me down and down and down.

WHAT ABOUT you and me? You might wonder that, here and now. The you and me of this book: The implied author and the real reader. Maybe you're doubting me, considering the possibility that Odin's publicity has been right all along. Despite cutting a somewhat comical, randomly dashing figure—despite my pretense as a reliable, relatable, even likable, narrator—I am evil, and I always have been. Maybe I really was the one who helped Hitler once upon a once upon a once upon a time…

Maybe this whole thing, whatever you want to call it… this *book*…can we even call it that if it's not done? Maybe this "book" has been one big, fat, phony apologia that I'm going to burn to the ground here and now.

Maybe, like a fake, Book of Revelation Jesus who took your pain but wants you to feel it all the same, I'll jump out from behind Daddy's robes just in time to shout, "Surprise! All that New Testament peace-and-love stuff was complete BS, guys. LOL and ROFLMAO. Now, fuck straight off to Hell!"

FANTASYLAND

HE SAID his goodbyes, saddened not at what he had done, but at what he had endured. A classic narcissist, Hitler's hatred for the people he'd wronged was legendary even then. And now, in history? Whatever is beyond legendary. That, I suppose, is what it would be.

Hitler hated the Jews and the Gypsies, the Slavs and the Blacks. He denounced them and hounded them. He beat them and jailed them. He tortured them and killed them. And these things happened over many years. They became his reason for living, an entire civilization's reason for being.

But for the people who loved him, for those who gave unerring devotion to his mad plans, Hitler gave special rewards, gifts to last forever or as near to forever as could be managed. To his dog Blondi and her pups, to Eva Braun and Joseph and Magda Goebbels and their six children, Hitler would give what he gave himself. He would give the swift sleep of morphine, the release of cyanide, the final gunshot at a soldier's hand.

And as the shot that killed him rang out in Midgard and Asgard—as it rang out across the Nine Worlds, I felt it too. I felt the loss of power, and I looked up. I looked up to see them falling through the gray and black and burning flack, one after the other, falling like birds that had mysteriously lost their power of flight.

ARMS AND legs, heads and feet, hammer, helm, shield, and sword. Odin and all the rest rolling through the roiling air, a high-speed caravan of dispossessed deities, gods whose time was over a thousand years ago, gods I knew would yet be hoping for a chance to live again.

They had fallen through dimensions and light centuries, fallen until they saw the globe of blue and white coming up on them. They knew where they were, where they were going. Then came the land in green and brown, the rivers like blue-silver veins, the mountains like the scales of a great, rocky serpent. They were over the Fatherland before they knew it, the place on which Odin had made them pin their hopes.

Berlin coming up fast. See it, now, the ruin of smoke and ash, fire and fury, gray rubble and settling dust. Hear the mortar rounds and machine gun patter, the grind of tank tread and boom of howitzer. The gods don't know whether they're safe or not. They're scared because they haven't been through this before, not once. Sure, I could have told them how it would go, but where would the fun have been in that? It was just too delicious to watch their fall, to hear their thuds…

They hit the ground in the Reich Chancellery courtyard. Old Adolf and little Eva were already charred, smoldering like the city around them, and the rest of the mess Odin had helped Hitler make. But the Russians were coming and so were the Americans. Odin knew this. He remembered in spite of the pain. Oh, yes, there was pain. Pain, but no death.

"Sudden falls are the worst, aren't they?" I called.

He looked up and I realized then that he'd changed physically, that they'd all changed, become lesser in stature and beauty. But he'd changed in other ways, too. Yes, he was naked. But he also had both his eyes.

"Loki?"

"It's me."

"You don't look the same."

"I assure you, neither do you."

"But your skin. You're black."

I looked down. I had indeed changed. I had, also indeed, lost my clothes. "Gosh, I guess you're right."

"Aren't you going to change yourself?"

"Meh."

"Oh, you can't do it anymore, the disguise stuff?"

"Poof," I said, changing into a black hermaphrodite, just to piss him off.

He sneered.

"Obviously, I can do it." I changed back. "But this form really seems to bother you, so I'll go with it."

"Change me, then. At least give me some clothes."

"Try yourself, maybe you can do it now, too."

He couldn't. "Well?" he finally asked.

I shook my head.

"Typical," he said. He looked around in disgust, adding, "So, this is Midgard, huh?"

"They call it Earth. And don't pretend you haven't been here before."

"Only as a projection. Never as a—"

"Corporeal being? The way you launched me time and again. I guess you know what it feels like now, don't you?"

"It hurts."

"Yes, it does."

"I don't know what…"

"Oh, but you do, don't you? You knew there was a chance

he'd betray you, that he'd decide to take fate into his own hands."

"Listen, son, let's forget about all that Hitler stuff. We need to work together, to get home."

"Home?"

"Yes."

"No."

18
RAGNARÖK

A DEARTH of stars in the winter deep, so few I barely notice dawn as it comes and goes, like an old flame sneaking into town, not bothering to say hi. Then, you're alone at a bar getting loaded, clicking your uPhone with practiced, anti-social determination, and some frenemy sidles over, tells you the old flame is around, that they didn't stop to say hi because they only came to town to fuck your best friend.

They've been fucking your best friend since before you knew either of them, says the frenemy, before giving you a disingenuous pat on the back and returning to their seat, where their real friends, their un-frenemies, await. All of them look at you—all the frenemies or frenemies' un-frenemies or whatever they are—they look at you and smile, big and bright and white, like a pack of jackals sizing up a wounded gazelle. And it's like all the lights in the world just came on. It's like waking up and opening your eyes only to find yourself staring at the sun. But, no, it's not the sun, not for me. It's only Sunshine, come to see me now, here at the end. Come, no doubt, to explain herself, to ease her conscience.

"What do you want?" I ask, through the bars.

"Aw, don't be like that, Trickster? You got played. It's not the first time. I mean, for you, it's *really* not the first time. You're sort of an expert in playing and in getting played both, aren't you? Funny how that works."

"It's not about me."

"Oh?"

"No. It's about them, the humans."

"Oh, right, your adopted species."

"Specifically, Bruder. Does she even know what's going to happen to her?"

"What's going to happen to her?"

"Well, let's see. Putting two and two together here. If Hitler killing himself resulted in the gods' power being trapped in the statue?"

"Yes?"

"And the Asgardians falling to Earth?"

"Yes?"

"And if you're going to reform the statue into Bruder's shape...to give the gods their power back...that must mean you're going to sacrifice her...that should release the gods' power and it should flow, automatically, back to them."

"Very good, Trickster. Don't forget, though, the power is flowing back to you, too."

"Fine, to me, too."

"So, perfect, right?"

"Except Bruder's sacrifice."

"Hey, if it's what Fate wants, who are we to stand in Fate's way?"

"And is it what Fate wants?"

"That's sort of a chicken and egg question."

"No chicken, no egg...Aren't you supposed to be one of Fate's handmaidens, y'know, sort of the source on what Fate wants or doesn't?"

She shrugs.

"And, again, does Bruder even realize what's going to happen? Do you even care?"

"Yes and no. She realizes something's going to happen. She just doesn't realize what."

"Don't you think she deserves to know? You're allowing the gods to meddle with the humans again."

"Really, Trickster, it's not me. This is up to Fate."

"But you're interpreting Fate."

"Hey, you know what they say, 'We report, Fate decides.'"

NO ASSHOLES. Three this day. Instead, it's the Robo-valks. They come in day's blinding wake. A squad of four, resolute and beautiful, in gleaming battle dress, and it's like the old days but only for a few seconds, only in my imaginings.

I don't even ask the Robo-valks their names, simply satisfy myself gazing upon the lustrousness of all that golden hair, the impressive spans of their big, strong, fluffy wings, the gleaming armor, the swords. I let them take me where they will and maybe I close my eyes for a second or two, maybe I think a naughty thought or ten. Nothing evil, though, nothing I'd be embarrassed to tell my mother, whomever or whatever she is...

They haul me back through the house, the toes of my shoes scraping the Earth. The murmur of speech grows as we turn towards the scene of yesterday's sham trial. The temperature rises with the building sound, the heat I always feel at judgment. The feeling of loss, of Odin's eternal disappointment and self-righteous anger. Sure enough, that's where we're going. And all those old feelings are there, in me, in the here and now.

Just like the day before, they bring me into the rising pitch of Aesir and Vanir, the massed feeling they have that this is fate, the fate they've been waiting for. I can feel it, too, like an ambience of destiny, everywhere, the taut expectation that this is how it should be. But is it fate, whatever fate is, if it keeps happening again and again? If something happens more than once, can it really be fate? You might think the answer is, "yes, obviously." If it's not a sole, final event, a true conclusion, can it really be what we, what *you*, think of as fate?

Because I have been here before. I've always thought all this trial and punishment stuff—all this being launched from Valhalla, sent sailing cross-dimensionally again and again—had nothing to do with reality. Even if there was Fate, real Fate, this was never what it was. Because the Norns never had anything to do with it. It was just Odin saying how he wanted things to be. He needed someone to beat on, someone to hate, and that someone was me.

This time is different, though. I stare at the Norns as the Robo-valks seat me and shackle me to the chair. Odin motions to them and Sunshine stands, in all her gowned glory, bright and beautiful and terrible. She stands like what dawn might be if I loved it. And like any dawn, like my sense memory of dawn, she betrays me.

"Loki Niflheim," she intones, smling, "you have been found guilty."

"Of what?"

Odin bangs Gungnir on the floor. *Boom, boom, boom.* Wolves bark. Ravens caw. The golden boar grunts, grunts again, then roars. Denunciatory murmurs, whispers of derision from Aesir and Vanir. Odin bangs his great war-spear again and finally there's quiet.

Sunshine clears her throat and continues, "Of meddling in the affairs of humanity. Of being the force of evil in Midgard and Asgard and all the Nine Worlds. Of plotting the end of existence from the day of your birth. Of causing the fall of the gods. Of being the darkness and everything it represents. Do you have anything to say before Fate passes judgment on you?"

"Sunshine, why are you doing this to me?"

But she doesn't answer. She turns towards the window, as though she's heard something. What a joke, I think. She can't even look me in the eye, here at the end.

Odin asks, "Does the defense have anything to say before we impose sentence?"

I want to die, give up, even as I realize the drapes are open a sliver. A flurry of movement comes in that moment, daylight's reflection dancing off metal and glass, an interplay of gleams and sheens that makes me think of Valhalla in the old days. One of the Robo-valks hovers over to Allfather.

Odin's sureness fails him. His self-satisfied smile falls, and the monocle follows, bouncing off the shiny, tile floor. He motions to Thor and Heimdall, nods at me, curtly, as if he'd like to give me a head butt instead. "Hide him."

"Where?" asks Thor.

"I don't know, maybe back in the dungeon, you idiot."

I can't help laughing.

Thor punches me in the side once, then again and again, and Heimdall is whispering all the while, bitter somethings about fate and truth, light and dark. He's trying to make me hurt, make me pay for being me. The murmur of speech grows as they haul me from the room.

Heimdall whispers, "You think this is going to be OK,

now, don't you? Like it always is for you."

"Why would I? I think you have me confused with someone else."

And Thor says, "Well, it's not," and punches me again. And more whispering, more sweet, hateful whispering. So, it goes as we wind our way back into the darkness.

THE FIRST camera crew shows up in a white, unmarked van, at the front gate of New Valhalla. The guards know Odin is busy. They know…everyone…is busy. When the guards won't let them in the crew decides to back the fuck up…then drive the fuck through the front, fucking gates and over The Fucking Rainbow Bridge. Okay, maybe they're not "just" deciding this. Maybe they're working on intel, a tip, if you will. Maybe, M-F has been sprung, maybe he's actually in the back of the van. Odin's guards on the other hand…well, intelligence is not their game.

Thinking this is just run-of-the-mill insanity, they call the local police who, to their credit, come directly. In the meantime, the rest of the VB shows up, on their bikes, rolling through the broken, battered gates like the gassed-up equivalent of a cavalry charge straight out of the thirteenth century. They head straight for the white van then surround it, creating a partition between van and house.

The cops don't take long quizzing Odin's guards. They're on the move towards the white van, the VB, and the house, even as camera crews 2, 3, and 4 show up. Odin's security guards follow haplessly in the wake of all those cops, neo-Nazis, and the few who are both. The VB are looking for Wrath X., and the cops are looking for Greta Bruder. The camera crews just keep coming: 5, 6, 7, 8…

Eventually, Odin changes into some more human attire and heads outside to manage the situation. All follow, except Greta Bruder who slips away. Soon, she's standing in front of Hel's cell door, much to Hel's surprise.

"What is going on up there?" Hel asks.

"What's going on is it's time to go."

Hel reaches my cell first, but Bruder's not far behind. They look like they belong together, as simple as that. And I begin to wonder, if we get out of this, whether they might be happy together, someday. Even if I can't be happy with Sunshine, even if I never see her again, something about the sight of Hel and Bruder feels right and good, even if it's complete speculation at this point, a reality that may never be born.

"I have never been so happy to see anyone!"

"Really," asks Bruder.

"No. It's an expression. Don't forget I'm thousands of years old."

"Let's go," says Hel.

"What the—"

"Don't—"

"Is going on up there?"

"A distraction."

And I say, "There's just one thing."

"What?" Bruder replies.

"The statue, of course."

"But they can't do anything without me."

"I'm not so sure about that. The only way to make sure is to take it with us."

"He's right," says Hel.

"Why is this my life?" Greta Bruder asks.

THE PLACE I was before, the place Odin had the Norns stashed, back when this was all just for shits and giggles, I know that's where he must have the statue. How do I know? I don't know, I just do. And the fun part is that's exactly where it is. Which is where the fun ends. The problem being he doesn't have just one statue there. He has two.

"So, which Hitler is fake?" I ask Hel.

"How should I know? I just saw this thing for the first time the other day."

"They do look identical," says Bruder, nodding in solidarity.

Hel smiles. "Who says we have to choose?"

"Okay, but what then?"

"You mean, how are we getting out of here?"

"Right."

"You mean, even though there's a diversion, who knows how long it will last?"

"Right."

"You mean, how are we really getting out of here once we leave the house?"

"Right, right, right!"

"Follow me," says Greta Bruder.

There's a tunnel leading out. They certainly didn't have one of these in the original Valhalla. When we get to the end I'm still wondering where we're going to go. But when we come out into the sunlight, I see precisely where. The giants are in the front seat of a BMW SUV, Fen between them, smiling a massive canine grin.

"Were you guys in on this the whole time?" I ask once the doors are locked again, and we're speeding away.

"I wish," says Surtur, "That trial sounds exciting, but someone had to stick around to rescue you from Odin."

"And the Norns, don't forget them. They completely betrayed you. What liars," Thyrm adds

Hel clears her throat. "Based on the way your time has gone, don't tell me you're really surprised."

"What happened to second chances? What happened to redemption?"

"I guess those only work for humans."

"If then," says Bruder.

"I still have no idea what we're going to do with her," says Hel.

"Hide her, of course," I reply.

Bruder shakes her head. "I'm not hiding anymore. I've got to get back to reality one way or the other. I've still got an election to win."

I look back as we drive away. I see New Valhalla there, now burning in the growing distance, sending up so much thick, coal black smoke that it leaves the sky in a slow-moving split screen, the light and heat of life itself juxtaposed against what can only resemble the end of all things.

VALHALLA A smoldering ruin, it's only a matter of time before Sunshine shows up with Odin in tow. Yes, I'll spend the rest of eternity carrying those Hitler statues around with me, never sure which one is real. That, or I'll sink them to the bottom of the ocean, bury them in a hole, hide them in a cave, something. The important thing is no one will be able to use them. At least then humanity will be safe and Bruder will be free, free for now, at least, now that she knows the truth. Odin may have the Norns. He may have won them over, but he can't do anything without the statue. No, it's not a foolproof plan but it's better than nothing. Then I realize I haven't seen Kurt.

"Where's Kurt?" I ask the group.

Surtur pipes up, "Still in his cell."

"Well, go get him. We have to take him with us."

"Hold on," says Bruder.

"What?"

"He's not there anymore. I let him go."

"Why?"

"It's not right to keep other people captive."

"I know, but…"

"But nothing…"

"When did you do this?"

"A few minutes ago, right after we got back. Honestly, he seemed pretty out of sorts, but I thought it was for the best."

"It was a bad decision to let Kurt loose."

"He was tied up. In a cell."

"It was for his own good."

"I mean, that just sounds like the conundrum of the criminal justice system, doesn't it? Is it helping? Is it not? You're not really sorry I let him go, are you?"

"It's the principle."

"Even after all I've done for you."

"I'm grateful, of course. Hey, wait a second, I just saved your butt back at Valhalla."

"It's Sunshine, open up!" I hear come through the intercom.

I stumble over to the front door, peer out. There she is, at the gate, alone.

I push the "Talk" button, "I'm supposed to believe you're by yourself."

"Oh, no, you shouldn't believe that. You should believe you're surrounded. That your old buddies Tyr and Frey have taken your boat."

"Boat?"

"Yeah, you remember that foolproof emergency escape plan you told me about, the reason the villa was *so* perfect?"

I hear the boat's motor start. I motion Surt to look. He hustles over to the window, turns back after a second, nods.

"Fuck!" he screams.

Sunshine laughs. "You've got no choice, Trickster. Time to come out and play Fate's tune."

"Don't you mean 'face the music?'"

"Don't tell me what I mean."

I hear Odin's booming voice then, coming through a megaphone. "It's Odin," he says, obviously, in that gravel and command tone, that I'm-not-fucking-around, All-Father nonsense. "I demand you come forth and treat with me."

I cross the room, peer out the window, see snow all around, a layer of soft white maybe a foot deep. The flakes are still coming big, white, and geometric, an army of holy pentagrams. Sure enough, there are three sets of headlights glaring back at me. They catch the flakes, seem almost to spike them in mid-air. "And?"

"I want them."

"You can't do anything with just the statues. Hasn't the last hundred years proven that?"

"I've got the Norns. All three of them, right here with me. If Bruder won't go along, I'll just find some other muttonhead."

"Like Reinhold Vekk maybe?"

"Maybe."

"Or you'll just lie to her, right? Tell her how great the power's going to feel."

"I guess."

"Well, she's right here. So much for that."

"Blah, blah, blah…You know this will happen eventually. Why keep fighting Fate?"

"Yeah," says Sunshine, "Why fight Fate?"

Bruder says, "Fine, I'll do it."

Sunshine laughs.

"What, why?" I ask. "You'll die. Is this like a whole Jesus thing? Have I not made it clear a thousand times? The dude is not real."

"I guess if you call doing the best thing for the greatest number of people a Jesus thing then that's what this is. Finally getting rid of you guys once and for all could make humanity a lot better. Could completely change things."

"Again, you'd be dead."

Bruder shakes her head, steps past me, and punches the button for the front gate. She opens the front door and walks out into the yard.

I stand staring at her, the door open. She turns back, motions for me to come. I shake my head but begin to walk anyway. I step out into the yard carrying the two statues.

Sunshine, Darkness, and Halflight are there, waiting for me in the middle of the courtyard. Odin and his massed troupe of gods loom beyond.

"I don't know how you're going to tell them apart, but I guess that's your problem."

Sunshine grabs greedily for the statues, tosses aside the one I was holding in my left hand. She does know the difference. I guess I was wrong about that, too.

"Perfect," says Odin, "Bring it here."

"No," says Sunshine, and it may be the most perfect word I've ever heard uttered, "Odin Allfather, we've known it was you for all these centuries, since we left you in Asgard. But we had to give you a true opportunity for redemption. It was what Fate decreed."

"But you said?"

"Yes, we said. We lied. You should be familiar with that by now, shouldn't you?"

She turns back to her sisters, nods, and they begin to chant, all in time, "*Var Ma'Rek'Tessora'Vay, Var Ma'Rek'Tessora'Vay, Var Ma'Rek'Tessora'Vay...*"

And I see it. I see the statue of Hitler begin to change. First the facial features become shallower, then the hair and the mustache are gone, the creature depicted becoming like some tiny, golden mannequin. The uniform fades, no more of those horrible swastikas to stare at. No more love of death.

"Loki Niflheim, will you accept kingship of the gods? Will you rule wisely, beyond the realm of men?"

"What?" Odin asks. "You can't be serious. You're leaving him in charge?"

"Not leaving, not the way you mean. This is the end, Odin. This is Ragnarök. Thus, will be your fate for eternity. Will you accept, Loki?"

"What, to be a god again, to have all that power? And to be forced to trust all these other monkeys with that power, to have to watch over them for the rest of eternity?"

"Yes."

I look down, pondering. "And to be able to launch him across the expanse of spacetime whenever I feel the urge," I say pointing at Odin.

"That, too."

I shake my head. "This is way more difficult than I thought it would be."

"What is?" Sunshine asks.

"Saying no to power."

And Sunshine smiles. She turns to her sisters. "I told you."

And the Norns speak as one, "So comes the Twilight of the Gods. From this time forward, you are as mortal as any human. Do with your lives as you will."

"But what about Valhalla? What about Asgard?"

"They are gone. Forever," say the Norns.

I see the statue has fallen to the ground and that it's growing. It's no longer metal, but something like pure energy. It's like a tiny sun, growing ever outward, brighter and brighter. Then the Norns begin to change. They begin to become light, to become one with the sun the statue has become.

I catch Sunshine's gaze. She smiles. But I can see she's sad. And I'm sure this is the last time I'll see her; equally sure I'll never stop hoping to see her again. Then in a flash of light and darkness together, of nothing and everything, of something we watched happen, but didn't, they're gone. The statue, the golden light, Sunshine, Darkness, and Halflight. All gone.

I WISH Sunshine were still alive, but I think I realized a long time ago that we weren't both going to make it through this. Truly, I thought it would be me who died, especially there at what felt like the end, on the grounds of New Valhalla, at what felt like it had to be Ragnarök.

A glorious death was what I'd been conditioned to believe in, a vision I'd lived with for so long. Whether in actualization or avoidance, the end dominated my thoughts, even over this last century, even over this time I spent pretending to be something I now really am.

Even now, I wonder why it wasn't me who died. I realize I will never get the answer, that in the end, I didn't really know any more than you. Or am I just forgetting, now; forgetting everything I knew when gods were real, and I was still one of them?

BY THE time we're driving back to the airport I've got a low-grade cold, one that graduates to mid-grade on the two-hour trip to Tegel. The giants are down, too. As for Hel, she's fine physically, but the final loss of our immortality seems to have hit her in a different way. She's been moping around the villa, finally tells me she needs time to think, says she'll take a later flight maybe, or travel a little. She does drive us to the airport, though I can't help thinking she just wants to make sure to keep the 6. She's gotten really into driving that thing. Bags unloaded, I'm talking to her through the lowered passenger's side window, and I say, "This wouldn't have anything to do with Greta Bruder, would it?"

"This what?"

"Staying behind?"

"What, you think I'm still fiddling around with politics?"

"I was thinking more along the lines of still fiddling around with Greta Bruder."

She nods her head, lights up a Gauloise, smiles at me one last time and peels out, the 6 torquing into a nice little mini-fishtail as she merges with traffic. Daddy's little girl is all grown up.

ON THE plane, we're waiting for coach to board, and the giants are making a complete scene. Stuffed up, sneezing, and calling mournfully for aspirin, water, and tissues, they sound like Dickensian street urchins panhandling for sixpence.

Fen's the only one of us who really seems OK. I got him the two seats behind me so he could really stretch out. He's already snoring, dreaming his new, final iteration of happy, doggy dreams. No more visions of scarfing the sun or taking off Tyr's hand. No more tales of dark glory to rule his nights.

This illness has me feeling closer to you guys, gives me an even better understanding of how tough it's been for you with all these low-grade maladies. It's easy to see how you lose days, even weeks at a time. I've got my head tilted back, trying vainly to cop some pre-take-off zzz's when I hear her voice.

"Excuse me?" she says.

I open my eyes, see Sunshine, a woman that looks like her at least. I wonder if this cold is actually some sort of hitherto undiscovered Level 8 virus, and I'm hallucinating. So, I reach out, touch her hand.

"Yes, it's really me," she says, smiling, "And that's my seat." She points to my left.

"I thought you disappeared, as in vanished, dematerialized. I thought you were..."

"Dead?"

"I guess."

"I was," she says, sidling by.

"So, now you're back? We're going to keep doing all that Ragnarök shit for the rest of time?"

"No, my sisters are gone for good."

"And you just came back to run things, keep an eye on us?"

"Nope. I'm mortal now, just like you, just like everyone else on this big, blue ball of potential energy."

"Why?"

"Why what?"

"Why come back?"

"I came back for you."

"But I don't want to go anywhere. I like it here."

"No, Trickster, I came back to be mortal, with you."

She leans in to kiss me.

"I've got a cold. And it's getting worse."

"I don't care," she says, finishing her swoop. Our lips touch. She kisses me, and I kiss her back. I let my mind float, let my soul try to find, to feel, hers. I can't do it of course, but it's the trying that matters.

I open my eyes, see her staring back at me. "Well, that was nice, wasn't it?"

"It was."

"Oh, Jesus, I just thought of something."

"What?" she asks.

"Kurt."

"At a time like this?"

"No, I mean…What about everything he knows? What about Bruder? And Vekk?"

"What can they say? And who's going to believe them if they do?"

"True. I guess you're pretty good at covering your tracks."

"Our tracks, Trickster. Now, kiss me again."

THE BABE IN A BASKET

I MAY never have been a Christ figure. That role, One-Eye monomaniacally reserved and jealously held. But I was a Moses figure, a babe in a basket, a woulda-been-shoulda-been-coulda-been king. If only things had worked out. The worst part is I remember it all.

Yeah, I know, you think just because you can't remember anything before the age of three or four or five, that's how everyone is. But it's not. See, technically, I don't even have an age. It's just that one day, an incalculable number of years ago, I popped into being. Poof.

There I was a teensy tine-sy baby giant in an exceptionally large basket, on the grand, front steps of Odin's golden Valhalla. Those steps are so high, you'd need climbing gear to get up them. It's true: Everything's grander on Asgard, especially at Valhalla. At least it was when Asgard and Valhalla were real.

Who'd brought me, who'd found me, who'd birthed me, who'd left me? No one knows any of it. Oh, sure, there were theories, *are* theories; but just like so much history, the reality was lost long ago. I can fill you in on the theories, though.

They say I'm the product of an illicit union between Odin and a giantess. They say I'm Odin's prize of battle from when he finally subjugated Jotunheim, a slave if you will; that my parents were the High King and Queen of Jotunheim, long before even the times of Surtur and Thyrm. They say Odin killed my parents, horribly, hideously, seemingly remorselessly. But he couldn't bring himself to kill little old me. They say that's all wrong. They say I brought myself into being, long ago, somehow, someway. They say so many things. Maybe one of them is true.

MY FIRST time in Valhalla's throne room, The Valheim, had me duly impressed. Gold and silver everywhere. The Valks, the Aesir, and the Vanir. That was when the gods were still a nuclear family more or less, multiple generations living under the same roof. There was happiness, love, and plenty of good cheer. Yes, it's true, there was love, even for me.

I guess one of the Valks must have found me on those grand steps and brought me inside, set my basket down on the dais before Odin. He reached down with those meaty paws of his and picked me up.

"Well, who have we here?" he asked.

Obviously, I couldn't reply. I was a baby. I goo-ed. I gah-ed. I guess he liked what he heard, though.

"Any idea who brought him?" he asked the Valk.

"No, All-Father."

"Well, we can't very well turn him away, can we? He's just a baby."

"But he's a giant!" Heimdall warned.

"He's a baby is what he is."

"But…"

"No, Heimdall, but since you're so interested, maybe you can help me come up with a name."

Heimdall looked down. He kicked at the floor. I was a

giant, so he couldn't even bring himself to give me a name. Disgusting was what it was.

"I know," said Frigga, crossing the hall, always looking to help Heimdall—her fave in those days—out of a jam. Yes, there were a story or two about Frigga and Heimdall, about secret tristes at the castle he kept overlooking Bifrost. Not that Odin really cared. Like I told you, what with all the giantesses, hot and cold running Valkyries, and a jaunt to Midgard or Alfheim every so often, he had his hands full. "Let's call him Linder-Heimdall."

"Little Heimdall?" Odin asked. "No, no, that won't do, wife."

"Why?" she asked.

Baldur piped up, "Well, it's not terribly lyrical."

Forseti nodded in agreement. Freya smugly seconded his head bobs.

Odin held up his hand for silence even though no one was talking. He was Odin, after all, the All-father. He had to be the idea guy. Even if he wound up eventually adopting one of your ideas, he'd convince himself, and everyone else, it was his.

"The child must have his own name. Let's call him…Loki." Odin said, looking at me warmly, misting a little, tears forming at the corners of his eyes.

Yes, they both worked then. I still remember how much love I felt that day, which makes it so hard to countenance the truth, a truth that evolved over time. The truth was that I was just a baby, taken in and treated with love, but I was destined to be hated, fated to destroy the nine worlds. Try that one on for size. Problems? Demons? Yeah, just a few…

Conflicted? Oh, hell, yes, I was. Still am, obviously. In spite of all the…what else could you call it but hatred? I know Odin loved me once. I remember.

But it was easy to doubt that as the millennia piled up. As

the bad memories just seemed to accumulate, the good paled. And I thought today was always and yesterday was gone.

Yes, I remember the love. How could I not? But I also remember something else was there, something like Fate maybe, and now I know what that means. I know that Fate would always be there, watching and waiting, looking for its chance.

19

LIQUID IN HIS VOICE

A FEW weeks after we get back, my uPhone's brand new, big bad bossa nova ringtone brings me screaming out of a dream I can't quite remember, leaves shadows of black and red dancing in my head even as my eyes fix on the nightstand and the phone's shiny, white lines and rounded, silver corners. I guess the bad dreams will never be gone for good, even now that I'm human. Bad dreams, though, are a small price to pay for life. Try to remember that, little ones.

The screen is its usual wrecky visage of distracting color splashes and phased disintegrations. The only cogent takeaway is that someone wants to talk to me but they're not willing to share their name. I pick up though I'm sure I shouldn't.

"They got Bragi," Odin says in this slow, hoarse whisper, the practiced tone of regret I've heard too many times to believe, yet still do on some level.

Sunshine stirs next to me, red-gold locks spilling over the top of the russet covers, the rustling of bedclothes refracting a shaft of sunlight that has fallen through a crack in the drapes.

I lower my voice, turn away. "And I'm supposed to care about this why?"

"He's your brother."

"They're all my brothers. Except the ones that are my sisters.

And they all wanted me dead a thousand times. Just like you. The last time was a few weeks ago, remember? Why am I even speaking to you?"

Sunshine turns towards me, eyes brightening with recognition. "That's not Odin, is it?"

"Why shouldn't it be?" he shouts in that tone of command he never needed to practice. "I'm the All-Father," he adds, entitlement practically liquid in his voice.

She turns away from me, burrowing into her pillow in an attempt to escape the noise.

"You were," I whisper.

"Were what?"

"Were the All-Father."

"Oh, I'll never stop being that. Believe me."

"Maybe, maybe not. But you'll stop being it for me."

"Meaning?"

"Meaning we're done, Odin. I never want to speak to you again. Go and live your life, enjoy whatever time you have left."

"And what if I refuse?"

"Vekk's coming for you, isn't he? And you want my help?"

"You've got the only Norn!"

"She can't do anything anymore."

"Has she tried?"

"Yes. It didn't work." I lie.

"What if he comes for you instead? Did you think of that?"

"You're the one who was lying to him, convincing him you were going to help clear the way for his take-over."

"I'm just saying you never know with humans. The only way to be sure is for us to team up, take him out, and clean up any evidence. Then we can go our separate ways."

"I am not helping you clean up anything. Ever again. You've got plenty of money. Find an island somewhere. Get some sun. Go skiing. Read a book. Write a book."

I kill the call, switch to answer-only, and set the thing down, realizing Odin is almost gone, like really gone, for good. Of course, Vekk will come for him. Win or lose, he's the kind of guy who'll see what Odin did as a betrayal.

ELECTION DAY comes and things immediately accelerate to the downside in Germany. While Bruder appears to have won, the results can't be certified for technical reasons: local voting irregularities, trouble with machines, software, and the like. In addition to that, there's apparently been some foreign interference, reports of it at least. Though the Germans seem desperate to blame the French, it looks more like it may be the Russians, the likelihood that they were helping Vekk, trying to at least.

The takeaway is that both sides, Bruder's and Vekk's, insist the other cheated and that the Russians helped them. There are streets protests from both camps, riots that get bloody and worse. The police have their hands full, so much that Merkel calls out the military, and starts imposing curfews in the major cities. I can't help thinking it's good Merkel is still in charge. But that won't last much longer.

Not that any of this should be a surprise to me, or you. From France to England, Ukraine to Syria, Turkey, Iran, and Iraq, the Russians seem to be meddling wherever they can. Call them a second-rate power, but they're doing first-rate damage. They're making up for their lack of economic might and dwindling military with cyberwarfare, espionage, and political dirty tricks. Fortunately, America's been spared, at least thus far. And maybe there's still hope, as long as America survives.

I briefly wonder whether Odin could be behind it. Whether he could be the one working with the Russians. Now, still, could he be playing his games, working all sides? Yes, I've changed, but maybe he can't. Or won't. I continue to hear from him, of course, over the intervening days: in cryptic DM's, voicemails, and emails about how "they're" after this or that Asgardian. No matter where I am, or what I'm doing, I'm screening everything and promptly deleting any messages Odin leaves. Yes, the family I spent thousands of years trying to be a part of is gone, but I've got Sunshine. The giants and Fen are safe and with me. Even though Hel isn't here, I know she's still out there, sowing her wild oats. She'll be back eventually. Yes, my heart feels truly full for the first time I can remember.

You guys—and I include myself in this, now—spend so much of your lives hoping for someone or something to save you from death. Family, money, love, art, science, and especially religion...you accumulate these things over your years, pile them atop each other like a wall of talismans, then you get to the end and realize none of them worked. You realize the wall may have been real, but what you'd hoped it would do was an illusion.

But that illusion is what you guys want. You want someone or something that can take care of all your problems, wipe away every tear. Maybe that's why you've become so infatuated with monotheism. That's one thing we never were able to promise, even though we were real in a way Jesus, Yahweh, and Allah aren't. We could never promise you everything. And, in the end, I guess, you're happier with a convincing lie than an awkward truth.

WINTER IN Boston. The days that follow are cold and sunny. More than that, they're precious in a way they never seemed before. Now that I can see an unavoidable, proximate end to my time, each fragment of it seems to have a hold on me in a way history's spent millennia never did.

Cups of hot chocolate and long walks with Sunshine. Fenris playing in the leaves: rolling, gamboling, acting like a puppy. He never was, you know; not before. In a way, that's one of my deepest regrets; the fact that he was never young and that he never will be. I guess, in a way, Fen's just making up for lost time. We all are. But I find myself wondering how long any of us have. That's the problem with really, truly, finally being mortal. The diseases I scoffed at, the ridiculous benders I didn't give a second thought...as a mortal, a true mortal, there's risk around every metaphorical corner. Too much caffeine, too much nicotine, too much sex—they take their tolls. They shouldn't. It's not fair. But they do. Oh, yes.

No, Odin wasn't able to intricate himself into your affairs— not in the way he wanted—but the bad guys won all the same. Vekk and his cronies are spreading, and they feel like the future in a way Old Adolf never did, even back then.

Old Adolf was evil, yes, but he was also sad and inept. Not least for the fact that he still needed us to help him carry out his wretched plans and that even then he couldn't make them work. But you don't need help anymore: Vekk's hunting the gods is proof of that. Just be careful, America. If it happened again in Germany, it could certainly happen to you.

Oh, sure, you still rely on your constructs—Allah and Yahweh, Buddha, Jehovah, and anything else you can get your hands on—but the power's really yours now. There's no witchcraft, or even wishcraft needed, no feeble second-rate gods like me, like I used to be, to run around magically meddling in your affairs.

Giving up? Oh, bite your fucking tongues. I'll never give up on you guys. Or, I mean, us guys. I may not be a god anymore. I may not even be what I was after I was a god, but I've seen human history and no one with a heart who's seen your history, not a century let alone millennia of it, can turn away. You have to accept the truth in experience. You have to give history its due.

I'VE BEEN avoiding calling Kurt since we got back. Honestly, I'd prefer to use magic, make him forget this whole sordid mess, but there's no magic left. Not even my paltry, disguise-y poofs have a bit of impact anymore. One day, though, he calls. I pick up, and it's time for answers.

"Gustav? Or, should I say, Loki?" he asks.

"About that."

"Completely forgotten."

"Literally?"

"Obviously not since I just called you Loki. I remember every last horrid detail. It'll make a great book someday, *Kidnapped by the Gods: A Memoir*. Speaking of which, I've actually got something for you to take a look at."

"Oh, yeah? Turns out I've got something for you, too."

"Well, of course you do. Email it over, give me a few days to read, and we can meet."

"Sunday in the Public Garden?"

"Perfect."

"There's just one thing. When you read, bear in mind, the ending still needs work."

SUNDAY. MID-AFTERNOON. Kurt's waiting when we arrive. I see him standing in the middle distance, posed against winter's early darkness. He's looking away from me, staring intently at the slow, meandering traffic on Arlington Street. Shades on, hands deep in the pockets of his black wool coat, he's smoking a Gauloise. Admittedly, he does look pretty cool with that black cancer stick hanging from his lips, cherry going intermittently red, like a lighthouse bringing in a ship. He looks as if he's imagining himself doing press photos for an album cover, something like that.

I turn to Sunshine, "Maybe you could get us some coffee?"

"Now I'm a barista for you and Kurt?"

"For you and me. For after I'm done. Unless you were hoping to say 'hi' to Kurt."

She chuckles. "What about Fen?"

"Oh, the giants can watch him."

"But who's gonna watch the giants?"

We both laugh.

"They'll be fine. I'll just be over there."

Sunshine walks away, bobbing her head side-to-side as though replaying the last lines of our conversation. She does that a lot, you know. Plays back conversations for herself. I guess once she finds a joke she likes, she wants to really get to know it.

I watch her make for the Starbucks across Beacon Street, with its tinted windows, deserted outdoor tables, and indestructible metal chairs. The wind blows from the north, whipping her hair to and fro as she crosses, making the green Starbucks awning flap in the biting breeze.

Kurt turns when I'm about halfway to him, watches as I cover the rest of the distance between us. I get a smile and a handshake. Firm, warm. "So, you and Sunshine still, huh?" He motions towards her retreating form.

"We're getting married."

"Takes the idea of a long courtship to a new level, doesn't it?"

"Indeed."

"Am I invited?"

I try to gage the likelihood of an objection at the wedding. But what's Kurt going to say, "He's the former god Loki, and she's a once-upon-a-Norn named Sunshine? Somebody call the Mythology Police!"

"Sure, man, what the hell. Maybe you can be the ring girl or something."

He laughs. "Flower boy!"

I fix on the manila envelope, folded double and sticking out of his coat pocket. "That's it? My book?"

He hauls out the envelope, thrusts it towards me. "*Twilight of the Gods*, notes and all."

"Initial thoughts?" I ask, looking down at the thing, realizing he's sealed the envelope. I won't really know what he's said until I get home.

"Thoughts? Well, you did what I suggested: You went epic."

"Right. And?"

"It's solid." He nods judiciously, his expression going cold. "You're right, though, the ending needs work."

Kurt smiles, opens his mouth to say more, but stops as he takes note of the menagerie in the distance. Fen is chasing the giants around in circles. He catches one, nips him in the leg, foot, or butt then goes right after the next. No, there's no blood. I told you, Fen is a sweetheart, especially now.

"They're a riot, aren't they?"

"They are. Except when they're contemplating killing you."

"You know they were totally joking about that, right?"

"I'm not so sure. Maybe I'll find out at the wedding? Or the bachelor party?"

"Maybe you will. I don't have long today, man. Did you have any more to say?"

"The ending needs something. You said it yourself. Overall, it's decent, even good. Of course, now that I know you're a god, I should probably raise my standards."

I decide this is the best I'm going to get. I'll take the manuscript back with me to Chateau Loki, chew through all his notes, read them forwards, backwards, upside-down. If I have any lingering questions, I guess I can always get Kurt on the phone. Who knows, maybe I will see him again? Maybe we'll be buddies until we're old and gray. "Here's yours," I say, handing him a similar manilla folder.

"Why didn't we just email each other?"

"You were the one who suggested it. I just went along."

"True. Thoughts on mine?"

"My first thought is...I *thought* it was going to be a novel."

"It was."

"So, what happened to *The Mists of Seeking*?"

"I don't know, maybe seeing what the world was really like left me feeling daunted, as if relying on my imagination was ridiculous because it could never compete with the simple cataloging of reality."

"You wrote all this since getting back?"

'Oh, no, I've had most of it in my pocket for a while."

"A memoir, though? Seriously? I thought you hated them."

"Well, there are definitely too many these days. But there

aren't too many good ones. So, I thought I might as well give it a try. See if I could write one of the good ones."

"All this is true? Even the stuff about the Turkish-Russian-French-Canadian-American girlfriend who ripped you off?" I say, motioning towards the manuscript. "She really owes you a million bucks?"

"Close to it. Unfortunately, she's completely real, and her name is Kader Kotumehmet."

"Not Drakonika Atatürk?"

"Right."

"Then this isn't exactly a memoir, is it?"

"I guess there are autofictional elements. But Kader's completely real. We spent two hellish years together and way more than that if you count our time in court."

"And your dad's drinking?"

"Yep. I may appear to have my shit together, but I'm actually a complete mess."

"I'm sorry, man. As you know, I've had my share of challenges as well."

"Oh, I know. Sleipnir. Jesus, that must have hurt."

I nod. It did. "You really got fired from your first job?"

"Yep."

"At a McDonald's?"

"Yep. They said I had a bad attitude. Which was completely true." He pauses, jaw setting in a smirk. "Speaking of which, you're doing a lot of hemming and hawing here, not that any of it surprises me now that I know who you really are. Come on, man, spit it out."

"Spit what out?"

"The verdict. On the book."

318

"It's good. Truly."

"You think it will sell?"

"I do. But you'd be better off letting Suzy-Sadie make that call."

"About that?"

"What?"

"Suzy-Sadie's not real."

"So, you don't have an agent?"

"Correct. Honestly, it's sort of the bane of my existence, not having an agent."

"How do you get all these books published then?"

"Man, I just, honestly, I don't know. It's not like I'm making bank or getting famous. Sure, I get stuff published. I guess that's something."

"Well, you should try to get an agent for that."

"I don't know, dude. I mean, again? I'm just sort of tired of it, all the query letters, all the hoops to jump through."

"How many times have you tried?"

"How many times did Odin throw you out of Valhalla?"

"Touché."

"Anyway, thanks," he says.

"Of course, man…just one thing?"

"What?"

"Well done with all that skullduggery about how you were working on a novel about Norse mythology. You really had me there. You sure you didn't at least suspect I was, well, me?"

"No skullduggery, man. I've got a bunch of books in various stages of incompletion. It's sort of a sad analog to the capitalist maxim, 'The one who dies with the most toys wins.'"

"I thought you felt daunted. Even after dealing with the reality of my life, you still want to write a novel about it?"

"Someday. Why not? By its nature the novel is constructed. I can make it whatever I want, in spite of reality. A writer can turn black into white or good into evil if he can somehow make it work. I'll get back to making things up again, someday." He pauses, looks down then back up quickly. "Really, though, Loki, you think the book works? You're not just blowing smoke."

I glance at his cigarette. "Cross my heart," I say. And I do, for emphasis.

That's not enough for Kurt of course. He's serious about this writing thing. All writers are. Just. So. Serious. Especially when they're young. And, as far as writers go, they're always young in a certain sense. They're young until they're dead.

Kurt goes on to ask me about the dialogue and the descriptions. He asks me about the pacing and the prose. He's devoting every scintilla of his mental energy to finding a hole in my critique, or at least something I *really* didn't like. I want to throttle him after a few minutes, but I go along. I know what I said about the wedding and being pals, but somehow, this feels like it might be the last time I see Kurt, and I owe him this much. I owe him a little honesty. Because he is young, at least compared to me. More than that, he's a writer. Even though you guys don't realize it—even though most of you think the opposite is true—artists really are like holy people, struggling for knowledge and understanding on behalf of you all. You should revere them. You should pity them.

THE COMMOTION comes from the trees beyond. I see a shape emerge: The eye patch, the frozen leer, and ample gut.

Odin looks right at me. "Help me, son. There's no one else."

"Uh-oh," says Kurt.

"You should go." I add a whisk-broom hand gesture and malevolently arched brow to make my point.

"You'll call?"

"I'll call," I say.

Kurt walks away as the first of the black shapes emerge from the trees. In the distance, I see Sunshine. I see she's heading my way, the cups of coffee borne before her. She moves slowly, stoically, as if part of a church processional.

The black shapes carry long, black guns, all except one. Slightly shorter, the seventh carries a pistol—a shiny silver pistol—but he doesn't look like he's going to use it for business. He looks like he's going to use it for emphasis, stand watching as the others deal with the mundanities of triggers and safeties and death. And I realize that man is Reinhold Vekk.

"Stoy!" he shouts, his accent thick, perfect Russian.

Odin freezes in place, the riflemen in their firing positions. I try to catch Sunshine's eye, but she keeps coming. The remaining space can't be more than fifty yards. She must see the guns, but she keeps coming.

"Vekk really was mobbed up with the Russians?" I shout at Odin.

"Yes," he answers.

"And they're here to kill you?"

"Maybe not just me."

"Poslushay, ya ne khochu etogo," I say, hoping my use of Russian will earn me more points than, "Look, I don't want any part of this," would have.

Vekk squints, smiles. "Herr Loki, I've been anxious to meet you since we spoke," he says.

And with that statement, half the guns are trained on

me. The Russians are all smiling now, thinly, preparing to do what they're paid to do, what they're fated to do. Their jobs, nothing more.

Sunshine is still closing, foolishly closing. I try to will her away with my gaze, but it's useless.

"Strelyate!" Vekk shouts.

And they do. Two of the guns that were on Odin swivel to Sunshine. One takes her in the leg, the other in the chest. Odin runs for the trees but one of the riflemen hits him in the back of the head. He falls face-first. And I'm running for Sunshine rather than my father. She's on her knees when I get to her. I catch her in my arms, cradle her, lay her on the grass. There's blood everywhere, my hands slick with it. I feel a new absence of hope, like the entire world is dying in slow motion before me. I feel like this is Ragnarök. This is what Fate has been all along.

Sunshine gives me a weak smile. "Fate," she whispers.

"Fate, what?"

"It's a lie."

"What?"

"A story."

"But The Wheel? All the magic?"

"The Wheel and the magic were real. Fate's the only lie."

"No, Sunshine, not now. Don't. You can't."

"Don't be sad, Trickster, I'll see you again. Promise."

The light behind her eyes goes dark, and I know she's gone.

HEART OF AMERICA

I SEE Kurt standing with the Russians. I worry at first that they think he's a witness, that they're going to kill him. But it's not true. He's laughing, chatting in Russian with Reinhold Vekk.

They look at me, the two of them, with their blond hair and blue eyes. And I know I shouldn't have given Kurt the real story, *my* real story. That's all a writer needs, isn't it? A real story? Once he's got that, he could care less about anyone or anything.

Vekk points at me. Kurt nods. The two of them begin walking my way, the six gunmen closing still faster. They come within ten feet, spread out in a broad arc. But they don't shoot. They wait. Kurt looks away and smiles thinly, as if he's not doing what he's doing. As if this had been determined by Fate or something like it.

"It was," he says, taking a drag on the Gauloise.

"Was what?"

He exhales. "Determined by Fate. Or something like it."

"This looks like choice to me."

"You know that's not true, Loki. I'm sorry, truly I am," Kurt says, "Of all the gods, you're my favorite. Good and evil, man and woman, misunderstood and mistreated, you're perfect in your way. But the world doesn't need gods anymore."

"I'm human now!"

"You may not be immortal. But you're still not human. It's

your memories of our sordid history, the volumes of stories that live in your head that make you so dangerous. That and your knowledge of Fate, of what it is, and what it means."

"Fate's a lie. Sunshine just told me that."

"Maybe it is. Or was. But we'll never know for sure. Because the magic's gone now, and it's not coming back."

"You're letting Vekk win. Here he is, killing me, and you're helping him. How long before he does this to Bruder or worse?"

"I'm not letting anyone win. This is just a story."

"This is real, and you know it. Fascism's taking over again."

"Nobody cares."

"People care. You saw them in Germany. Bruder may still have won."

"Germany's not the problem, Loki. You knew as well as I did Vekk would come to America. Humans crave answers, can't seem to give up the needs for absolution and absolutism, no matter the dangers. And Americans may be the worst of the lot, because we've had it so good for so long."

I hear Vekk shout, "Strelyate," and they open fire. I'm hit more times than I can count; stomach, arm, leg, but none in the head. I fall to the grass, the frozen blades digging into my cheek, the ground hard and cold, like a premonition of real, physical death.

I hear Kurt and Vekk speaking, and I hear Vekk's voice change. He's speaking perfect American English now, without a trace of accent. You'd think he'd been in America all along, hiding, waiting to reveal himself until it was too late to stop him.

"Now for reality," Vekk says as he brings the pistol flush with Kurt's forehead, fires once, twice.

Dual exit wounds, twin jets of crimson spray, an anti-baptism of sacred red, flesh, and bone across the dead, winter grass, and the envelopes containing the two manuscripts, envelopes now spattered with reality's deep, dirty substance.

Kurt stumbles back, falls, and lands with a thud, a few feet from me. Reinhold Vekk drops his shiny silver gun. Without a word, he walks away, into the heart of America.

THE END

ACKNOWLEDGMENTS

Sincere gratitude to my friend and editor James Reich of Stalking Horse Press; my gracious blurb providers Mark Doten, Jonathan Evison, Sequoia Nagamatsu, Iris Smyles, Amber Sparks, and Matthew Specktor; and my fearless early readers Tobias Carroll, Leland Cheuk, Seb Doubinsky, and Ted Fauster.

ABOUT THE AUTHOR

Kurt Baumeister's writing has appeared in *Salon, Guernica, Electric Literature, Rain Taxi, The Brooklyn Rail, The Rumpus, Vol. 1 Brooklyn, The Nervous Breakdown, The Weeklings,* and other outlets. An acquisitions editor with 7.13 Books, Baumeister holds an MFA in creative writing from Emerson College. *Twilight of the Gods* is his second novel.

Printed in the USA
CPSIA information can be obtained
at www.ICGtesting.com
JSHW021030310824
69050JS00004B/16